THREE MONKEYS
A DCI Jack Callum Mystery

LEN MAYNARD

First published as *No Evil* in 2015 by Joffe Books
First published as *Three Monkeys* in 2019 by LMP

This edition published in 2020 by Sharpe Books

DEDICATION

Hugh Maynard 1925 - 1958

AUTHOR'S NOTE

Certain liberties have been taken with the geography of Hertfordshire for the benefit of the story. Hopefully the residents of that beautiful county, home for many years, will be forgiving.

CONTENTS

Chapters 1 – 39

1

SUNDAY AUGUST 10th 1958

Frances Anderton let herself out of the Blainey house and took a deep lungful of the warm, summer air. She walked down the crazy-paved path, through the gate and out into the tree-lined street. It was early, not yet seven. Hopefully, she would be home before breakfast.

She walked briskly along the street, before turning into Glendale Road, an equally leafy thoroughfare. A milkman trundled by, milk bottles rattling in the crates stacked on his float, but apart from him there didn't seem to be anybody about. She crossed the road and took the small lane that led to Riverdale Avenue, a few streets away from her parents' house.

She was regretting the argument she'd had with her father the previous evening that led to her being sent away by her mother to stay with family friends. It was to keep her out of the way of her father's unpredictable temper – not that he'd ever hit her, but last night he had come very close to it. All because of that stupid dress, her desire to wear it, and his unreasonable demand that she should not.

It wasn't as if she was a child. She was fourteen, for heaven's sake. She should be allowed to dress how she liked, not be confined to the gymslips and ankle socks which, if her father had his way, would be all she was ever allowed to wear. She wouldn't, couldn't, stay his precious little girl forever. He should let her grow up. Her older sister hadn't had these problems, she was sure. Fiona was wearing what she chose, going out to parties, mixing with boys, and father didn't make *her* life miserable.

Along the road a young man was crouching down beside a gleaming, two-tone blue motor scooter. He appeared to be tinkering with the engine.

"Hello," the young man said as she walked past. "It's Frances, isn't it?"

She was taken aback for a moment. "Yes," she said, hesitantly. "How do you know who I am?" He was smartly dressed in a fawn jacket and cream slacks. His fair hair was short, neatly parted and combed, and he was very good looking. He was smiling at her, *at her*. She was not at all confident with boys, remaining very much in her sister's much more glamorous shadow. Suddenly she was very aware of the wire braces on her teeth, her freckled face, and her unruly shock of ginger hair.

"You're Fiona Anderton's sister, aren't you?"

"Are you a friend of Fiona?" she said.

"Yes, Fiona and I go back a long way. Derek Webster," he said, and stuck out a hand.

She shook the hand. "Very pleased to meet you," she said.

"Likewise, I'm sure. What do you think of the scooter?" he said. "I've only had it a few weeks."

"It's very…smart," she said.

"It's more than smart," he said. "It's a *Phoenix,* designed by the great Ernie Barratt, made with an all steel body and a 150cc engine. There're not many of these around."

She made a show of admiring the motor scooter, but not really sure what she was supposed to be admiring.

"Would you like a go?" he said.

"I…I don't know how."

He laughed. "Not to ride it," he said. "I'll take you for a spin, if you like, on the pillion."

She shook her head. "I'd better not," she said.

"Don't you trust me?" he said. "Don't you think I can ride it properly?"

"No," she said. "It's not that. I'm sure you ride very well."

"Then where's the harm?"

She glanced down at her *Timex* Alice in Wonderland wristwatch, and felt immediately embarrassed by the childish timepiece. She pulled down the sleeve of her blouse to hide it. "I don't want to be late for breakfast," she said.

"You worry too much," he said. "Your sister doesn't…" He let the sentence fade away.

"All right then," she said, rising to the unspoken challenge. "Take me for a ride on your wonderful *Phoenix*."

"Well done," he said. "Just hop on and hold onto my waist. I'll have you home in time for breakfast." He straddled the

2

machine and steadied it as she climbed aboard.

Once she had settled behind him on the pillion, and wrapped her arms around his waist, he kick-started the scooter and eased it forward off its stand. Moments later they were heading down the street.

"Not too fast," she called above the engine's noise.

"Just relax," he called back, "and when I lean into a bend, follow my lead and lean the same way."

Within minutes they had left the leafy streets behind and were heading into a part of town she didn't recognise. The neat houses with their tidy gardens were replaced by warehouses and factories guarded by yards of chain-link fencing.

"Where are we going?" she called.

"Away from traffic," he called back. "I want to show you what this beauty can do." He twisted the accelerator. The engine rose in pitch and she felt herself pushed back by the sudden turn of speed. She held onto his waist even tighter.

The scent of his hair oil was strong, almost overpowering, and she turned her face away from his neck to take a lungful of fresh air.

"I think I've had enough now."

He didn't answer. They had entered a long straight stretch of road and he increased their speed still further.

"I'd like to go home," she said, but her words were whipped away on the air buffeting her face.

Still he was ignoring her.

Seconds later they were leaving the chain-link behind and entering more streets with houses.

"I want to go back, now," she called.

Finally he acknowledged her. "Yes, of course." They were slowing down to a more sedate speed. "I just have to make a stop and then I'll take you straight home."

"Thank you," she said with relief.

He steered them along a tree-lined avenue and then took a left turn, into a drive belonging to a large Victorian house that stood alone from its neighbours, surrounded by high privet hedges. He drew up outside the house and switched off the engine.

"I just have a call to make,' he said, pulling the scooter up on its stand and dismounting.

"Should I come with you?" she said.

"No, you wait here. I'll only be a moment."

She watched him as he trotted up the steps to the front door of the house and inserted a key in the lock.

The door swung inwards and he disappeared inside.

She sat there on the pillion of the scooter and looked at her watch again. It had only been twenty minutes since he had offered her a ride, but to her it seemed much longer, and she was starting to wish she had never accepted his offer. She wanted to be at home, enjoying breakfast with her mother and sister, and building bridges with her father. Being a rebel didn't sit comfortably with her.

She glanced at her watch again and was just about to dismount to see how long he was going to be. She had one foot on the ground when she was grabbed roughly from behind and something, a rag or a pad that smelled sweet and sickly, was clamped tightly over her nose and mouth. She tried to cry out, but whoever had grabbed her was too strong, and she was hauled backwards off the scooter. She flailed her arms and kicked out with her sandaled feet, her foot connecting with the rear end of the scooter, gashing her toe.

She was trying to pull air into her lungs but the sickly sweet aroma was all she could smell, and it was making her head spin. Gradually, as several minutes passed, her struggles grew weaker and her strength ebbed away from her. As she was dragged back over the ground her feet kicked weakly, but her arms just hung uselessly at her sides. Consciousness was slipping away, and her eyes started to close, until all she could see was the green blur of the privet hedges, and the crisp blue of the sky above her. And then they closed completely, and she sunk down into darkness.

Webster walked from the house, unfolded the wad of crisp one-pound notes, slipping them into his wallet, then he straddled the scooter, eased it forward off its stand and kick-started it. Seconds later he was steering out of the drive and onto the street. At the gateway he paused and looked back at the house. The front door was now closed and the place had an empty, almost abandoned, feel about it. For a second a slight pang of guilt made him shiver, and then he felt the reassuring weight of the calfskin wallet in his pocket, and the thought of the money, so easily made, banished the guilt from his mind.

"Until the next time," he said softly, twisted the accelerator on the handlebar, and rode off to properly start his Sunday. He was hungry, and looking forward to his eggs and bacon breakfast. All this activity had given him an appetite.

As Derek Webster walked into the ABC café the smaller of the two youths waiting for him rose from the *Formica*-topped table and went across to the counter where a fat, balding, middle-aged man wearing a creased white shirt and scruffy grey trousers was dispensing tea into white enamel mugs from a large stainless steel pot. "Three teas," David Neville said.

"Wait your turn," the man behind the counter said and nodded towards the two people queuing

"Yes," Neville said. "Of course."

Webster walked the length of the café until he reached the table where the larger youth was sitting, pulled a chair out from under it and sat down. "All right. Pete?" he said.

Peter Lamb folded his face into something resembling a smile and nodded his head. "Davy's getting the tea," he said.

"I want more than just tea this morning," Webster said. "I've had a busy morning so far." He looked at the blackboard fixed to the wall at the back of the counter. A menu was written on the board in neat, precise capital letters. "I think I'll have a full-English breakfast."

Neville came back to the table, carrying a tray with three mugs. Tea slopped out of the mugs as he set it down on the table.

"Hey! Careful!" Webster said and picked up an enamel mug, wiping the drips of spilled tea on the edge of the black Bakelite tray.

"So?" Lamb said. "How did it go?"

"Like clockwork," Webster said. "Piece of cake." He picked up the glass dispenser from the table and poured a steady stream of white sugar into his mug.

"Was Gavin happy?"

"He seemed so," Webster said. "But you'd know better than I would on that score."

"What do you mean?" Lamb said, the smile sliding of his face, eyes flaring dangerously.

Neville watched the exchange with interest, "Well, you two are…" he said, but Lamb's hand shot out from beneath the table and gripped him around the throat, hauling him from his chair.

"We're what?" Lamb said, tightening his grip.

"Friends," Webster said hurriedly, watching as Neville's face turned a vivid crimson. "He meant you were friends, good mates, that's all. That's right, isn't it, Davy?"

Neville managed to nod his head. Lamb's fingers were digging into his throat, cutting off his air supply.

Lamb drew in a breath and released his grip. Neville collapsed back into his seat, his trembling fingers clawing at the top button of his shirt.

"When does he want us to get rid of her?" Lamb said, calm once again.

"He said he'd telephone," Webster said.

"It's your job," Lamb said.

Webster smiled. "I know," he said. "I know just the place to dump her."

Neville picked up his mug and took a noisy gulp. It hurt to swallow.

Lamb glared at him. "You get rid of the next one," he said to him. "So put your mind to it."

"I know, Pete. I know," Neville said, wiping tea from his lips with back of his hand.

"Good," Lamb said and turned to Webster. "Did he pay you?"

Webster smiled, took out his wallet and set it down on the grey *Formica* tabletop.

When Peter Lamb had first approached him and asked if he wanted to make some easy money, he had jumped at the chance. He'd had his eye on the *Phoenix 150* for some time, but financially the scooter was out of his reach. These little jobs he was doing for his old school friend Lamb and, by extension, Gavin Southland, gave him the security to put a down payment on the *Phoenix* and meet the weekly payments. He'd been reluctant at first to bring David Neville into the game but it was Lamb's suggestion, probably brought about by the fact that Neville had access to his father's car, and Gavin Southland that seemed to warm to him when he and Lamb had taken Neville round there to introduce him to the man. Webster guessed it was Neville's "pretty boy" looks that had impressed the older man.

Lamb was staring down at the wallet on the table. "Well?"

With an easy chuckle Webster picked up the wallet and flipped it open. "Same split as usual?" he said.

"Why shouldn't it be?" Lamb said.

Webster took out the wad of one-pound notes and started counting them into three equal piles. "Money for old rope this," he said.

"I told you it would be," Lamb said, scooping up his cut and jamming the notes into the pocket of his jeans.

Webster picked up his mug and raised it. "Here's to the next one. May they keep coming," he said.

Lamb and Neville touched mugs and joined him in the toast.

2

SUNDAY

The *Last Train to San Fernando* barrelled down the stairs carried on Johnny Duncan's nasal whine. Jack Callum sighed, laid down his newspaper and went out into the hall. Tennessee Ernie Ford had been bad enough last-year, singing about *Sixteen Tons* and what it could get you, but at least his rich bass/baritone voice was easier on the ear than this skiffle nonsense.

"Eric!" he called up the stairs. "Turn that racket down!"

"Oh, leave him alone, Jack." Annie, Jack's wife, came out from the kitchen, wiping her hands on a tea towel. "Weren't you ever fourteen?"

"Yes, Annie, I was, and I remember that I had a better taste in music."

"So *you* say," she said with a smile, and dabbed the end of his nose with a floury finger.

"Hey!"

"Dinner in ten minutes," she said.

"Something nice?"

"Roast pork with crackling and apple sauce."

"It smells delicious," he said. For the past hour the aromas floating out from the kitchen had been making his mouth water. Upstairs the volume was lowered slightly.

Jack went back to his armchair in the sitting room and picked up his newspaper. Spurs had lost again. The fixture was only a pre-season friendly against the Portuguese side, Benfica, and Terry Medwin had scored the Spurs' only goal – a real belter – but, nevertheless…. It was becoming a depressingly familiar result, and it didn't bode well for their season opener against Blackpool in a couple of week's time. He had followed Tottenham Hotspur football club since childhood. Growing up in North London's Edmonton district there hadn't really been an alternative for him. A few of his friends supported the Arsenal but he had always considered that to be treachery on an epic scale. Even when he moved from London and came up here to live and work in this part of rural Hertfordshire, his footballing heart and soul still resided at White Hart Lane. If he were a stick of rock he'd have Tottenham Hotspur written all the way through him.

The telephone in the hall started to ring and he glanced up at the clock on the mantle. It said ten to one. He was curious. Who would be phoning at this time on a Sunday afternoon?

"I've got it, Jack," Annie called, and the ringing stopped. A few moments later she stuck her head around the sitting room door. "It's for you. Sergeant Brewer."

"Andy? On a Sunday? What on earth does he want?"

"Well, you'll never find out sitting there with your head buried in the sports pages."

With a sigh, he climbed out of his armchair, blew a kiss at his wife's departing back, and went to take the call.

He picked up the receiver from the hallstand. "Andy," he said. "To what do I owe this dubious pleasure?" "I'm sorry to disturb your Sunday, sir," Desk Sergeant Andy Brewer said. "But you're going to have to come in. The balloon's gone up."

Jack raised his eyebrows. Brewer was a past master at exaggeration. "What colour?"

"Sorry, sir?"

"The balloon, Andy. What colour is it?"

"Oh, red, sir, definitely red. The Chief Super's on his way in as we speak, and *he* was in the middle of a golf tournament. Wasn't best pleased to be called in, I can tell you."

"Don't worry about it, Andy. You've probably saved him from his regular humiliation ritual on the links. He'll thank you for it one day."

"I doubt that, sir. So, shall I send a car?"

"Don't trouble I'll drive myself. It will give me time to brood about the Sunday dinner I'm missing."

"So, I'll tell them you're on your way?"

"Yes," Jack said. "You tell them that."

"Was it something nice, your dinner that is?"

"Pork, roast pork."

"Ah, I can't touch pork. Gives me the belly ache."

9

"Philistine," Jack said, and rang off.

He grabbed his coat from the rack and went out into the kitchen.

Annie saw the raincoat clenched in her husband's fist. "Oh, no, Jack. Not today. Not now."

"Sorry, Annie, they need me."

"Well, they certainly need something, but that something isn't you. How long are you going to be?"

"I can't say. I'll be back later."

"What's going on?" she said.

"I don't know. As my Sergeant so eloquently put it, *the balloon's gone up*."

"Andy Brewer always did have a way with words."

Jack looked across longingly at the shoulder of pork resting on the counter. The aroma was even more delicious in such close proximity to the joint. "Save me some," he said.

"Of course I will," Annie said. "But it won't be the same. The crackling will be leathery."

Jack winced. The crackling was his favourite part.

"I shed hot tears of pain at the promise of a gastronomic treat so badly thwarted," he said.

Annie threw the tea towel at him, "Get along with you. We have two children who will happily devour your share if you don't want it."

"Speaking of which, where *is* Rosie?"

"In her room. Mooning over a boy. She thinks she's in love," Annie said.

"Again? We've been down that road before."

Annie nodded. "I'm afraid so."

"It'll pass. It always does."

"Always?"

He crossed the kitchen and wrapped her in his arms, kissing her cheek. "There are exceptions to any rule."

"Stay safe," Annie said, and pecked at his lips.

"Cross my heart," he said, and went outside.

He unlocked the car and sat behind the wheel. He'd had the series three Morris Oxford for a little over a month now and had been telling himself he would take Annie and the kids out for a spin. A picnic perhaps – sandwiches, sausage rolls and hard-boiled eggs, all washed down with hot sweet tea from his *Thermos* flask. So far he hadn't managed it. Something always came up. He'd left London and taken this posting in the hope it would give him more time to spend with his family. Fat chance. Agreed, the crimes here tended not to be so violent and potentially dangerous to investigate, but there were just as many of them. There were as many criminals out here in the sticks as in town, but they tended to be better behaved.

It took him ten minutes to drive to the station and he parked in the car park next to Chief Superintendent Lane's gleaming, ivory-coloured, Rover. There was another, unfamiliar, car parked next to the Rover – a Bentley Continental. "Now, there's a car I'd like," he mused. "But I probably wouldn't get the chance to enjoy it," he added ruefully.

"Sorry about this, sir," Andy Brewer said as Jack pushed in through the station door.

"Not your fault, Andy," Jack said. "Where's the party?"

"In your office, sir," Brewer said. "Chief Superintendent Lane stormed in and seconded it."

"Bloody cheek," Jack said. "What's wrong with his own office?"

"The decorators arrived yesterday to spruce it up. It's all dustsheets and emulsion paint in there. *Taupe*, I ask you."

"What the hell's taupe?" Jack said.

"It's the colour he's having – a sort of brownish grey, or is it greyish brown? I'm not sure."

"Why can't he have sludge green like the rest of us?" Jack said.

"Because he's the chief super," Brewer said.

Jack shook his head in mock despair and made his way up the stairs to his office on the first floor. It wasn't much – a desk, a couple of chairs, a filing cabinet and a hat stand – but it was his, and he'd worked long hours to get it. To have it taken over without a by your leave rankled.

"Ah, Callum, good of you to come in at such short notice," Lane said. He was a large, balding man with a ruddy complexion and a paunch, barely concealed by his neatly pressed uniform.

There was another middle-aged man in the room with the chief superintendent who looked vaguely familiar. Lane turned to him. "Warren, this is the officer I was telling you about. Detective Chief Inspector Jack Callum, one of my finest. Jack, Warren is a close, personal friend of mine."

The man, Warren, was a tall, athletic-looking man with sallow skin and a dyspeptic demeanour. He took a step forward and stuck out his hand. "Warren Anderton," he said.

"Warren's the managing director of Anderton Plastics," Lane said. "But you knew that, of course."

"Of course," Jack lied.

Anderton sat down at the desk next to Lane. "So you'll help me?" he said.

Jack remained standing. "Yes, of course, if you tell me what it is you need help with."

Anderton's face crumpled and he dabbed at his eyes with a handkerchief. "Fourteen! She's only fourteen."

Jack shot Lane a questioning look.

"Mr. Anderton's daughter seems to have gone missing," Lane said. "She went to stay with some friends last night and didn't come home this morning."

"Is it usual for your daughter to stay overnight with friends?" Jack said. He certainly wouldn't let Rose stay out all night, Saturday or not, and Rosie was two years older than this girl.

"They're very good friends of both my wife and myself," Anderton said, and then bridled. "What are you implying, Chief Inspector? That I let my daughter run wild?"

"No, nothing of the sort, sir."

Lane laid a hand on Anderton's arm. "Calm yourself, Warren. I know Inspector Callum didn't mean anything by it."

"She's a good girl, my Frances. She doesn't misbehave."

Jack doubted that. Frances Anderton was a fourteen-year-old girl. All fourteen-year-old girls misbehaved to some degree or another. They're genetically predisposed to cause their fathers as much anxiety and heartache as possible. He was sure he'd seen that written somewhere.

"Do you have a photograph of her, sir?" he said.

Anderton reached into the pocket of his jacket, took out an 8x6 inch colour photograph, and smoothed it out on the desk in front of him.

"That's her. That's my Frances."

Jack picked it up and studied it. Frances Anderton was a fairly plain, freckled-faced girl with a shock of curly ginger hair and wire braces on her teeth. She was smiling in the photograph, a smile of youthful innocence. Perhaps Anderton was right. He could not imagine a girl with those angelic features causing any father grief.

"When did you last see her, sir?"

"When I dropped her off at Pam and Richard's last night."

"Pam and Richard?"

"Pam and Richard Blainey. Richard's my Finance Director and Jessica, my wife, has known Pam for years. They went to school together. St Theresa's convent school."

"And you say she didn't return home this morning. What do Mr. and Mrs. Blainey have to say about it?"

"Frances told them she'd walk home by herself. It's only half a mile."

"Is that something she normally does?" Jack said.

Anderton looked at him blankly.

Jack tried again. "Does she usually walk home, by herself, when she visits the Blainey's?"

Anderton shook his head. "I can't really say. You'd have to ask my wife. She'd know."

"Yes," Jack said. "I'll do that. Is your wife at home at the moment?"

"Where else would she be?" Anderton snapped. "She stayed behind in case Frances shows up."

Jack nodded. "Yes, of course. Very wise."

"So what are you going to do to find her?" Anderton said.

Jack took a breath. "Does your daughter have any friends she might have gone to see on the way home?"

Another blank look from Anderton.

"Yes, I see. I'll ask your wife," Jack said. "Perhaps I should go and see Mrs. Anderton now."

"If you think that's appropriate, Chief Inspector," Lane said.

"It's hardly *inappropriate*, sir," Jack said. "It would seem that Mrs. Anderton has most of the answers to my questions."

Anderton bridled again at Jack's implied criticism and opened his mouth to say something.

"I'd like to interview the Blaineys as well," Jack said before the man could speak. "Perhaps I can do that once I've spoken to your wife?"

"Very well," Anderton said. "I'll telephone them and tell them to expect you."

"If you would, sir. That would be very helpful."

"Give Eddie Fuller a ring, Andy, and tell him I'll pick him up outside his house in twenty minutes," Jack said when he went back downstairs.

Brewer winced. "He won't thank you for that, sir," he said. "He was on a promise last night – Judy, the barmaid from the *Dog and Duck*. He's been trying to ring her bell for weeks."

"My heart bleeds," Jack said. "And tell him to shave. We're interviewing a managing director's wife. We can't turn up there with him looking like he's been up all night – even if he has."

Detective Sergeant Eddie Fuller climbed into Jack's car and a cloud of heavy scent wafted in after him. "Ye gods, Eddie, you smell like a tart's boudoir," Jack said as Fuller settled in beside him.

"I was told to shave before meeting you, sir," Fuller said. "It's just my aftershave, that's all."

"Have you got shares in the company, or do you buy it by the gallon?" Jack said. "Jesus Christ, it smells like you've bathed in it. Open a window."

"What's the S.P.?" Fuller said as he wound down the window.

"A child's gone missing, and the chief super wants us on the case."

"What makes this one so special? I thought you had the weekend off."

"I did," Jack said. "I'm giving up a perfectly good shoulder of pork to be here, and Chief Superintendent Lane gave up his golf tournament. It's a missing child, and not just any ordinary missing child. This is one Frances Anderton, the fourteen year old daughter of Warren Anderton, managing director of Anderton Plastics, and a personal friend of the chief super."

Fuller lit a cigarette and flicked the match out through the open window. "I figured it had to be something a bit unusual when Andy told me he'd had to call Lane in from the links. What do we know about her?"

"Not a lot, but then neither does her father, which is why we're paying Mrs. Anderton a visit. We'll see if she knows her daughter any better than he does."

"Nice car," Fuller said as they picked up speed. "Is it new?"

"New to me," Jack said. "Bought it from a friend of a friend with 20,000 miles on the clock."

"I won't ask you what you paid for it."

"I wouldn't tell you if you did," Jack said. He took out a scrap of paper from his pocket and handed it to Fuller. "That's the address."

Fuller opened a street map and spread it out on his knees. After a couple of wrong turns they found themselves in a wide, tree-lined street with large, well-to-do houses on each side.

"Plastics you say?" Fuller said as he watched the salubrious houses pass by. "Christ, I'm in the wrong game. There it is. Number seventeen. The one with the gates."

3

SUNDAY

The door was opened at the first ring by a rather beautiful young woman, dressed in a conservative grey suit, her blonde hair neatly secured in a French pleat. She stood in the doorway and stared at the two men with ill-concealed contempt.

Jack took out his warrant card and showed it to her. "Chief Inspector Callum. This is Sergeant Fuller. I think Mrs. Anderton is expecting us."

The young woman stood aside. "Come in and wait here."

She was well spoken and assured, and she left them standing in the large hallway, disappearing into one of the adjoining rooms. A few moments later she re-emerged. "Mother will see you in the morning room. This way."

"Why do I get the feeling I should be tugging my forelock?" Fuller said quietly as he followed Jack across the deeply carpeted hallway. "I bet you're glad I wore the aftershave now. Bound to impress the ladies."

"If you say so."

The woman who stood to greet them was an elder version of the young woman who had met them at the door. She stepped forward, extending a neatly manicured hand dripping with expensive-looking rings. "Jessica Anderton," she said. "You've met my eldest daughter, Fiona?"

Jack nodded. "Callum," he said. "Chief Inspector. I have a few questions, if you don't mind."

"If it means the safe return of Frances then I don't mind at all." She went back to an elegant burgundy chesterfield and sat, crossing her ankles demurely.

"Has anyone been in touch with you regarding your daughter?"

She shook her head, gasped and put her hand to her mouth. "You don't think someone might have taken her?"

Jack raised his hands. "No, no. Let's not get ahead of ourselves here. These are just the type of questions I have to ask."

Jessica made a visible effort to calm herself, taking a few deep breaths and exhaling through her nose.

Jack let her settle for a moment before he spoke again. "I'm interested to know if Frances has ever done anything like this before," Jack said.

Jessica shook her head again. "No. This is totally out of character."

"Frances is a swot," Fiona Anderton said as she crossed the room and sat down beside her mother.

"Fiona! She's not a swot, just studious. She appreciates the value of a good education, that's all."

"Meaning that I didn't?" Fiona said.

"Meaning that she won't be able to rely on her looks to ease her way through life."

The tension between the two women was crackling. Fuller stared down at the floor. Jack pressed on.

"Are there any friends Frances might have visited on her way home from the Blaineys?"

Again Fiona answered. "She doesn't have friends."

"Mrs. Anderton?" Jack persisted.

Jessica shook her head. "We only moved here a year ago, when Warren was made MD. Frances hasn't had a chance yet to pursue any meaningful friendships."

"It hasn't stopped *me*," Fiona said.

"Frances isn't like you, Fiona. You're five years older than her. She's still a child," Jessica said. "Unlike you, she doesn't find it easy to…" She let the sentence die. "Frances is a shy girl, Inspector. It's why I was so happy when she was invited to stay with the Blaineys. They have a daughter a similar age to Frances. They go to the same school and study together."

"Sarah Blainey's a little swot too," Fiona said. "They're like two peas in a pod."

"Have *you* any idea what might have happened to your sister, Miss Anderton?" Jack said.

"Have you tried the library?"

"It's Sunday," Jack said. "Libraries don't open on Sundays."

"Really?" Fiona said in a bored voice.

"If you don't mind me saying, Miss Anderton, you don't appear to be very concerned by your sister's disappearance."

Fiona looked at him steadily. "I just don't think it's high drama." She turned to her mother, "I mean, involving the police. I really don't know what Daddy was thinking."

"Your father's worried about her, Fiona."

"He's never worried about me like that," Fiona said. "But his precious Frances, his baby, goes missing for a few hours and he's calling in the cavalry."

Jessica threw up her hands. "Oh, Fiona, you're impossible. Your father cares for you both equally. He doesn't favour…"

The doorbell rang.

"That will be Pam and Richard," Jessica said. "They knew you wanted to see them so they said they'd come over."

She stood up from the couch and went to answer the door.

Fiona busied herself screwing a Dunhill cigarette into a long ivory holder. "Do either of you have a light?"

Fuller produced a silver lighter from his pocket and offered her the flame. Fiona took his hand and guided the lighter towards the end of her cigarette, sucking in the smoke and blowing it out in a thin stream.

"I take it you don't get on with your sister," Jack said.

"We get on," Fiona said. "I just don't like a fuss, that's all. Frances lives in her own little world. She's probably gone to the park or something and lost track of the time. You'll find her somewhere, I'm sure, her nose buried in a book."

"Your parents seem very worried."

"Fiona! I told you before about smoking in the house. If you're going to use those filthy things at least have the good grace to do so in the garden." Jessica Anderton came back into the morning room flanked by another couple. "Chief Inspector, this is Richard and Pamela Blainey."

As Jack shook hands with the Blaineys, Fiona got to her feet and walked huffily to the French doors, throwing them open and stepping out into the garden.

Jack turned to Fuller. "Smoke them if you've got them, Sergeant."

"What? Oh, yes. Miss Anderton, do you mind if I join you?"

18

Fuller said, and followed her into the garden.

"These young people," Jack said to the others. "Money to burn."

"So, Chief Inspector," Richard Blainey said. "Have you had any news yet?"

"You have a daughter I understand," Jack said, ignoring the question.

"Sarah, yes."

"And Frances didn't happen to mention to her where she was going when she left your house?"

"No. As far as we were all concerned, Frances was coming straight home."

"Did she seem bothered about anything at all?"

"Not to me," he said. "Pam? Do you think Frances had anything on her mind?"

Pamela Blainey was in her mid-forties, a small mousey woman with tightly permed hair and pale skin. "She didn't seem to have a care in the world. Besides, if Frances had something on her mind, I'm sure Jessica would have told me. That's right, Jessica, isn't it?"

"Of course, Pam." She turned to Jack. "Chief Inspector Callum, I'm not sure where you are going with this line of questioning, but I feel you're on the wrong track. You seem to be implying that my daughter may have run away because she was worried, or troubled by something. I can assure you, that simply isn't the case. Frances is a happy child. She works hard for the marks she gets at school, but that's *her* choice. My husband and I don't put her under any pressure. There's no imperative to achieve in this house. We feel our children should be free to enjoy their childhood."

"Commendable," Jack said. Having met Fiona he doubted there was much in the way of parental control of any kind in the Anderton household.

"Is there anywhere she likes to go, perhaps to spend some time alone?"

"Apart from the library, and the church, no," Jessica said.

"What church would that be?"

"St Stephen's. It's on the Helton road. My husband and I

19

attend whenever we can."

"You go there as a family?"

"As I say, whenever we can, though sometimes it isn't easy to find the time."

"Mr. Anderton is a very busy man," Blainey said, "as I'm sure you can imagine, what with his business duties. Running a company is no easy feat. There's not a great deal of free time available to him."

"So, Frances sometimes goes there alone?"

"Sometimes, but I phoned Reverend Foster at St Stephens to see if she was there, but he hasn't seen her since last Sunday."

"Well," Jack said. "I don't think I have any more questions for the moment. Unless you can think of anything else that may be relevant."

Jessica shook her head and Blainey shrugged.

"Well, there is this," Pamela said. "But I'm not sure it has anything to do with Frances." She was delving into her handbag and produced a small blue envelope.

"What's that?" Blainey said to his wife.

"I found it, propped up against the door when I brought the milk in this morning."

"And you didn't think to mention it?" Blainey said.

Pamela shook her head. "I was busy getting breakfast so I just popped it into my handbag. I thought it was probably a note from the milkman. Of course, then we got the call to say Frances hadn't made it home and it just went out of my mind."

"May I see? Jack said, holding out his hand to take the envelope from her.

She handed it to him and he held it by the edges. He took a pen from his pocket and slipped it under the flap, peeling it back. Inside was a folded sheet of paper, the same blue as the envelope. Carefully, without smudging any latent fingerprints, he unfolded the paper and looked at it.

It looked like a child's drawing, nothing more. Three small figures, in the middle of the page, drawn in what looked like green ink.

"What are they? The three bears?" Blainey said. He was peering at the picture over Jack's shoulder.

"I don't think they're bears," Jack said.

"What then?"

"I think they look more like monkeys. I'm afraid I'll need to take this back to the station with me," he said to Pamela Blainey. "I'll get my people to take a closer look at it."

"Do you think it has something to do with Frances going missing?" Jessica said.

"Too early to say," Jack said, folding the letter away and slipping it into his pocket. "Of course, if it leads us anywhere, you'll be the first to know. I'll send an officer round to take your fingerprints is that's okay. For elimination purposes only."

"Did you enjoy your cigarette?" Jack said when they got back in the car.

"Now there's a girl with a huge chip on her shoulder."

"Yeah, I thought as much. It's why I wanted you out there in the garden with her. I thought she'd be more likely to open up to you, you being more her age."

"Closer in age but not in social standing," Fuller said. "It was as much as I could do to get her to talk to me at all."

"What did you learn?"

"That she has no respect for her parents, and thinks it's a huge joke that her father was made managing director – she says that if he runs the company the way he runs his household they'll be bankrupt within a year. She refers to her mother as a doormat, and doesn't like her sister very much."

"A productive chat then," he said.

"Oh, once she started talking she wouldn't stop," Fuller said. "All she did was spew out vitriol and bile, directed at her nearest and dearest, and I'm not really sure what they've done to deserve it.

"Spoilt little rich girl," Jack said.

"I was about to say rich bitch," Fuller said.

"Steady."

"I'm sorry, sir, but girls of that type make my blood boil. They have it all laid out for them on a plate and then all they can do is to complain about how hard their spoilt little lives are. Oh, she has a boyfriend by the way."

"Is that significant?"

"Only insofar that mummy and daddy don't know and wouldn't approve of him if they did."

"Sounds like a minor rebellion to me. Does he have a name, this boyfriend?"

"Adam, but that's all. No last name."

"Not very helpful," Jack said. "Does she have any idea what might have happened to her sister?"

"She thinks she might have run away. It seems her visit to the Blaineys wasn't all it seems. There were major ructions in the house yesterday concerning Frances and her father. Jessica Anderton sent her to stay with the Blaineys until things calmed down. Apparently it's not the first time it's happened."

"Any idea what the row was about?"

Fuller shrugged. "Your guess is as good as mine, sir. But if Fiona is to be believed, not everything in the Anderton household is as perfect as Warren Anderton and his wife like to present."

"Ah well, food for thought. Good work, Sergeant. I'll even forgive you the aftershave…just this once."

He drove them back to the station, dropping off Fuller on the way, left the envelope and drawing with one of the boffins in the forensic department, and went home. There was little more he could do today. He'd pick up the investigation tomorrow once he had his full squad assembled

It was just after six as he walked into the kitchen. A large saucepan of water was simmering slowly on the cooker, his Sunday dinner on top, caught between two plates, steaming away all its flavour. It wasn't the first ruined meal he'd had, and he was pretty sure it wouldn't be his last.

"Go and wash your hands, Jack," Annie said. "I'll serve up. I've kept it warm as best I can."

He pecked her on the cheek. "I'm sure it will be delicious," he said as he walked from the kitchen.

"It won't be," she called after him.

She was right. The crackling was like chewing old cowhide.

Later that evening, when the kids had gone to bed, he told her about his day.

"Do you think she'll turn up?"

"I think she might. Everything I've learned so far leads me to think that Frances Anderton has run away from an unhappy home life."

"Poor Mrs. Anderton, she must be going through hell, her daughter going missing like that."

Jack nodded as he sipped his cocoa. He knew from bitter experience what Jessica Anderton was going through and it was something he wouldn't wish on his worst enemy. "Early night?" he said to Annie.

"How can I refuse?" she said.

4

MONDAY AUGUST 11th 1958

Police Constable Alistair Kirby buttoned up his uniform and looked at himself in the mirror. The uniform had just been cleaned and pressed. The trouser creases were knife-sharp, and the trouser cuffs hung the requisite half an inch above boots that were polished and buffed to a mirror finish. Satisfied with his reflection he brushed a small piece of lint from the sleeve of his tunic, adjusted the black fabric belt around his waist and took the leather dog lead from the hook on the back of the door.

Walking from the dressing room he snapped an order, "*Satan, come!*" From out in the hallway came a low bark, and a large, black Alsatian emerged from the shadows.

Kirby dropped his hand and let the dog nuzzle it with its snout. "Good boy," Kirby murmured, and clipped the lead to the dog's collar. "Heel!" he snapped again, and the dog dutifully fell into step beside him as he walked from the house.

The morning air was fresh, with a slight autumnal feel, even though it was still early August, and Kirby breathed in deeply, filling his lungs. It was a new day and a new adventure. Patrolling his beat had become as much second nature to him now as eating and breathing.

With his ramrod straight back and impeccably smart uniform, Alistair Kirby was a well-recognised and formidable figure in the town. Ordinary civilians rarely approached him and his dog, and the local tearaways and ne'er-do-wells actively avoided him. "Copper" Kirby was as much a legend on these streets as Regimental Sergeant Major Kirby had been on the parade grounds of the many army bases he'd been seconded to during his illustrious career with the Royal Fusiliers, and that was how he liked it. He'd joined the police force for that very reason. Twenty-five years of military service had left him ill-equipped to deal with civilian life. The police force gave his life order and purpose. He had never pursued a higher rank in the force. Being a "beat bobby" was a more than adequate occupation, and feeling the collar of a local villain, or arresting someone for being drunk and disorderly, was all the job satisfaction he needed.

He turned left into the park to follow his beat, along the path leading down to the small circular lake, around the lake to the tennis courts and past the pavilion where they sold ice creams and soft drinks, and across the cricket pitch. Then down into the small woodland area where he could pause to let *Satan* do his business, and back up to the play area that, during the summer months, was alive with children, riding see-saws, spinning on the roundabout, or propelling themselves skywards on the wooden swings that hung from stout steel chains. Or simply sailing their model boats on the boating lake and splashing through the calf deep water of the paddling pool.

He'd noticed that when children were playing here, a certain hush fell over the playground until he had passed by, which gratified him. Respect, it was all about respect, and leaving the army had done nothing to diminish that, as he'd feared it might. Respect was a byword for his life-blood and he couldn't exist without it.

He took the leaf-strewn path that led into the small wood and unclipped the lead from the dog's collar. The Alsatian remained at his side until he gave the order, and then it bounded off into the trees. Kirby removed his peaked cap and ran a hand through his severe crew cut, counting the seconds before he could call the dog back to him. He had undertaken much of *Satan's* training himself, filling in the gaps left by the instructors at the training school. They could train any Alsatian to become a police dog and to respond to a pre-set number of commands, but no training school in the world could make a dog truly his. That was a task that took countless hours, building a rapport with the animal and forming a bond that was unbreakable. He felt he had achieved that with *Satan*, moulding the animal into something more than just a police dog, more an extension of himself.

He checked his wristwatch, watching the second hand sweep past the time he'd allotted for *Satan* to do his business, and stared out through the trees. He replaced the cap on his head and called, "*Satan?*"

The second hand made another revolution and he struck out in search of his dog. "*Satan*?" he called again as he stomped over bracken and crushed brambles beneath his boots. An answering bark sounded in the distance. "Come, boy," he called, but there was no sound of the animal crashing through the undergrowth towards him, only another distant bark.

Kirby pushed through a large expanse of dense rhododendron that blocked his path, and heard the dog bark yet again, closer this time. He was coming up to a point where woodland thinned out into scrubland on the perimeter of the park. It was then he saw the Alsatian. The dog was standing over what looked like a pile of rags as if on guard, turning its head left and right as it strained to see and hear its master approaching.

"What is it, boy?" Kirby said as he drew close. "What have you got there?" And then he saw the mud-streaked mop of orange hair and the half-naked body of a girl. "Oh, good grief," he said quietly. "*Satan* stay!" he ordered the dog, and then turned and started to run, retracing his steps, back to the park gates and the emergency police box that stood just outside of them.

Detective Sergeant Eddie Fuller rang the doorbell of the large semi-detached house on Rupert Street and checked his watch. He was running early this morning and there was every chance the governor would not be ready.

Annie Callum opened the door and greeted him with a bright, "Good morning, Eddie. Jack's not come down yet. Come through. We're in the kitchen."

Fuller followed her through the house to the kitchen at the back.

"Morning, Eric, morning, Rosie,' he said to the Callum children as he entered the sun-filled room. The kitchen overlooked Jack Callum's beautifully kept garden. Dahlias rubbed shoulders with chrysanthemums, whilst tall spikes of hollyhocks jutted up from the soil in a rainbow of colour.

"The garden's looking lovely, Mrs. C," Fuller said.

"Jack's work, not mine," she said. "I look after the weeding and dead heading, nothing more. Take a seat, Eddie. Toast?"

"Don't mind if I do," Fuller said, and took his place at the table between Eric and Rosie. "Have you been on your paper round yet, Eric?"

"Long since," Eric said, and spooned some more cornflakes into his mouth. "Two rounds today," he added.

"Are you saving up for something?"

Eric nodded and swallowed. "Dad said that I can have a guitar if I buy it myself."

"Do you play?" Fuller said.

"I want to learn."

"What kind of music do you like?"

"Lonnie Donegan. Skiffle."

"I like him," Fuller said.

"Have you heard his new record?"

"I've got it."

"Really?

"I play it all the time. I think it probably drives my landlady crazy," Fuller said. He lived in one room above the greengrocer's in town. It wasn't much, but with the shared bathroom and kitchen it was enough for him at the moment.

"What kind of guitar do you hope to buy?" he said.

"A cheap one. I've saved just over a pound," Eric said.

"If you save another ten shillings, you can buy my one from me," he said. "It's not an expensive one like Lonnie plays, but it's nice. It's a Hofner. Twin f holes, single cutaway, low action. It plays like a dream."

"And you'd let me buy it from you?"

"I don't see why not. But I want thirty shillings for it, not a penny less," Fuller said.

"Eddie," Annie said. "That really isn't necessary. Eric can buy one down the market when he has enough money."

"It would be my pleasure, Mrs. C. I've been meaning to sell it on for some time now. I'm afraid my skiffle days are long behind me. If I sell it to Eric here, at least I'll know it's going to a good home and, besides, it would be nice to know I'm fostering new musical talent."

"Some hope." For the first time, Rosie added her voice to the conversation. "He doesn't know how to play."

27

. "Well, I can show him the three basic chords. After that I'm sure he'll pick it up as he goes along."

"Did you ever play in a group?" Eric said. "For a while. There used to be a skiffle club in a room above the *Dog and Duck* in town. I used to play there once a week." Fuller smiled at the memory.

"And you'd teach me?" Eric said, his eyes wide with excitement.

"Yes. Why not?"

At the cooker, Annie filled the toast rack and took it across to the table. "There's honey, jam or golden syrup. *Marmite* or *Bovril* if you'd prefer something savoury," she said.

"Just butter is fine for me," Fuller said.

Jack smoothed shaving soap over the lower part of his face and then scraped off the lather and stubble with his new safety razor. The razor had yet to convince him that it was a worthy successor to the straight blade he usually favoured, but it was a birthday present from Annie so, in deference to her, he persevered. From downstairs he heard the telephone ring followed by the sound of someone running up the stairs.

"Dad," Rosie called through the bathroom door. "It's for you. Work."

With a silent curse he wiped the remaining foam from his face with a towel and went to see who was disrupting his normally sacrosanct morning routine.

"Callum," he said, and listened carefully, scribbling notes on a pad by the phone as he went along. He rang off and went out to the kitchen. Eric and Rosie were both eating from bowls of cereal, Annie was at the cooker and Fuller was pushing the last corner of toast into his mouth.

"Dad, Eddie said I can buy his guitar for thirty shillings," Eric said excitedly as Jack walked into the kitchen. "And he's going to show me how to play some chords."

"That's nice," Jack said. "And is he going to put you up at his place while you're learning to caterwaul? Good morning, Sergeant, I didn't hear you arrive. That was the station on the phone. They've found a body."

At the cooker Annie gasped and put a hand to her mouth. "Oh no, Jack. Not that poor girl."

"It looks like it might be," Jack said, and pulled the last slice of toast from the rack, spreading it liberally with butter.

"We'd better head in then," Fuller said.

"If the girl's dead then she won't be any less so in the time it takes me to eat a slice of toast and drink a cup of tea."

"Fair point, I suppose," Fuller said.

Annie came across to the table and picked up the teapot. "A top up, Eddie?" she said as she poured the steaming liquid into their cups.

"Don't mind if I do," Fuller said. "That's if you have no objections, sir."

"No, go ahead," Jack said and took a bite out of his slice of toast.

"Did they say how the poor girl was killed?" Annie said.

Jack shook his head. "No. They just said the circumstances were unusual."

"What does that mean?" Fuller said.

"You know as much as I do, Sergeant." Jack said. "I suppose we won't know for certain until we get to the station."

Outside, in Fuller's car Jack said, "I got it wrong, Eddie," Jack said. "Yesterday I believed it was just a child running away from a dysfunctional family, and now this."

Fuller glanced around at his boss. Jack Callum's face was a mask of despair and his hands were shaking slightly. He'd never seen his DCI this upset before.

"I wasn't being coy in there, Eddie, but what they told me does not make for good conversation over the breakfast table." He shook his head. "So wrong."

"You mustn't blame yourself, Jack. I thought the same as you." Fuller said as he started the car and pulled away from the kerb. "So was it bad?"

"They found her half naked body in the park," Jack said. "Her mouth had been sewn shut, as were her eyes, and something that appears to be candle wax was poured into her ears."

"Bloody hell," Fuller said. "I can see why you didn't want to talk about that stuff in front of your wife and kids."

"Indeed," Jack said.

"There are some sick people out there," Fuller said.

"Yes there are," Jack agreed. "Unfortunately it falls to the likes of you and me to see that they're put away for a very long time."

"A policeman's lot…"

"Is not a happy one," Jack said. "Not a happy one at all. We'd better head straight to the park. They won't be moving the body until the doctor's signed it off."

"Right you are," Fuller said, and indicated a left turn.

They pulled in through the park gates. An ambulance was there already and a couple of ambulance men were preparing a stretcher. Also there, standing just inside the gates was PC Alistair Kirby. He approached the car as they climbed out and saluted.

"I found the body, sir," he said to Jack. "Or rather *Satan* here did." He cast a fond look down at the ferocious looking Alsatian that sat obediently at his heel. "I'll take you down there," he said. "This way."

Kirby set off at marching pace and the two detectives had to trot to keep up with him.

5

MONDAY

"Help me out here, Sergeant," Jack said as he stared down at the mutilated body of Frances Anderton. "What kind of person can do this to a child?"

Fuller didn't answer.

"A monster, sir. Pure and simple," Alistair Kirby said. He was standing a respectful distance from the crime scene, watching four CID officers scour the area for clues, but he was listening to all that was going on around him.

Jack turned to him. "Have you experienced anything like this before, Constable?"

Kirby shook his head. "I was on the Western Front during the war, and saw many atrocities, but no, sir, nothing like this."

"If it's any consolation." Doctor Barry Fenwick was still crouched over the body. "The damage to the eyes and the mouth occurred post mortem. Judging from the lack of blood I'd say that her eyes and mouth were sewn shut after she was killed. As for the paraffin wax poured into the ears I can't say whether that was done post or anti mortem."

"Any idea how she was killed?" Jack said.

"Strangulation. There's a ligature mark on her throat. Thin twine or cord, I'd say. Of course, we'll know more when we get her back to the mortuary."

"Any idea who's performing the post mortem?"

"I would guess Hepton," Fenwick said.

"Maurice Hepton?" Jack said.

"*Sir* Maurice Hepton. He was knighted in the birthday honours."

"Really? I had no idea."

"Well, if you cross his path make sure you remember to call him *Sir Maurice*. One of my colleagues forgot and received a fierce tongue lashing for his pains."

"Should I bow as well?" Jack said.

"It wouldn't do any harm," Fenwick said with a smile. "But

31

seriously, Hepton's a damned fine pathologist, up there with Sir Bernard Spilsbury and Keith Simpson."

"Simpson hasn't been knighted," Jack said.

"It's not what you know," Fenwick said. "It's who. I hear Hepton's wife plays bridge with various minor Royals, and Violet Hepton is a force to be reckoned with, by all accounts."

"Barry, your depth of knowledge about such patent rubbish never ceases to astound. Any idea on the time of death?"

Fenwick returned his attention to Frances Anderton's body. "From the temperature of the body I would estimate time of death to be somewhere between nine am to one pm yesterday. Can't be more precise, I'm afraid. Establishing time of death can be awfully tricky."

"But if you're right, Barry," Jack said. "Frances Anderton was killed before we even started looking for her." He turned to Kirby. "And this is how you found her, Constable?"

"Yes, sir."

"Then I'm surprised no one found her before you did, out in the open like this."

"That part of the park was closed off yesterday, sir," Kirby said.

"And why was that?"

"Routine maintenance of the rides in the playground, sir. Can't have the kiddies playing here when that's going on."

Jack thought for a moment. "So you have a group of workers performing maintenance on the slides and seesaws, and someone dumps a girl's body a hundred yards away, and no one sees anything." He turned to Fuller. "Get onto the council. I want a list of names and addresses of all those who were working here yesterday."

"Very good, sir."

Back at the station he found Chief Superintendent Lane still camped in his office.

"Have you given Anderton the news?"

Lane nodded grimly.

"How did he take it?"

"Not well. Not well at all. They've taken her body to North

Herts Hospital. Sir Maurice Hepton will perform the post mortem. Anderton will have to go along to make a formal identification once Hepton's finished his work. Eyes sewn shut." He shuddered.

"And lips, with candle wax poured into her ears," Jack said.

"But why?" Lane was wringing his hands.

"See no evil, hear no evil, speak no evil," Jack said. "It ties in with the sketch left on the Blainey's doorstep this morning."

"Sketch?"

"The lab boys have it now," Jack said. "I think it's a picture of three monkeys. See no evil, hear no evil, speak no evil. The sketch didn't make any kind of sense until I saw Frances Anderton's body. Now it does."

"So you think whoever committed this awful crime is sending a message of some kind?"

"It would appear so, sir."

Lane shuddered again. "Sometimes, Jack, I wonder what kind of sick and twisted world we're living in."

"I'm afraid the Japanese tore the blinkers from my eyes when I was stationed in Burma. Up until that point I didn't believe that someone could treat their fellow man with such cruelty, all in the name of an evil and perverse philosophy."

Lane picked up a pen from the desk, tapped it against his teeth. "Do you think this could be somehow connected to Warren's firm? I hear he's a tough man to do business with. A disgruntled customer or supplier?"

"It's something I'll be considering," Jack said. "All we can hope is that this crime was a one off, and not the start of something more sinister."

"What are you suggesting?" Lane said.

"This has all the hallmarks of a ritual killing."

"But you have no evidence to support that."

"The mutilation of the body and the sketch of the three monkeys left at the house. That's your evidence," Jack said.

"But all we have is one murdered girl."

"So far," Jack said. "Let's just hope it stays that way," he said, but in his gut he feared the worst.

"Why do you think the sketch was left on Blainey's doorstep

and not at the Anderton's?" Lane said.

"Yes, that's been bothering me too, and I don't have an answer for you. It could be a simple case of practicality. There's no easy access to the Anderton's house. It has a high wall and iron gates guard the entrance. No easy feat for our killer to sneak in there and leave a letter on the doorstep. From what I understand the Blainey's home is open to the street."

"And you think Frances Anderton was the intended target and not the Blainey girl?"

"I'm not deciding anything yet, sir. It's too soon to tell. Once the investigation is seriously underway, we might get a clearer picture."

"We have to find this monster, Jack, and find him soon," Lane said.

"I couldn't agree more, sir. Couldn't agree more."

He excused himself and found Fuller at his desk. "How's that list coming?"

Fuller looked up. "Six names, six addresses. The council were most forthcoming."

"Good," Jack said. "Take DC Grant and go and check them out. See if any of them saw anything yesterday morning."

"Okay," Fuller said, and called across to Detective Constable Harry Grant who was carrying a cup of tea back to his desk. "Harry, get your skates on, you're coming with me."

Grant took a mouthful of tea and set the cup down on his desk. "I was enjoying that," he grumbled to himself and followed Fuller out of the office.

"Where are we going?" Grant said.

Fuller handed him the sheet of paper with the names and addresses. He scanned through them quickly as went down to the car park. He climbed behind the wheel of a black Wolseley and started the engine, passing the sheet of paper to Fuller as he climbed in beside him. "I know where most of these streets are," he said.

"We'll probably find most of the names are out at work," Fuller said. "But we'll track them down. The council also gave me their work schedules, so finding them should be easy enough."

"Is this about Warren Anderton's daughter?" Grant said.

"Yes."

Harry Grant shook his head. "If we find the bastard who did it, I'll rip his arms off."

"Join the queue," Fuller said. "The gov'nor gets first shot at him, with me running a close second."

Grant eased the nose of the Wolseley out of the car park and onto the High Street. "It always gets to you when kids are involved."

Fuller nodded. "It certainly does, Harry."

Jack picked up the phone and dialled through to the switchboard. "Hello, Helen. Can you get me the number of Tottenham Grammar School?" He replaced the receiver and waited for it to ring.

Helen on the switchboard found the number quickly, called him back and read it out to him. He dialled it vigorously.

"I'm trying to get in touch with Doctor Poole, Alan Poole. He used to be head of your history department," he said to the woman who answered the phone.

"I'm afraid Dr. Poole retired three years ago."

"I see," Jack said and introduced himself. "Do you have any idea where I might find him now?"

"He moved away from the area," the woman said.

"Do you have a number for him?"

The woman obliged.

He recognised the prefix. Poole was living near here in Hatfield. He replaced the receiver and picked it up again, dialling the number he'd been given. The phone on the other end of the line rang twice before a voice said, "Yes?"

"Is that Dr. Poole?"

"Yes."

"This is Detective Chief Inspector Callum of the Welwyn and Hatfield police. I was wondering if I could come and see you?"

Poole lived on a leafy street, in the older part of town, and away from the New Town development programme.

His house was large and detached, with a front garden given over mostly to shrubs and conifers.

Jack pressed the doorbell, and Poole emerged from around the side of the house. "I'm working in the back garden," he said. "Come through."

Jack followed him along a path that gave onto a space that was nearly half an acre of sweeping lawns and mature trees, with three large island flowerbeds, and an ornamental fishpond.

"It's an impressive garden," he said, as he walked the path beside the old man. Alan Poole was much as he remembered him from his school days, just older, greyer, and slightly shorter, but that was probably because he walked with a pronounced stoop. The man must be in his seventies now.

"Glad you like it," Poole said. "It's a bit of a passion of mine."

"Mine too," Jack said. "But my garden's not a patch on this."

"I consider myself to be very fortunate. It was the garden that sold me on the house. After living in London all my life, this seemed like paradise."

"Yes, I can imagine," Jack said. He felt the same about his own house.

"What do you grow?" Poole asked him.

"Vegetables mostly, but dahlias and chrysanthemums for colour."

"Fuchsias are my weakness, I'm afraid," Poole said. "I have over thirty different varieties."

They pulled up at a small circular paved area that had a round wooden table and four chairs surrounded by flowerpots of various sizes all containing various varieties of Poole's beloved fuchsias.

"You sit there," Poole said. "Would you care for a cup of tea? I was just in the middle of making one when you arrived."

"That would be grand," Jack said.

"Right, I won't be long," Poole said, and walked back to the house, reappearing five minutes later carrying a tray. He set the tray on the table and proceeded to pour tea from a brown earthenware teapot.

"Biscuits?" he said, pointing to four digestive biscuits laid out neatly on a china plate.

"Thanks," Jack said, helping himself to one.

"Well," Poole said. "This is very nice, very sociable. I don't get that many visitors. What can I do for you, Chief Inspector?"

Jack sipped his tea.

"I want to pick your brains, if I may," Jack said. "I remember, years ago, during one of your lessons, you spoke of the legend of the three wise monkeys."

"One of my lessons?"

Jack nodded.

"Were you a pupil of mine then?"

"Back in 1924 and '25."

"Good heavens. You *are* turning the clock back." Poole sat back and took a long look at Jack. "Yes, I think your face is vaguely familiar. Callum, you say? John Callum?"

"Most people call me Jack these days."

"Very good on the industrial revolution, I seem to recall. Had a bit of a passion for early machinery, if my memory serves me correctly."

"It does indeed," Jack said. He was a good thirty years younger than Poole but his memory wasn't half as sharp. "The three monkeys?" He jogged the teacher back to the subject.

"You remember that? It's gratifying to know that some of my lessons stuck in the mind. Sometimes, when you were teaching a class of teenage boys, you felt that your words were just being sucked away into the ether and having no effect at all. Anyway, the three wise monkeys, what do you want to know?"

"I remember you telling us that the legend was open to interpretation."

"Yes, yes indeed it is." The old man sipped his tea, sat back in his chair and closed his eyes. "The three monkeys embody the proverbial principle to *see no evil, hear no evil, and speak no evil*. Their names are *Mizaru*, who covers his eyes and sees no evil; *Kikazaru*, who covers his ears and hears no evil; and finally *Iwazaru* who covers his mouth, thus rendering himself dumb – speak no evil, you see? The legend is Japanese in origin, and, as I say, open to a few interpretations.

"In the Buddhist tradition, the proverb is about not dwelling on evil thoughts but, here in the West, both the proverb and the image of the three monkeys are often used to imply a lack of moral responsibility on the part of people who refuse to acknowledge wrongdoing – looking the other way or feigning ignorance. I've also read of it signifying a code of silence in criminal gangs, but I think you'd be better placed than me to speculate on that. Is that of any use to you? I take it this has something to do with one of your investigations."

"Yes, it's helpful and yes, it does have some bearing on a case I'm currently investigating."

"Would you care to enlighten me?"

Jack told him.

"Oh, how very distressing," Poole said. "That poor child. So do you think she was killed because she witnessed something she shouldn't have?"

"That's one of the avenues I'm going down," Jack said.

"Well, it's not really faithful to the legend, but I can see your reasoning. More tea?"

Jack spent another thirty minutes with the old man, which included a tour of his greenhouse.

"Stay in contact, Jack," Poole said, shaking Jack's hand vigorously. "Feel free to drop in any time. I've got all this knowledge up here…" He tapped the side of his head. "…and nothing to do with it. It just rattles around in there and, I'm sure the facts fall out of my ears and vanish if they're not being used."

Jack said he would stay in touch and took his leave.

6

MONDAY

Jack closed his book and glanced up at the clock on the mantle. "Rosie, turn on the wireless. It's nearly seven. Give it a chance to warm up."

"*Journey into Space?*" Eric said hopefully from the dining table that was partially covered by his homework.

"Not tonight. Mantovani and his Orchestra from the Savoy ballroom," Jack said. "I need some music to relax by. It's been a long day."

Eric pulled a face and went back to his algebra.

"Mother," Jack called through to the kitchen. "It's nearly seven."

"Coming," Annie called back. "Just drying the saucepans."

Rosie turned on the radiogram and went back to ironing the tabard she wore at her job in the local baker's. "I think I'll go upstairs when I've finished this," she said, "and play some records."

"No, you won't, young lady. It's Monday night, and Monday night is?"

"Family night," Eric and Rosie answered together reluctantly.

"All done," Annie said as she came into the room untying her apron. "Rosie, must you do that in here? It's what the kitchen is for."

"*You* were in the kitchen, Mum. I didn't want to get in your way," Rosie said.

"You could have done the drying up. That wouldn't have been in my way." Annie said.

"I'm doing the ironing," Rosie protested.

"Yes," Annie said. "In the *living room*."

The radio broadcast started, and the cascading strings of Mantovani's orchestra filled the air.

"May we listen now?" Jack said patiently. Family nights were important to him. They were an escape from the world of crime. "Mother," he said to Annie. "Sit yourself down and enjoy the music."

Annie took off her apron, draped it across the back of a dining chair and sat down in the armchair opposite his. "This is nice," she said. "Eric, how are you getting on with your homework? Do you want your dad to help you?"

"Nearly finished, Mum. Only three questions to go."

"Shhh," Jack hushed them, closing his eyes and humming along to *Charmaine*.

As the tune approached its coda the doorbell chimed. Jack snapped his eyes open and sat forward in his seat. "Ye gods! What now?"

"I'll get it," Annie said.

Jack held up his hands, "No, Mother. You've just cooked the dinner *and* washed up. You just sit and relax. I'll go and see who it is."

He went out into the hall and opened the front door.

For a moment he stared open-mouthed at the young woman in the gabardine mackintosh and with bleached, Marilyn Monroe hair.

"Joanie?" he finally managed.

"Hello, Dad," the young woman said.

Without another word, Jack turned on his heel and walked back to the living room, leaving Joan, his eldest daughter, standing on the doorstep.

"Who was it, Dad?" Annie said as he came back into the room.

Jack sat down heavily in his chair, shook his head and said nothing.

"Jack?" Annie persisted. Eventually she gave up waiting for him to reply, pushed herself out of her seat and went to see who was at the door.

"Good God," she said as she reached the front door. "Joanie. Three years without a word and now you turn up, out of the blue. Why now?"

"It's Monday night, Mum," Joan said with an uncertain smile. "Family night."

Jack sat in his armchair and stared into the empty fire grate.

Mantovani was serenading with strings but he wasn't listening. He was thinking about Joan, his first child, born three months prematurely, and just inside wedlock.

1939, a momentous year for many reasons – 30,000 souls lost in a Chilean earthquake; the outbreak of the war with Germany, with him entering the army to fight for King and Country, and Joan taking her first living breath. Those early weeks were fraught. Medical opinion was divided on her chances of survival, but he'd never had any doubts. He knew his daughter was a survivor, a fighter. Likewise the name was never an issue – it had to be Joan. He named her after Joan of Arc, the Maid of Orleans, and for years he'd called her his little *Jeanne d'Arc*, another fighter.

Throughout her childhood she had always shown a fiercely independent streak, and he'd encouraged it, admiring her passion for life and her ability to meet it head on, on her own terms. So it should not have been a surprise to him when she met and fell in love with a man a good few years older than her – Ivan, a Czech émigré who had come to England during the war to fly with the RAF, and stayed to make his life here. The age gap between them was worrying for both him and Annie, and they had tried hard to discourage the romance, but as Joan asserted her independence their home started to resemble a war zone, with weekly battles and daily skirmishes, and the day after her sixteenth birthday she crept out of the house when everyone was sleeping, and eloped with Ivan.

Jack had not seen or heard from her since that day, until five minutes ago when she rung the doorbell.

He listened as his wife's conversation moved from the front door to the kitchen.

"Who was at the door, Dad?" Rosie said during a pause in her ironing

Jack was still deep in thought. "Eh? Sorry."

"Who was at the door?" Eric echoed from the dining table.

"Your sister," Jack said.

"Don't be silly, Dad," Eric said. "Rosie's right here."

The skin around Jack's eyes tightened. "Your other sister."

"Joanie?" Rosie squealed incredulously and rushed out to the

41

kitchen.

Eric was more taciturn. He rose from the table, ambled across to where Jack was sitting and rested a hand on his shoulder. "Don't worry, Dad, I'll go and see what all the fuss is about."

The Mantovani program had finished before he pushed himself out of his armchair and walked to the kitchen. In the doorway to the kitchen he paused. In the centre of the room the four of them stood, locked in a tearful tableaux of reconciliation. They didn't even look his way to see him standing there.

He turned away, grabbed his coat from the hallstand and walked from the house.

By the time he entered the park the light was fading from the sky. As he took the path down to the woodland area he passed the park-keeper's hut. A grey-haired old man in a threadbare, blue-serge uniform was emerging from the hut, clutching a large bunch of keys. He looked up as Jack went past. "I'm closing up," he called to him. "You've got half an hour before I lock the front gates."

Jack ignored him and carried on walking. Eventually he came to the spot where Frances Anderton's body had been discovered yesterday, and stood, staring down at the flattened bracken.

He had never expected to see Joan again. After the initial pain of her leaving, he'd steeled himself, convinced that his precious *Jeanne d'Arc* was lost to him forever, and even told himself that he could live with that, and that if she ever showed her face again he would have nothing to do with her. Nothing could have prepared him for the pain he was feeling now.

A light suddenly flared in his eyes. "Okay, and what do you think you're up to?"

Jack put his hand up to shield his eyes. "It's all right. Police."

The light was switched off immediately. "Sorry, sir. I didn't recognize you at first," PC Kirby said.

Jack lowered his hand. "Don't you ever rest, man?" he said.

"The villains don't, so why should I?" Kirby said. "Are you feeling all right, sir? You look pale."

"Had a bit of a shock, that's all," Jack said.

"I'm still feeling it after yesterday," Kirby said. "That poor child. Her poor father."

"Do you have children, Constable?" Jack said.

"Just the one daughter, sir. My Gillian. You?"

"Two…three," Jack said. "Come on, let's walk. The park-keeper is doing his rounds, locking the gates."

They walked away from the woodland and headed back through the park.

"How old is your daughter, Constable?"

"Twenty-four, sir."

"And she still lives with you?"

Kirby nodded and tugged the dog's lead, bringing *Satan* to heel. "I dare say she'll meet a fine man one day, get married and settle down with him, but for the moment there's just the two of us. It's been that way since Mrs. Kirby passed five years ago."

"Does she work?"

Kirby nodded. "Yes. When I left the army, my wife and I pooled our savings and bought a small livery stable out on the Weston Road. Caroline, my wife, used to run it for a while, at the same time as bringing up Gillian. What we made from it, which wasn't a great deal, supplemented my police salary, but we rubbed along pretty well. But then, of course, the cancer got her and I had to make other arrangements. I didn't really want to sell up. The stables had been our home for nearly ten years by then, but Gillian had the bright idea of starting a riding school. She'd been brought up with horses and was comfortable around them, and was, and still is, a pretty fine horsewoman. So over the last few years she's built the school into the best in the area. We've still got the livery side of the business so what she makes with the school is *her* money. She's growing a nest egg, and one day, as I said, I'm sure she'll meet someone and settle down, but for now, I treasure every moment she's part of my life."

"You're a very lucky man," Jack said.

Kirby nodded again. "I know I am. It's why I feel so much for Warren Anderton. He has wealth, a fine house and the final say in how his company's run, but I'm sure he'd give it all up tomorrow to have his daughter back, just for one day."

They reached the park gates.

"Thank you, Constable," Jack said as they started to go their separate ways. "You've helped me see the wood for the trees."

Kirby looked at him curiously. He gave a small salute. "Happy to oblige, sir. Happy to oblige."

Jack entered the house through the back door but the kitchen was empty. The clock above the door read ten past ten. Probably everyone was in bed. Rosie had an early shift at the baker's tomorrow and Eric had to catch the bus to school at eight in the morning. Jack made himself a cup of cocoa and took it through to the living room.

"Did you make me one?" Annie said from the armchair. The standard lamp in the corner was on, giving the room a very subdued light, and casting a shadow over most of her face. He couldn't read her eyes.

"Have this one," he said. "I'll make myself another." He set the cup down on the small occasional table beside her.

"Thanks," she said. "Where have you been?"

"Walking. I needed to get some things straight in my mind. Walking helped."

He sat down in the armchair opposite hers. Cocoa could wait. They needed to talk. "Joanie?" he said.

"Sharing with Rosie tonight. I'll clear out the box room in the morning so she can have a bedroom of her own. We still have the put-you-up. It will do until we can buy a bed at the weekend."

"I didn't think we'd ever have to," Jack said.

"She's come home, Jack. Our girl's come home." She leaned forward in her chair, reaching out her hand to him.

He took it and squeezed it lightly. "Why?" he said.

Annie sighed. "Ivan's left her. Gone back to Czechoslovakia."

"Why?" Jack said again.

Annie shook her head. "I don't know all of the details. You'd be better asking her yourself."

"So we're having her back…after what she did?"

"We can't turn her away, Jack. She knows she's been a very foolish girl, but we can't punish her. She's been through enough."

"When did Ivan leave her?"

"Six months ago. They were renting a flat over a shop in Palmers Green. She kept up the rent for as long as she could by working as a barmaid at a pub, but when the landlord got over-friendly she left. Eventually her savings ran out and she couldn't afford to keep the flat on. She was scared, coming back here. She didn't know how you'd react."

Jack stared blankly at the tiles in the fire surround. "I didn't do very well, did I?"

"Who could blame you? You were shocked," Annie said.

"You could say that," he said. "I'll speak with her in the morning."

"Be gentle with her, Jack."

He smiled. "When she left, *the way she left*, it broke my heart, Annie," he said. "I thought I'd never forgive her."

"There was blame on all sides, Jack. We could have tried to be more understanding. I mean, she was in love. I remember, when I first met you, thoughts of you consumed me. You were the only thing I could think about for months. I used to drive mum and dad up the wall, just mooning over you. I should have remembered that feeling when Joanie first told us about Ivan."

"Yes," Jack said. "Being in love is like a sickness. It addles your brain and makes you behave irrationally. I'll speak with her tomorrow. I'll be kind."

Annie rose from the armchair and picked up her cocoa. "I'm all in. I'm taking this up." She came over and bent to kiss the top of his head. "You're a good man, Jack Callum," she said.

"I'll be up shortly. Warm my side of the bed."

"I'll make it as warm as toast for you," she said.

"As any dutiful wife should," he smiled at one of their mutual jokes.

He sat for another few minutes before venturing upstairs himself. Outside Rosie's room he paused before quietly opening the door and looking inside.

The two girls were laying top to bottom in Rosie's single bed. Their breathing was a soft susurration. Moonlight poured in through the window, kissing their faces with silver lips. He took a step into the room and stared down at Joanie. A lump was forming in his throat and tears were pricking at his eyes. "Welcome home, my little *Jeanne d'Arc,*" he said softly, and with his finger, gently brushed a blonde curl away from her eyes. "Sleep tight."

"Ssstight," Joan mumbled sleepily without waking.

He left the room as silently as he had entered and went to his own room.

7

TUESDAY AUGUST 12th 1958

Annie was standing at the cooker making scrambled eggs when Jack came down for breakfast.

"Are the girls up yet?" he said.

"Rosie's was up early, and she's gone to work," Annie said. "I'm letting Joanie sleep in. The eggs are for Eric. He's just finishing off the last of his homework in the living room."

"He should have done that last night. When you asked him about it he said he only had three questions to go."

"Yes, well, things didn't exactly go according to plan last night, did they?"

"I suppose not."

"Are you going to speak to Joanie before you go to the station?"

He buttered a slice of toast and checked his watch. "Not unless she gets up in the next ten minutes. Eddie will be here in…" The doorbell rang. "In fact he's here now." He took one bite of toast and washed it down with a mouthful of tea. "Got to dash," he said.

Annie frowned at him. "Jack, you *will* speak to her, won't you?"

"Yes, of course I will…but later." He went out to the hall, grabbed his coat and opened the front door. "A bit prompt today, aren't we, Sergeant?"

"I'm chasing up Douglas Madison. He was on the council's list but I couldn't get hold of him yesterday. He was working over Hitchin way but nobody knew quite where. If you don't mind stopping off on our way in, I thought we could go to his house and try to catch him before he leaves for work."

"Good idea. Where does he live?"

"Just off of Birchwood. It will only take us a couple of miles out of our way."

On the way there, Jack told Fuller about his meeting with Dr. Poole the day before. "So now you know as much about this case as I do," he said as Fuller parked the car in front of a row of terraced cottages with cream stuccoed walls, their windows flanked by green-painted, louvered shutters.

The woman who answered the door looked to be in her forties, wearing a pink nylon overall and dark blue carpet slippers. She had stringy, mud-coloured hair and watery blue eyes in a doughy face. The eyes narrowed into suspicious slits as she read Jack's warrant card. "What's Dougie done now?" she asked in a tired voice.

"Nothing, as far as we know," Jack said. "We just need to ask him some questions."

"You'd better come in then," she said, and yelled up the stairs, "Douglas Madison, get your lazy arse down here! People to see you!" She turned back to Jack and Fuller. "Come through," she said, and led them into a small, cramped kitchen.

Something was bubbling away in a large aluminium pot on the ancient gas cooker, filling the room with a noxious odour. "Excuse the stink," she said. "Just boiling some fish heads for the cat. Sit yourselves down."

Jack and Fuller sat down at the scratched and bruised table, avoiding the smears of tomato ketchup and drying puddles of spilt milk.

"Dougie!" she yelled again, and listened to the thump thump of feet on the floor of the room above. "'S'all right. He's up," she said, and buried her arms in a sink full of washing up.

Jack took in the room, from the yellowing wallpaper to the sticky strips of flypaper that hung from a cobwebbed ceiling. "Can I get you a brew?" she said.

Jack stared at the grey and grimy cloth she was using to clean her plates and said, "No thanks. I've not long had my breakfast."

Fuller too was staring at the cloth and shaking his head. "I'm fine," he said.

A small man with thinning hair, pomaded to a brilliant shine, and dressed smartly in sports jacket and fawn slacks came into the kitchen. He walked across to the table and extended a pink, freshly scrubbed hand.

"Douglas Madison," he said. "And you would be the gentlemen here to see me?"

"Detective Chief Inspector Callum," Jack said. "This is Detective Sergeant Fuller."

"Delighted to make your acquaintance," Madison said, shaking Jack's hand enthusiastically. "Always pleased to meet members of the local constabulary."

"Pour yourself a cuppa, Dougie, though it's probably stewed by now. I made it ages ago."

"Thank you, dear. You've met my wife," Madison said to Jack. "Susan, did you think to offer the gentlemen a cup of tea?"

"Yes, she did, and we're fine," Jack said

"Well, that's splendid," Madison said, and squeezed into the extra seat at the table. Jack glanced at Fuller who had suddenly taken a deep interest in the fly-speckled strip hanging down from the corner of the ceiling.

"So what can I do for you, Officers?" Madison said.

"You were at work on Sunday, at Norton Park. Maintenance of the playground rides, as I understand it."

"Yes, that's right."

"Well, I don't know if you've heard, but a young girl has been murdered and her body dumped in the woodland area of the park, some time during the day on Sunday."

The colour seemed to drain from Madison's face. "Murdered you say? That's dreadful."

"Yes," Jack said.

"So we were wondering," Fuller said, his pencil poised above an open notebook, "if you saw anything untoward that day?"

"What? Like someone dumping a dead body, you mean?" Madison said. Suddenly the precise vowels and clipped diction had deserted him and his voice rang with a Middlesex accent. "I think I would have noticed something like that, don't you?"

"Which of the rides were you working on?" Jack asked him.

"The witch's hat. I was greasing the bearings."

"And the witch's hat is?"

"It's that upside down cone that spins like a roundabout and goes up and down," Fuller said helpfully. "A friend of mine broke his leg on one of those, years ago. Caught his leg between the seat and the ground. Nasty."

"Yes, thank you, Sergeant, for that insight," Jack said, and turned his attention back to Madison. "The witch's hat is in the far eastern corner of the playground, am I right?" he said. "That's no more than fifty yards away from the wood, isn't it?"

Madison said nothing, but nodded his head,

"You're not suggesting that my Dougie had anything to do with a murder, are you?" Susan Madison said, moving away from the sink and standing over her husband protectively while she dried her hands on a tea towel as grubby as the dishcloth she'd been using.

"We're suggesting nothing of the kind, Mrs. Madison. It's just that we're very short of witnesses and your husband was in the immediate area when the girl's body was left."

Madison was shaking his head. "I don't know what to say. I didn't see anything, apart from…" His voice tailed off.

"Apart from what?" Jack pounced on the unfinished sentence.

Madison looked flustered. "I thought he'd gone into the trees to relieve himself."

"Who, Dougie?" Jack said.

"A man, just a man."

"Can you describe this man?" Fuller said, pencil hovering, waiting to write.

Madison sat back in his seat and thought for a moment. "I really didn't get a close look at him. I was at the top of the pole, greasing the bearings. Tricky things witch's hats. You have to get the lubrication just right or the bearings grind against each other, and that can lead to…"

"The man you saw?" Jack prompted.

"Yes, right. I didn't get a good look at his face because he was wearing a hat, a trilby, and had the brim pulled down over his eyes. I thought it was because he didn't want to be seen, I mean, taking a Jimmy Riddle in a public place, with the gentleman's lavatory not a hundred yards away."

"What time was this?

"About four. The chaps and I had just had our afternoon tea break."

"Height?" Fuller said.

"Medium."

"Weight?"

"Uh, medium, I'd say."

"Hair colour?"

"He had the hat."

"Young? Old?"

Madison shrugged. "I'm not being a lot of help here, am I?"

"So far you've described someone of medium height, medium build, who could be young or old, and wears a trilby, so no, Dougie, you're not. In fact I'd say you're about as much use as a witness as a bread roll," Jack said.

"Well, there's no need to be insulting. He's trying to help," Susan Madison said defensively.

"Did you see anyone else while you were up the pole?" Fuller said.

"Apart from the park-keeper, no."

"And was the park-keeper near the wood? Could he have seen the man you failed to describe?" Jack said.

Madison shook his head. "No. He was at the wood a while before I saw the man in the trilby. It was while I was drinking my tea. He was pushing a wheelbarrow into the wood."

"What was in the wheelbarrow?"

"How would I know?" Madison said. "Whatever it was, it was covered by a tarpaulin."

Jack sat thoughtfully for a moment. "How long after you saw the park-keeper did you see the man in the trilby?"

"I can't really say...I suppose about half an hour or so. I remember thinking that he was lucky the park-keeper didn't catch him taking a wee."

"Describe the park-keeper," Jack said.

"About thirty or so, I'd guess, medium height, medium build, hair...covered by a park-keeper's hat..." His voice trailed off. "You're thinking it might have been the same man?"

"I saw the park-keeper last night when I went to the park," Jack said. "He's seventy if he's a day."

Madison lowered his eyes. "Oh. I see."

"So is there anything else you can tell us about the park-keeper? Fuller said.

"Sorry," Madison said. "You know I'd help if I could."

Jack got to his feet and handed Madison a card with the

station's number printed on it. "Well, thank you for your help, Dougie. If you think of anything that may be of use to us, you can reach me on that number. We'll see ourselves out."

Back in the car Fuller said, "Strange couple. An odd match."

"It takes all sorts, Sergeant," Jack said. "So what have we learned?"

"Well, it would appear we're looking for a man in his thirties, who wears a trilby and impersonates park-keepers. That narrows the field somewhat," he added with heavy sarcasm.

Jack shook his head. "You and Grant go back and speak to the others who were working at the park that day. See if any of them can describe the park-keeper." He paused for a moment and then said. "What happened to the wheelbarrow?"

"What?"

"Madison said he saw the park-keeper pushing a wheelbarrow into the wood. Let's assume he had Frances Anderton's body in the barrow, covered by the tarpaulin."

"But he made no mention of the wheelbarrow when he saw the man in the trilby emerging from the woods after taking the supposed leak," Fuller said.

"So what did he do with the barrow? And the tarpaulin for that matter," Jack said. "Let's go back to the park."

"I'll radio the station and tell them we're going to be late in," Fuller said.

They stood near the spot where the body was discovered and looked about them at the surrounding landscape.

"Four of our boys gave this area a pretty good going over yesterday," Fuller said.

"Agreed," Jack said. "But they weren't looking for a wheelbarrow, were they?"

"Very true."

"What's that through there?" Jack pointed through the trees.

"It looks like a shed of some kind."

Built from creosoted timber the small shed stood fifty or so yards from the area searched yesterday. It had a pitched roof covered with grey roofing felt, and in one wall was a small window, caked in grime so thick the glass was opaque. The door was secured by a simple butterfly catch. Jack spun the catch and prodded the door open with the toe of his shoe.

"I'm sure they must have searched this yesterday," Fuller said.

The interior of the shed was as dirty as the window. Dust and dead leaves covered the floor, and spiders had built their homes in the thick webs that covered the walls. Jack looked at the spiders and shuddered. He hated spiders.

"And what would they have found, Sergeant?" Jack said as he took a breath and stepped inside. "A spider infested tool shed with a couple of rusting spades, a broken rake and very little else. Apart from a wheelbarrow and an old tarpaulin. Not enough really to register on anybody's radar."

Fuller stared at the old wheelbarrow propped up on its end, leaning against the wall of the shed. "Well, I'll be blowed," he said running his fingers through his hair.

"You'd better call this in and get a couple of officers back here," Jack said and, with one eye on the spiders, crouched down and lifted the edge of the tarpaulin. "Let's see what else they missed."

8

TUESDAY

"You have your office all to yourself," Andy Brewer said as Jack entered the station later that day.

"Has the chief super got his own office back?"

"The decorators are moving their stuff out now," Brewer said, nodding to a man dressed in paint-splattered overalls, carrying a stepladder down the stairs.

"Good," Jack said.

"Did you want to add a *riddance* to that, sir?"

"You know me better than that, Andy. I would never be so rude," Jack said with a smile. "I'll be in *his* office if you need me."

"Ah, Jack," Lane said. "What do you have to tell me?"

"We have a witness who saw a man wheeling a barrow into the woods Sunday afternoon," Jack said, "dressed as a park-keeper, but *not* the park-keeper. We've found the wheelbarrow and have two men down there now, dusting for fingerprints and checking for any other evidence."

"Do we have a description of the man?"

"Only a very vague one. I have Fuller on it now, sir, interviewing the men doing the maintenance work on Sunday for the second time. He can ask more useful questions this time around."

"Good," Lane said, and sat down behind his desk. "I don't need to impress upon you, Jack, that we need a positive outcome on this one. And a very speedy one."

"We're doing what we can, sir."

"Yes, I'm sure you are. Do you realise how many people in this town rely on Warren Anderton for their jobs? He's a very important figure in this area. The Chief Constable was on the phone to me this morning asking how the investigation is going – he belongs to Anderton's Lodge, and of course he's very upset that such a thing could befall a fellow Mason. I stalled him but he's ringing back this afternoon. I'd like to have something positive to tell him."

"When *I* have something positive, you'll be the first to know."

"And *I* know you won't let me down, Jack," Lane said.

Jack went back to his office, feeling depressed. No one wanted to solve this case as much as he did, but he and his men could only do so much, especially if all the witnesses turned out to be as useless as Douglas Madison.

He took a briar pipe from the drawer of his desk, filled it from a round tin of *Bondman* tobacco and tamped it down, before lighting it with a match. He rarely smoked but sometimes sucking in tobacco smoke and rolling it over his tongue helped him concentrate. "Well it worked for *Sherlock Holmes*," he said to himself.

"We have three people who saw the park-keeper on Sunday," Fuller said. He'd been gone for most of the morning.

"Descriptions?" Jack said.

"We have a few more details to go on," Fuller said. "All three put his age at nearer twenty than thirty. All agree he was fairly good looking. One of them saw him without his cap and said his hair is fair to mousey."

"Fair to mousey?"

"That was the best he could do."

"And he's in his twenties." Jack said. "Closer to Frances's age, I suppose."

"Do you think the age is significant?" Fuller said.

"It might be. It could be someone within her social circle."

"Unlikely, sir. At that age the gap between fourteen and someone in their twenties is huge."

"But not when you're nineteen," Jack said. "What do we know about Fiona Anderton's secret boyfriend?"

"Apart from his name, Adam, nothing at all. She's playing her cards very close to her chest on that one."

"Then I'm going to see her," Jack said. "Find out what she can tell me about him. There must be a reason why she's keeping him a secret from her parents."

"Do you want me to come, sir?" Fuller said.

"No, you stay here and wait for the boys to get back from the park. I'll handle this alone."

"My parents are out," Fiona Anderton said as she opened the door. "They've gone to arrange the funeral."

Jack stood on the doorstep, his hat in his hands. "First, let me offer my sincerest condolences."

She shrugged. She looked different from when he saw her last. Her face was makeup free, her hair was down, curling about the shoulders of a black roll-neck sweater, and her legs were sheathed in tight, but neatly pressed, black slacks. On her feet was a pair of black satin pumps. Somehow she looked younger and, strangely, more vulnerable.

"Actually, it was you I came to see, Miss Anderton," Jack said. "May I come in?"

She stared at him imperiously for a moment and then stood aside to let him enter. "Come through to the morning room," she said, and led him through to the same room he'd been in before.

She went across to the fireplace and took a cigarette from a box on the mantle, screwed it into the ivory holder and lit it with the flame from a chrome table lighter standing next to the box. She inhaled deeply and blew out the grey smoke through pursed lips. "Well, what can I do for you, Chief Inspector?"

"Do you mind if we sit down?"

"It's a free country," she said, and sat down on the chesterfield, within arm's length of a marble ashtray that rested in the centre of an oak coffee table.

Wondering what had happened to Jessica Anderton's no smoking rule, Jack sat in an armchair opposite her and crossed his legs. "Forgive this intrusion," he said.

She shrugged again. "I have the time," she said. "It's not as if I can go anywhere until they get back." She drew in smoke from the cigarette and blew it, almost defiantly, up at the ceiling.

"Oh? Why is that?"

"Well, you know how it is, Chief Inspector, all hands to the pumps in time of crisis. I have to guard the telephone to make sure my father doesn't miss some important message from some underling." There was quietly repressed anger in her voice. Her relationship with her father certainly seemed fractious. "So, what can I do for you?" she said.

"Your sister must have come as a terrible shock," Jack said.

She sucked in smoke again. "Do you mean her death, or her birth?"

He was flummoxed for a moment, not sure how to answer.

Fiona gave a brittle laugh. "I'm sorry, Chief Inspector. I didn't mean to put you on the spot like that. I don't suppose you're used to the petty rivalries of teenage girls."

"I have two daughters myself, Miss Anderton, of a similar age to you and Frances. I don't think there's much you can say that would shock me."

"*Touché*," she said. "I suppose I deserved that. Please, carry on with your questions."

"Apart from the petty rivalries, did you and your sister get on?"

"As well as most sisters, I expect," Fiona said. "She was five years younger than me so there were never any issues of her borrowing my clothes without asking."

"Or boyfriends for that matter."

Her eyes narrowed and her nostrils flared. "What do you mean by that?"

Jack smiled. "Well, I know with my girls that Rosie, my youngest, regularly had crushes on the boys her elder sister brought home. I wondered if the same thing applied to you and Frances."

"It might have. I never asked her."

"So you wouldn't describe your relationship with your sister as close?"

"It was as close as I chose it to be. She was a child, Chief Inspector. There were certain things about my life that I had no desire to share with her."

"Like the boyfriend you keep secret from your parents."

She stubbed the cigarette out furiously in the ashtray and stood up. "I think you should leave now."

Jack remained in his seat. "But you do have an ongoing secret relationship?" he said.

"That's none of your damned business."

"It *is* my business if it could have some bearing on your sister's murder."

The word *murder* made her blink. She reached for another cigarette and lit it, not bothering with the holder this time. She sat back down on the chesterfield.

"My friendship with Adam had nothing to do with Frances. She only met him once and that was by sheer chance."

"Adam who?" Jack prodded gently.

She hesitated before answering. "Adam Channing."

"And how long have you known Mr. Channing?"

"*Professor* Channing. He's a lecturer at the London School of Economics. I studied under him for a year after leaving school."

"And now he's your boyfriend?" Jack said.

"He's my *lover*," she said, tilting her chin defiantly, as if determined to shock.

Jack was unmoved. He knew how to play her game. "I can see why your parents wouldn't approve," he said. "A man like that, in a position of trust, taking advantage of a young woman."

"Oh, please don't kid yourself, Chief Inspector, it was I who took advantage of him. He tried to resist, but when I've made my mind up that I want something, I generally get it."

"I'm sure you do," Jack said, thinking that what she wanted was a good shake to bring her into the real word. "Is he married?"

"Unhappily, yes he is."

"Unhappily for him or for you?"

"Both of us really. His wife's an invalid. It's not a proper marriage but he can't leave her."

"Can't or won't?"

She shrugged. *She's enjoying this*, Jack thought. *She's probably pleased to finally tell someone about it.*

"So when did Frances meet Professor Channing?"

"At an end of term party," she said. "I understood he couldn't attend because of his wife, so I invited Frances along. You can imagine my surprise when Adam showed up. His wife was staying overnight in hospital having some tests, so he was up there for her and staying at an hotel."

"Doesn't he live up in London?"

"No. He has a house near Stevenage, hence the hotel."

"Let's get this straight," Jack said. "His sick wife was in hospital undergoing tests, and so he decides to go to a party at the LSE."

"He was at a loose end," Fiona said. "He was bored, at the hotel by himself, so he thought he'd come along and show his face. It was a surprise, I can tell you, albeit a lovely one."

"Charming," Jack said sardonically. "And you introduced him to you sister?"

"No, of course not. Do you think I'm totally irresponsible?" The nostrils were flaring again. "No, Adam just sat at our table. She met him then."

"How old is Professor Channing, Fiona?"

"Forty-five, or is it six? I can never remember."

"And the age gap doesn't bother you?"

She shook her head. "Not a jot. Adam's a man, Chief Inspector, not like boys of my own age. They're so immature. He's a brilliant, kind, compassionate man."

"Try telling that to his wife," Jack said, getting to his feet. "I'll see myself out."

Fiona walked to the door with him anyway. "You won't tell them," she said. "My parents. You won't say anything to them about Adam."

"It's not my place to do so, Miss," Jack said. "But I would advise you to tell them. Sooner rather than later."

"They'd never understand."

"Sometimes parents can surprise you," Jack said, and climbed in behind the wheel of the pool car he was using. As he drove away he saw her watching him from the doorway, biting her lip pensively. "Silly girl," he muttered, and drove out through the gates.

Once back at the station he went up to see Superintendent Lane to tell him of the recent developments, not that there was much Lane could pass on to the Chief Constable, but Jack would let his boss worry about the internecine politics.

"Take me home, Sergeant," he said to Fuller when he went

downstairs. "I've had enough for one day."

"How did it go with Fiona Anderton?" Fuller said as they walked to the car.

"The boyfriend's not our man, but we'll check him out anyway." Jack said. "His name's Professor Adam Channing and he's a lecturer at the London School of Economics. He and his wife live in Stevenage. But he's too old to be our park-keeper, and we're looking for someone who lives locally, or at least has local knowledge and has somewhere he can keep the girls he abducts while he does what he does to them, prior to dumping their bodies."

"Girls?"

"I have a bad feeling about this one, Eddie. I think Frances Anderton was just the first. Call it a hunch."

"I hope you're wrong, Jack."

"So do I, Eddie So do I."

9

TUESDAY

Jack arrived home to find everyone in the back garden. Annie had got the deckchairs out from the shed and they were all sitting, enjoying the late afternoon sun, even Eric, who was usually bored by things that didn't involve climbing trees or kicking a football around. Jack's three girls were wearing flowery sundresses. Annie had her chestnut hair tied up in a ponytail, which gave her a girlish look, and took him back to their courting days.

"Sit yourself down, Dad," Annie said. "Rosie has made some lemonade. I'll fetch you a glass." She vacated her deckchair and went inside.

Jack settled himself into the gaudily striped canvas chair and slipped off his shoes. Despite the informality of the setting, the atmosphere in the garden seemed tense. His two youngest kept switching their gaze from him to Joan, anticipating the emotional explosion that seemed likely to occur at any moment. Annie came back with the lemonade and handed the glass to Jack.

"Eric," she said to her son. "You have your homework to do. Get yourself inside and get on with it. I don't want a repeat of yesterday. And Rosie, I want you to give me a hand with dinner. You can peel some potatoes."

The grumbles of protest were met with a curt, "Now!" from Annie, and both children got obediently to their feet and followed her back into the house.

The ensuing silence in the garden was finally broken by Joan who said, "Mum isn't very subtle, is she?"

"She tries her best," Jack said. "I don't think this situation has been easy for any of us."

"I suppose not," Joan said. "Where did you get to last night? I was expecting a tongue lashing…a dressing down at least."

"You were right to expect it," Jack said. "Which is why I went for a walk – to clear my head…"

"And   calm   down?"
"If you like."

"Would an apology make any difference?"

Jack took a sip of lemonade. It was very sweet and he grimaced. "It might, if I thought you meant it."

Joan sat forward in her seat. "But I do apologise, Dad. I really do," she said, her voice catching in her throat. "You can't imagine how hard it was to come back here yesterday, not knowing if you could bear to even look at me, let alone talk to me. When you took off last night I feared the worst, even though mum assured me things were going to be all right."

"Your mum knows me pretty well," Jack said with a fond smile. "Better than I know myself sometimes." He lapsed into silence again.

"Mum said she told you what had happened with Ivan," Joan said.

"I should knock his block off," Jack said, his voice a low growl.

"It's not really his fault."

"Whose fault is it then, Harold MacMillan's?"
"I don't think Ivan realised what he was taking on, Dad. I was a brat, a sixteen year old brat who thought she knew everything about the world."

"How long before you realised you didn't?"

"When we moved into the flat above the shop and I had to behave like a wife." She planted her fingers in her platinum hair and tugged. "Mum made it look, *makes* it look, so easy; juggling the home finances, the cooking and the cleaning, looking after a husband and catering for his needs. I soon found out it isn't easy. I was only sixteen and I wanted to be out in the world, going to parties, going to the *Palais* and dancing until dawn."

"And he didn't?"

"Ivan had a job as a builder's labourer, working on a site in Holborn. By the time he'd get home in the evening and have his dinner, all he wanted to do was to sit and listen to the wireless. I suppose I couldn't really blame him but, as I said, I was young and a brat, so we argued. We argued a lot, violently.'

"Did he ever strike you?"

She lowered her eyes. "Only if I really deserved it."

Jack reached out and took her hand. "No woman deserves to be hit by the man she loves, no matter how much she thinks she might, and any man who raises his hand to a woman is a coward, nothing more, nothing less. I'm glad it finished before he could do any permanent damage."

"One day he just upped and left," she said. "He packed his bags, went down to the docks and boarded a tramp steamer to Marseilles. At least that's what Radek told me."

"Who's Radek?"

"Another Czech, and a friend of his. They used to work together on the building site. Radek was the one who got me the job at the *Queen of Diamonds*. It was his local and he knew the landlord."

"Mum told me how that worked out for you," Jack said.

Joan lowered her eyes. "I've made some bad choices, Dad."

"Yes, yes you have. But you're lucky to have come out of it relatively unscathed. You could have got yourself into trouble. At least you didn't have an unwanted child to…"

Joan started to cry, fat tears welling in her eyes and rolling down her cheeks.

"Oh, Joanie," Jack said getting out of his chair, squatting down at her side and wrapping his arms around her. "What happened to the child?"

She shook her head. "There was a woman," she said through the sobs. "In Hackney. She provides *special services* for unmarried mothers."

Jack felt his anger rising. "People like that are parasites," he said bitterly. "Taking advantage of young girls, trading on their misery and desperation."

"I didn't have a choice, Dad. We could barely afford to feed ourselves, let alone a baby." She gripped the sleeve of his shirt. "Please don't tell mum," she whispered urgently. "She doesn't know."

He took a handkerchief from his pocket and handed it to her. "I think we'll keep that just between us," he said. "She longs to be a grandmother. If she ever finds out that you…well, it would just about finish her off, and I don't want her to suffer any more than she has. She's a good woman, your mum, one of the best. You could learn a lot from her."

"Will you give me the chance to try?" Joan said, wiping her tears away.

"Take as long as you need," Jack said. "This is, and always will be, your home."

She wrapped her arms around his neck "I love you so much, Dad," she said.

They stayed like that for a long moment.

Unconditional love.

Until Joan was born, he had no idea what that term meant, but from the moment he stared down at the pink and wrinkled infant, lying vulnerable and defenceless in the hospital crib, he understood, and now, with his daughter hanging from his neck, with her tears soaking through the thin cotton of his shirt, he was feeling it acutely.

"I don't like it, by the way," he said softly in her ear.

"What?"

"The hair. It makes you look like a tuppenny tart."

She smiled. "Yes," she said. "Not one of my smartest decisions. I had it done when I was working at the pub. I thought it was more in keeping with my new job. Don't worry though, mum's friend Avril is coming tomorrow to put it right."

"First you come back and disrupt our lives and now you're turning my home into a hairdressing salon."

"Sorry," she said.

He wrapped his arms around her and hugged her tightly. "Apology accepted," he said, and kissed the top of her head.

10

TUESDAY

Sandra Duncan packed her books in her haversack and threw the strap over her shoulder.

"Before you all disappear for the night," Miss Havelock, her evening class tutor, said, "remember that, next week, we'll be looking at nutrition, and how we can provide a balanced diet to those children in our care. If you can all read chapter eleven of your text book in preparation."

As the class filed out of the room a few of the girls were making arrangements to rendezvous at the local pub. "Are you coming, Sandra?" one of the girls said as she passed her in the corridor.

"Not tonight, Diane. I have to catch my bus," Sandra said, pleased that she had been asked to join them. Despite all the empty promises by her school friends to keep in touch, she had lost contact with most of them when the school gates closed behind them for the last time. The girls she worked with at the bank were a fairly tight bunch and so far hadn't welcomed her into their club. She told herself it was because she hadn't been there that long, but it was months since she'd left school and gone to work there, so she doubted that anything was ever going to change. It was why she preferred to be with children. They were, on the whole, non-judgemental, and tended to treat her as an equal.

It was why this evening class in childcare was so important to her. Her dream was to leave the bank and go abroad, to work with children, maybe as a governess or a nanny. She'd chosen France as her primary destination, partly because she was fluent in the language, and partly because she could no longer see a happy future for herself in England. She hoped that in a different country, where nobody knew her, she would have the chance to build a better life than the one she had now. She could start afresh, a clean slate.

Her bus was waiting at the stop as she came down the stone

steps from the school. "Blast!"

She started to run, but she knew before she had taken half a dozen steps that she wasn't going to make it. As she ran out onto the street the bus was already pulling away. After a few more strides she stopped running and walked dejectedly to the bus stop. She looked at her wristwatch. The next bus would not be along for another thirty minutes.

There was a bench a few yards away. She sat down and opened her haversack, took out her textbook and found chapter eleven. By the orange light of the sodium lamp behind her she could just about read the words. It wasn't ideal but at least it would pass the time until the next bus came along.

"Can I give you a lift?"

She looked up from the book at the young man standing in front of her. He was casually dressed, but his clothes looked clean and pressed. His hair was short and neatly cut, fair, almost blond, with a side parting.

"I'm waiting for the bus," she said.

He smiled at her. "I thought you might be… as you're sitting at a bus stop."

"I just missed one."

"My sympathies," he said. "You're in for a long wait. The buses are all up the spout tonight. Something to do with an accident in town."

"I didn't realise," she said.

"So, would you care for a lift?"

She looked beyond him, looking for a car. She hadn't heard one pull up.

"I don't see your car," she said.

"Ah."

"So how do you intend give me a lift?"

He sat down next to her on the bench. "Look over there." He was pointing across the road. Fifty yards from where they were sitting a motor scooter was parked at the side of the road.

"You're offering me a ride home on that?"

"Yes, why not?"

"Because I value my life?"

He laughed. "It's perfectly safe. *I'm* perfectly safe. Scooters aren't like motorbikes. They haven't got the speed for one thing, and I never take risks with it, especially if I have a passenger."

"Thanks," she said. "But I don't think so."

"Have you just come from the school?"

"Night school," she said.

"I thought so, from the book. What are you reading?"

"It's a book on childcare."

"Really? You don't look old enough to have a child."

She felt herself blushing. "No," she said. "I mean, I don't have children of my own. I want to look after them though…as a job. Perhaps abroad."

"Derek," he said, sticking out his hand.

"Sandra," she said shaking his hand. "Sandra Duncan."

"Very pleased to meet you." He looked along the street. "Are you sure you wouldn't like a lift?" he said. "You could be stuck here for hours yet."

"No, really I…"

"Come and have a look at my scooter. You can see for yourself how safe it is." He got to his feet and stood waiting for her to respond. When he showed no sign of moving on she sighed, slipped her book back into her haversack, and stood up. "All right then. Just a look."

He smiled at her. He had kind eyes, she decided.

They crossed the street and walked along to where the scooter was parked. As they reached it he said, "It's a *Phoenix* 150. Only three months old. You can't really see in this light but it's blue, two-tone."

"It looks very nice," she said.

"Sit on it. Try it for size."

"I don't think…"

"Where's the harm?" he said, cutting across her refusal.

She shrugged and climbed on.

"Now, hold the handlebars and put your feet up on the footrest."

She did so.

"See how comfortable it is?"

"Yes, it is," she said. "Very comfortable." She glanced back along the road. There was still no sign of an approaching bus.

"Hours, you say, for the bus."

"One at least, possibly two. It's very snarled up in town."

"And you really don't mind giving me a lift?"

"It would be my pleasure, Sandra. Where do you live?"

"Gleave Road. Do you know it?"

"Know it? I was born and raised two streets away. North Avenue."

"I don't recall ever seeing you around."

"No, my family moved when I was six. Not far away though. We're still in the area."

"So it wouldn't be taking you out of your way."

He shook his head. "Not at all."

She thought for a moment. "All right then," she said. "I accept your offer."

It was not as if he could do anything to her while she was sitting behind him on the scooter, and she really did want to get home tonight.

"Splendid," he said. "I can be your knight in shining armour on his gallant steed, or actually, your knight on his shiny blue motor scooter."

"Two-tone blue motor scooter," she corrected him,

"Exactly," he said. "Move back onto the pillion, and off we go."

She shuffled back onto the pillion seat and he climbed aboard and kick-started the machine. "I just have to make a stop on the way," he said. "It will only take a few seconds." He felt her hands grip his waist and he smiled as he eased the scooter away from the kerb.

11

WEDNESDAY AUGUST 13th 1958

"There are people here to see you," Andy Brewer said as Jack and Fuller walked into the station. He pointed with his pen at the middle-aged couple sitting on the bench beneath the notice board. "Their names are Duncan, Mr. and Mrs. Duncan."

Jack went across to them and introduced himself. "So, Mr. and Mrs. Duncan. How may I help you?"

Duncan got to his feet. He was a thin, balding man wearing horn-rimmed glasses and a sports jacket with leather patches on the elbows. "It's our daughter, Sandra, Chief Inspector. She's missing."

Jack felt a hollowness in the pit of his stomach. "When you say *missing*, what do you mean exactly?"

"She didn't come home last night. She went out to her evening class at half past seven. My wife and I aren't what you would call late birds, so by nine o'clock we were in bed. When Allison took Sandra a cup of tea this morning, her room was empty."

"Her bed hadn't been slept in," Allison Duncan said. She was a petite woman who wore her auburn hair in a tightly lacquered shampoo and set. Her clothes were mostly tweed and wouldn't have looked out of place at a local gymkhana. She sat on the bench, staring up at Jack, her face a strained mask as she bit her lip to stop herself from crying.

"Have you called her friends to check that she didn't stay with one of them overnight?"

"We tried that," Duncan said. "But no one's seen her since she left the school at nine thirty last night."

"Which school would that be?" Jack said.

"St Clements. She's taking a course there in childcare. She has this misguided idea in her head that she wants to be a nanny…with a French family of all things. She's fluent in the language, you see?"

"How old is Sandra, Mr Duncan?"

"She's eighteen."

"And is there anywhere she might have gone, after finishing her evening class?"

"She always gets the bus straight home," Allison said. "Sandra's a good girl. She takes her studies very seriously and never stays up any later than half past ten. Staying out all night...well, it's just unthinkable."

"Come up to my office," Jack said. "I have several things I need to go over with you. A cup of tea?"

Both of them nodded. Jack went back to the desk. "Andy, could you see that a tray of tea is sent up to my office? And alert Superintendent Lane – tell him that we might have another missing girl."

"Will do, sir," Brewer said.

"Another missing girl, Jack?" Lane said.

"It certainly looks that way. Sandra Duncan, eighteen years old, didn't return home from yesterday evening's evening class."

He laid a colour snapshot on the desk of a fairly plain girl whose brown hair had been severely cut into a blunt pageboy style that did nothing to enhance her meagre looks.

Lane was shaking his head as he looked at the photograph. "It won't do, Jack. It simply won't do. We're stretched enough as it is, searching for Frances Anderton's killer, without this to contend with. We've even got the national press asking questions. The *national press*. What am I supposed to tell them?"

"Tell them that our investigations are progressing."

"But they're not, Jack, are they? We're no closer to finding the killer than we were twenty-four hours ago."

"I think you're being slightly unreasonable, sir."

Lane slammed the palm of his hand down on the desk, making the pencils in the desk-tidy rattle. "Damn it, Chief Inspector, I don't think it's unreasonable to expect you to do your job."

Jack said nothing. Lane was under pressure from all sides. He needed a whipping boy, and Jack was filling those shoes at the moment.

"No, sir," he said.

Lane was struggling to bring his temper under control. "I'm sorry, Jack. I realise you're doing your best. I just feel we should be doing more."

"I'll go back over the evidence," Jack said. "We might have missed something."

Lane took off his glasses and started cleaning them with his handkerchief. "Yes, do that. And keep me apprised of your progress with the missing Duncan girl."

"Yes, sir," Jack said and went back downstairs.

He walked over to the notice board fixed to the wall and pinned the photograph of Sandra Duncan next to the picture of Frances Anderton.

"Gather round," he called to the officers in the room.

Gradually they stopped what they were doing and joined him at the notice board.

"We have another missing girl," he said, pointing to the picture. "Sandra Duncan, eighteen, works at Lloyds Bank in town. Before that she was a pupil at the County School. She was last seen leaving her evening class at St Clements at about 9.30 pm last night. She never arrived home."

"Perhaps she went out with friends after her class," Harry Grant said.

"That has been suggested to her parents, but they assure me she would have gone straight home. They say she is a *good girl*."

"All parents say that about their children," Grant said. "It doesn't mean that she is."

"That's a fair point, Harry, and one that I agree with. The lenses are always rose-tinted when parents look at their kids through them. So, we'll assume nothing about the girl's character. Frank and Trevor, I want you to check out St Clements, get a list of the other students and interview everyone on it."

Detective Sergeant Frank Lesser and Detective Constable Trevor Walsh exchanged glances. "That could take all day, sir," Lesser said.

"Is there somewhere else you have to be, Sergeant?" Jack

said.

"No, sir."

"Good. St Clements it is then. It will save you hanging around here and cluttering up the place. Myra?"

WPC Myra Banks got to her feet.

"Myra, I want you to cut along to the bank. Have a chat with the manager and see what you can find out about our missing girl, and speak to the members of staff, especially the female ones, and see if they can give us a broader picture of her than the one provided by her parents. Some people have completely different personalities at work to the ones they show at home."

"Yes, sir," Myra Banks said. She was young, out of uniform and on secondment to CID, but what Jack had seen of her so far was impressive. He didn't think it would be that long before she was ready for a probation period, and after that he could envisage her becoming an important cog in the machine.

"Eddie, take Constable Grant and go down to the County school. Talk to her old teachers and any of her classmates still at the school."

Jack sat down at a desk as the officers filed out of the room and went off to their various assignments. He stared up at the clock on the wall. The minute hand ticked onto eleven. Five to ten. He couldn't shake the feeling that all their efforts were going to be too late, that Sandra Duncan was already dead. With a sigh he opened the Frances Anderton file and started reading through it again.

Myra walked into the bank and went straight up to the counter. "I'd like to see the manager," she said to the cashier through the brass grille. The cashier, a young man with a bad case of acne looked up from the pile of pound notes he was counting. "Of course," he said. "Who shall I say wants to see him?"

"WPC Banks, Welwyn and Hatfield Police," Myra said.

"And can I say what it is concerning?"

"I think that's between him and me, don't you?"

The young man slid off his high stool. "Yes. Yes, of course. I'll go and fetch him to the counter." He turned, walked past the other cashiers to a door at the back and rapped on it with his knuckles. Myra heard the barked, "Come in," out in the vestibule. The young cashier let himself into the office. A few moments later the door opened again and a middle-aged man emerged. He was tall, dressed in an immaculate navy, pin striped suit over a crisp white shirt, set off by a red and blue striped tie. He walked out into the small vestibule. "WPC Banks? Cecil Marsh. I'm the manager. What can I do for you?"

"Good morning, sir," Myra said. "I'm making enquiries about a girl who works here, Sandra Duncan?"

"Yes," Marsh said. "Miss Duncan. She's not long been with us. Joined the bank about six months ago. Is she in any kind of trouble?"

Their conversation was attracting the attention of the four cashiers behind the counter and a little old lady with a bulldog on a lead. The dog was lying under a small table in the corner, where the old lady sat, filling out a form.

"Do you think we could go somewhere and speak in private?" Myra said. "Your office perhaps?"

"Of course," Marsh said, and opened the door he had just come through. "This way." He turned to look at the cashiers. "Please, get on with your work. All of you," he said, and led Myra through to his office, ushering her inside and closing the door behind them.

"Take a seat, Officer," Marsh said, indicating a small straight-backed seat, the opposite side of the desk from his own brown leather office chair. He sat down at the desk and picked up a telephone receiver from a wooden box with lights and switches. "Hold my calls, Deirdre, until further notice." He replaced the receiver. "Right, Officer, you were saying?"

"Sandra Duncan. I was wondering what you could tell me about her?"

Marsh stood up, went across to a wooden filing cabinet in the corner and pulled open a drawer. He glanced round at her. "Staff files," he said by way of explanation. He thumbed through the files and took out a manila folder, bringing it back and laying it down on the large blotter on his desk. He resumed his seat, opened the file and started to read from it.

"Sandra Duncan, born the fifth of June 1940. She joined us in

January this year." He read on in silence for a moment. "Quite an impressive list of exam results. Hobbies include languages, reading and knitting. Lives with her parents at 21 Gleave Road, Hatfield. Her parents' names are Arthur and Allison. He is an insurance actuary, she is a prominent member of the parish council. Regular churchgoers. I actually know them quite well from the Rotary club. A very pleasant couple."

"And Sandra? How would you describe her?"

Marsh closed the file and frowned. "A wallflower is the term I think best describes her."

"A wallflower in what way?" Myra said.

"Well, she doesn't mix much with the other members of staff. Generally takes lunch by herself, in the staff dining room, and generally has her nose buried in a book of some kind. I'm not speaking out of school but I've heard some of the other girls here pass catty remarks about her."

"What kind of remarks?"

"About her clothes and choice of hairstyle – or lack of one – and …well, I'm not sure this is relevant…"

"Shall I be the judge of that?" Myra said. For all his stiff formality, Cecil Marsh seemed like a bit of an old woman, a gossip.

He leaned forward across the desk in a conspiratorial manner. "A rumour went around the bank a little while ago that Sandra was involved with a man. A man who was a number of years older than herself."

"Does he have a name, this man?"

Marsh shook his head. "Not that I've heard." He sat back in his leather chair. "Would you mind telling me why you have such an interest in Miss Duncan?" he said.

"She's missing," Myra said. "She didn't come home after her evening class last night."

"Oh, good gracious. Arthur and Allison rather dote on her. They're probably beside themselves."

"They're very concerned, yes." Myra said. "We all are."

"I'll give Arthur a call to see if there's anything I can do."

"I'd like to talk to the rest of your staff," Myra said. "Perhaps we can use this office to carry out the interviews."

"And perhaps not," Marsh said. "I appreciate you have your job to do, Officer Banks, but I am very busy man and my appointment book is full for today. I need my office. There's a room upstairs you can use. It's the staff rest room but I'm sure no one will complain if you set up store in there."

"Thank you," Myra said.

12

WEDNESDAY

DS Frank Lesser came out of the school secretary's office and trotted down the stone steps, clutching a folded sheet of foolscap paper.

"Did you have any luck?" DC Trevor Walsh said, as Lesser climbed into the Wolseley beside him.

"I have this," he said, holding up the paper. "There's no one here from the evening classes during the day, but the secretary's given me a list of everyone who shared Sandra Duncan's class last night. There's only eight in the class plus the tutor, so it shouldn't take us all day to track them down."

"If you don't mind me saying, Sarge, you seem to be in a bit of a rush today. Is something wrong?" Walsh said.

"There's a show on tonight at the Granada in Edmonton."

"Are you fighting?"

"Keep it under your hat but, yes, I am. Third on the bill, so if I get my skates on today I can make it."

"What would the governor say if he found out you were moonlighting as a wrestler?"

"He'd probably throw a fit, so we keep mum about it, right?" Lesser said, reached behind him, took a brown leather Gladstone bag from the back seat and unzipped it. In the bag was a pair of wrestling boots, a black sequinned cape and something that looked like a balaclava.

"So the Black Phantom fights again," Walsh said. "I'll have to come and see a match some time."

Lesser pulled the balaclava over his head. There were two holes for the eyes and one for the mouth but apart from that his entire head and face were covered. "What do you think?" he said.

"I think that if I saw you out in the street wearing that thing I'd probably arrest you."

Lesser pulled off the mask, stowed it back in his bag and threw the bag onto the rear seat, then he unfolded the piece of paper the secretary had given him and ran down the list of names with his finger. "Eunice Havelock, the teacher. She's the closest. We'll go and speak with her first. Park Drive. You know it?"

"Yes, I know it. We'll be there in five minutes. It is all fake, isn't it, the wrestling?"

"Try telling that to the grannies who sit at ringside. They would terrify some of the villains I've nicked in my time. Hatpins, pointed combs...one old girl clobbered me with her handbag once. The problem with that was she had half a house brick in it."

"Ouch," Walsh said.

"Indeed. Nearly laid me out I can tell you."

"But the matches themselves..."

"Don't strain your brain over it, Trev. Just look at it this way. There are six matches plus an intermission, but the show ends at ten thirty on the dot. The results are pre-determined but a lot can go wrong if someone doesn't do their job properly. It's why I train so bloody hard. One wrong or badly timed move and I could break an arm or a leg, and my cover would be blown, mask or no mask."

They pulled into Park Drive. "Here we are," Lesser said.

Eunice Havelock lived in a bungalow with a pink, Montana Rubens clematis almost hiding a front door painted bottle green. The rest of the front garden was similarly overgrown and wild, but a riot of summer colour.

Walsh twisted a small key on the front door and a bell sounded loudly.

Eunice Havelock was dressed for the garden in voluminous khaki trousers, a plaid shirt and her shoes were covered by black rubber galoshes. "Yes?" she said querulously as she opened the door.

"Mrs. Havelock..." Lesser began.

"It's Miss. Miss Havelock."

"Sorry," Lesser said and showed her his warrant card. "I understand you take evening classes at St Clements' School."

"Indeed I do, young man. How does that concern the police?"

77

"It concerns one of the students you were teaching last night, a Miss Sandra Duncan."

"Oh, yes, Sandra. Lovely girl. She shows great promise that one. I understand that she wants to work with children, possibly abroad."

"So we're led to believe," Lesser said. "May we come in and ask you a few questions."

"Yes, of course. Nothing's happened to Sandra has it? I worried all night, seeing her going off like that, on a motor scooter of all things."

Lesser and Walsh exchanged looks, eyebrows raised.

The bank's rest room looked like it hadn't been decorated since the nineteen thirties. There was a very plain wooden table with four chairs surrounding it, and a threadbare sofa that looked like it might have been fashionable when Stanley Baldwin was prime minister

Myra sat at the table, took out her notebook and waited for the first member of staff to arrive. There was a tap on the door and an overweight, fussy woman in a peach-coloured knitted twin set scurried into the room.

"Please take a seat," Myra said.

"Battle," the woman said.

"Sorry?"

"Battle. Phyllis Battle. Mrs."

"Thank you for sparing the time, Mrs. Battle," Myra said.

"Only too pleased to help," Phyllis said. She was wearing wire-framed spectacles and each time she spoke her head nodded and the glasses slipped down her podgy nose. She pushed them back with a jab of her index finger.

"I want to talk to you about Sandra Duncan," Myra said.

"All right," Phyllis said. Nod, slip, jab.

"How well do you know her?"

"Not well at all." Nod. "She hasn't been here that long." Slip. "She came here just after Christmas last year." Jab.

"Would you describe her as a friendly girl?"

"Not especially," Phyllis said. "Personally I found her quite sullen...morose even."

"So there's not much you can tell me about her personal life?"

"Nothing at all. As I say, I barely knew her. You'd be better off talking to Charlie."

"Charlie?"

"Third cashier, Charlie Simpson. I think he was quite sweet on her, but then Charlie's sweet on anything in a skirt. Quite the lady's man, is our Charlie."

"Well, perhaps you can ask him to come in on your way out."

"Is that it?" Nod, slip, jab.

"For the time being," Myra said brightly. "I'm only really interested in talking to people who know Sandra."

A frown crossed the woman's face. "Sorry I'm sure. If I knew I was wasting your time I wouldn't have bothered to come in to see you."

"No, really. I want to speak with everyone who works here. The slightest piece of information, however minor you consider it, could be a great help to us with our investigation."

Slightly mollified, the woman got to her feet. "I'll send Charlie in next," she said, and bustled to the door.

"Thank you," Myra said. This looked like it was going be a very long morning.

"Tell us about the motor scooter," Lesser said as they sat around the kitchen table dinking cups of tea.

"What do you want to know?" Eunice said.

"Did Sandra make a point of going home on a motor scooter?"

Eunice laughed. "Good heavens, no. She was a bus girl, like me. Sometimes we'd travel home together."

"But last night she rode her motor scooter?" Walsh said.

Eunice shook her head. "Perhaps I didn't make myself clear," she said. "She took off on the scooter, but she wasn't driving it…is that the correct term? Do you actually drive a scooter? I don't know. Anyway she was a passenger, sitting on the back, the pillion I think they call it."

"I see," Lesser said. "Did you see who was driving it?"

"Not really. I'd just come out of the school and was standing in the doorway when I heard the scooter start up. I looked across the road and I saw it pull away with Sandra sitting on the back of it. I knew it was her because of her rather unusual haircut, but I couldn't really see who was on the front seat, though I got the impression it was a man, and that surprised me because in the time I've known her she's never mentioned a boyfriend."

"I'm pretty sure she didn't have one," Lesser said.

"Can you describe the scooter?" Walsh said. "Colour? Make?"

"Make? I really have no idea," Eunice said. "I can't even recognise the makes of cars. As for the colour, that's difficult because of the street lights, but I would guess green or blue."

Walsh made a note on his pad.

"You say you worried all night about her," Lesser said. "Why was that?"

"Because it was *Sandra*. Like I say, we used to travel home sometimes on the bus and we'd chat. She seemed, how to put it, a little naïve. For an eighteen year old, she didn't seem very worldly wise. In some ways she was just a little girl. I sometimes wondered if her desire to look after children, especially babies, was just an extension of a childish desire to play with dolls. It's strange this class I take. It attracts all sorts, from young mums just starting out on the road to parenthood, to experienced mothers looking for some pointers to make their lives easier, to girls like Sandra who treat the care of children as a sacred calling, a vocation if you like."

"Is there anything else that you can tell us about her?" Lesser said.

"Only that I think her desire to go and work abroad was more an escape than anything else."

"An escape from what exactly?"

Eunice sipped her tea and stared at the two policemen over the rim of her cup. "Have you met her parents?" she said.

"Not personally," Lesser said. "But I understand from those who have that they care about their daughter very much."

"Perhaps a little too much," Eunice said. "I haven't met them myself, but from the way Sandra spoke about them, I got the impression that they are very controlling, hardly allowing the girl to have much of a life of her own. I know they are very churchy. Good Christian stock," she added quite contemptuously.

"And that's a bad thing?" Walsh said. As a regular churchgoer and a devout Catholic himself, he was fairly sensitive to any criticisms of his faith.

"Not in itself," Eunice said. "Although I've never found the need to believe in some kind of omnipotent, imaginary friend to sustain me – spending time in my garden, tending my plants, convinces me of the awesome power of Mother Nature, and that's all the sustenance my soul needs. But for a young woman, forced by her parents to live by the constraints of the Christian belief system, I think, would be very…suffocating. Thus her desire to go abroad and get away." Eunice finished her tea and set the cup back down in the saucer.

"And there's nothing more you can add?" Lesser said.

"No, I don't think so. Is Sandra all right?" she said.

"We don't know," Lesser said. "She didn't make it home last night."

"There wasn't an accident, with the scooter?"

"Well, now you've told us about it, it's one of the avenues we'll be pursuing."

Eunice was wringing her hands. "Oh, I do hope nothing bad has happened. Sandra is a dear girl, with all her life laid out in front of her. It would be a tragedy if she were involved in a terrible accident of some kind. You hear such awful stories these days."

"Well, let's not get ahead of ourselves," Lesser said. "I'm sure there's some fairly mundane explanation for her not going home last night, and I'm sure we'll soon find out what it is."

"I hope so," Eunice said as she walked them to the door. "If there's anything more I can do, please let me know."

"It's a shame you haven't got an imaginary friend you can pray to," Walsh said, earning him a reproving look from his sergeant.

"Good day, Miss Havelock," Lesser said.

"Keep it buttoned in future, Constable," Lesser said as they climbed back into the Wolseley.

"What do you mean," Walsh said.

"You know full well what I mean," Lesser said. "Just because someone doesn't share your beliefs, it doesn't mean they're wrong and you're right."

"My faith is very important to me," Walsh said.

"Yes, and I respect that, but just remember for next time we're interviewing a witness, that faith is not knowledge. It takes all sorts, Trevor."

Walsh fell silent and started the car. They didn't speak again until they reached the next address on the list.

13

WEDNESDAY

Charlie Simpson was in his early twenties, and a sharp dresser. His charcoal grey suit was immaculately tailored, and looked like it cost a week's wages. His hair was dark brown and blow-dried into an elaborate quiff. Myra watched him as he strolled casually into the room and sat down at the table, adjusting the knees of his trousers to stop them bagging. Here was a young man to whom appearances were important. She hoped he would have more interesting information to impart than Phyllis Battle.

"Hello," Myra said. "WPC Banks."

"Very apt."

"Sorry?"

"Banks, in a bank. Very apt...sorry. Charlie Simpson. Third cashier."

"What can you tell me about Sandra Duncan?"

"Mouse."

"Sorry?"

"*Mouse*, Sandra, it's what I call her."

"Doesn't she mind?"

"I think she's just pleased that I notice her."

"And that's something she would cherish? The fact that Charlie Simpson notices her?" Myra stopped and shuffled the papers in Sandra Duncan's work file, distracting herself before she said something rude to this arrogant, conceited little... "How well do you know Sandra?" she said.

"Not very well, but better than most. The other people here, well, they're very tight knit. They don't accept newcomers easily."

"But she's worked here for six months," Myra said.

"And Mouse isn't the easiest person in the world to get along with."

"But you do?"

"I took her for a drink when she first arrived here, but it wasn't a great success. She wanted me to take her home at nine. She said her parents would worry if she were out any later." He shrugged his shoulders. "After that I didn't really want to repeat the experience. I know a lot of girls. I tend to go out with the ones who know how to enjoy themselves."

"You're a real charmer, Charlie, aren't you?"

"Hey, I'm a gentleman. I respect women."

"Yes, I'm sure you do," Myra said tiredly. "Getting back to Sandra, do you know if she had anyone special in her life…a man?"

Simpson laughed. "Mouse? A man? You have to be kidding me."

"I understand a rumour went around the office a little while ago, that Sandra was seeing a man a lot older than herself."

"Rubbish," Simpson said. "I know where that came from – Linda Kramer, one of the typists. She's always making stuff up about people. She likes to stir it, does Linda. She's married to a real bore. Making up gossip is just her way of brightening her day. She's a sad case really. Someone should buy her a wooden spoon."

"So there's no truth in it?"

"Mouse, with an older man?" he said scornfully. "No. The only older man in her life is her father. Why do you want to know about her anyway?"

"She's missing. I'm trying to build up a picture of her. What she's like, the people in her life, that sort of thing."

Simpson leaned back in his seat and regarded her cockily. "Well, you're asking the right person," he said. "As I said, I know her better than most, and believe me, outside of the bank, Sandra doesn't have a life, social or otherwise. She lives like a nun."

"Did you happen to see her last night?"

He thought for a moment. "What was last night? Oh, Tuesday. Sorry, Tuesday is singles night at the *Palais*. I never miss singles night."

"No. I'm sure you don't," Myra said, snapping her notebook shut. "Thank you, Mr. Simpson. It's been most illuminating. Perhaps, on your way out, you could send the next person in."

"Do you get out much?" Simpson said, remaining in his seat. "I wouldn't have thought it's easy for a policewoman to find a date, and Wednesday nights at the *Palais* are usually good."

"Thank you, Mr. Simpson. That will be all."

He stood up and shrugged, "You really don't know what you're missing."

"You know, Mr. Simpson," she said with a smile. "I really think I do."

Linda Kramer was in her mid-twenties but dressed a lot older. Her blonde hair was worn in a short poodle cut, and the horn-rimmed glasses she wore were swept up at the sides, as if she were going for glamour in her spectacles if nowhere else.

"It's said that you started the rumour that Sandra was seeing a much older man."

"It was the truth," she said defensively. "No word of a lie." She seemed on edge, perched forward on the seat, her fingers clenched together. "It was Charlie Simpson, wasn't it, who told you I was responsible?"

Myra said nothing but waited for her to continue.

"He's a fine one to talk – constantly gossiping about people."

"What made you so sure about Sandra?" Myra gently nudged her.

"I saw them, in the park, sitting on a bench together. They seemed to know one another very well."

"Did you recognise the man?"

"I know his face – he might have been in the bank a few times – but not his name."

"Can you describe him?"

"About forty something, dark hair, swept back. Very good looking – a bit like that actor, Ray Milland."

"And what were they doing on the park bench?"

"Arguing," Linda said bluntly.

"How can you be sure?"

"Because he was holding the sleeve of her blouse very tightly and he had a face like thunder."

Myra made a note on her pad.

"I don't suppose you happened to hear what they were arguing about?"

Linda shook her poodle cut. "I was too far away," she said. "I'd just bought myself a cup of tea at the pavilion and had taken it to one of the tables. They were over by the tennis courts."

"How long did you watch them for?"

Linda bridled. "I wasn't spying on them, if that's what you're implying."

Myra smiled. "I'm sure you weren't," she said. "Just one colleague looking out for another."

Linda leaned forward still further in her seat and put her hands on the desk. "Exactly. That was it exactly. I could see the man was very angry with her and I didn't know what he was likely to do."

"And how did Sandra seem during this argument?"

"She looked scared."

"Scared?"

"Like he might attack her at any moment. In the end she pulled away from him and stormed off towards the gates. She passed me as I was sitting drinking my tea, but she didn't seem to notice me. She was crying."

"And what of the man?"

The poodle cut shook again "I don't know. When I looked back he'd gone."

"So when you got back to the bank did you ask Sandra about it, check to see if she was all right?"

"It was none of my business," Linda said. "Besides, Sandra and I aren't friends, inasmuch we don't talk."

"I see," Myra said. "How long ago did this take place?"

"A week ago last Thursday."

"You're sure about that?"

"Definitely. I always take my lunch to the park on Thursdays, and it wasn't last week, so it must have been the week before."

"Thank you, Linda. You've been very helpful."

For the first time, Linda Kramer seemed to relax. She smiled and sat back in her seat.

"That will be all," Myra said.

"Oh, right." Linda got to her feet and left the room.

Myra read through her notes. If Linda was to be believed,

Sandra Duncan was not as shy and timid as people had suggested. Arguing with an older man, in a public place, was not the behaviour of a shy, retiring wallflower. Chief Inspector Callum would find this interesting.

The telephone on the desk started to ring. Jack closed the folder and picked it up.

"It's the desk, sir," Brewer said. "Arthur Duncan's here to see you."

"I'll come down." Hopefully it was good news and Sandra had turned up. He could do with something positive today.

It wasn't good news.

He knew that as soon as he saw the fretful face of Arthur Duncan and spied the pale blue envelope clutched in his hand.

"How can I help, Mr. Duncan?" he said.

"I found this on the front doormat a little while ago," he said as Jack approached, and stuck out the hand holding the envelope.

Jack took the crumpled envelope and flattened it out on the desk. The sheet of paper inside was almost identical to the one left at the Blaineys – a fairly childish drawing of three monkeys. This couldn't be good.

He kept his face neutral as he said, "Did you see who delivered it?" There was no address on the envelope and no stamp. So it was obvious it had simply been pushed through their letterbox.

"No," Duncan said. "I heard the letterbox go and thought it may be Sandra coming in. We keep a spare door key hanging from a piece of string by the letterbox, just in case one of us forgets our keys, then we can get in."

As can half the burglars in the area, Jack thought. People's stupidity astonished him sometimes.

Arthur Duncan was still talking. "…but it wasn't. It was just that, lying on the mat." He stared down at the monkey picture. "What does it mean, Chief Inspector? What are those things? They look like monkeys"

"Three monkeys, yes, Mr. Duncan. We've yet to ascertain their significance."

"So you've seen something like them before."

"Yes," Jack said, mentally kicking himself for underestimating Arthur Duncan's perspicacity.

"When?" he said.

"We saw them in relation to another case we're working on."

"This case?"

Duncan reached into his pocket and took out a folded copy of the local newspaper, slamming it down on the desk.

The headline screamed up at Jack.

WARREN ANDERTON'S DAUGHTER FOUND DEAD.

Damn! he thought. He wasn't expecting the press interest to escalate so quickly.

14

WEDNESDAY

Calming Arthur Duncan down had not been easy, but eventually Jack convinced him he should be back with his wife in case Sandra came home. All he could do now was to wait for the reports to come in from his team. Seeing the Duncan's three monkeys sketch confirmed that Frances Anderton's abduction and murder was not an isolated incident. It was his worst fear made real.

When Fuller and Grant got back to the station from the County School they had a few pieces to add to the puzzle. The headmistress remembered Sandra Duncan but only in an "I think I taught her once" kind of way, and none of the remaining teachers could add much more. Of the girls who had shared classes with her, only one of them offered any concrete information about her, and that was only in the form of a few bitchy remarks about her former school friend's plainness and lack of personality. "When Sandra entered the room it was like someone had just left it," was Barbara Dawson's only contribution of note.

"She just didn't really make an impression on anybody," Fuller said.

"The invisible girl," Harry Grant added. "Sad really."

"Even more so when you consider that this was left on the Duncan's doormat this morning," Jack said.

Fuller grasped the significance of the sketch immediately. "You're thinking we're too late," he said. "Like Frances."

"That was my first thought when I saw it this morning," Jack said.

A gloomy silence settled over the room that only lifted when Myra arrived back from the bank.

"We need some good news, Myra," Jack said, picking up a pencil and chewing the end of it.

"Well, I don't know about *good* news, but I've found out a little more about her."

"And that would be?"

"A couple of weeks ago Sandra was spotted in the park, having an altercation with a man."

"A man?" Jack said. "That flies in the face of everything we've learned about the girl so far. Tell me more."

Myra produced her notebook and gave him a pretty much verbatim account of the Linda Kramer interview.

"That's the best description she can give? Dark haired? Good looking?"

"She says he looked like Ray Milland."

"Oh, that's all right then. We'll go and arrest *him*. I'm not that sure his Hollywood career is that wonderful at the moment, so it shouldn't inconvenience him too much." He threw the pencil he was chewing at the wall. "Why can't people be more bloody observant?"

Myra stared down at the floor. "Sorry, sir."

Jack shook himself. "No, Myra. It's not your fault. I apologise for my outburst. You did good work here. At least it's moved the investigation forward. Could any other members of staff corroborate Miss Kramer's story?"

"*Mrs*. Kramer," Myra corrected him. "And no. Most of them thought she was making the whole thing up. I'm afraid she has a bit of a reputation as a gossip monger."

"So this could just be tittle-tattle," Jack said.

"I don't think so," Myra said. "I think I'm pretty good at reading people and I didn't get the feeling that she was lying."

Jack leaned back in his chair and thought for a moment. He trusted Myra Banks' instincts. He had learned from past experience that a good copper's instincts were usually more valuable than dubious evidence. "Okay," he said. "We'll start trying to track *Ray Milland* down."

"I asked those at the bank if they recognised the description but no one was forthcoming," Myra said.

"Then go to the park and check with the owner of the pavilion. Take Sandra's picture with you, and see if he saw her and this dark haired man together. If he has, he might have some idea who he is, or at least provide us with a better description of him."

"Bit of a long shot, don't you think, sir?" Fuller said.

"Yes, Eddie, I do," Jack said, "but sometimes long shots are all we have, and sometimes they pay off."

It was after four when Lesser and Walsh returned from their interviews with the evening class students.

"A motor scooter?" Jack said. It seemed the more he discovered about Sandra Duncan the less he and everyone else knew about her. "They say it's always the quiet ones," he mused. "How reliable a witness is Miss Havelock?"

"She's very level headed," Lesser said.

"Can she describe the driver?"

"She was too far away to see clearly."

"But she's sure it was Sandra she saw on the back of it."

"Oh, yes, she's certain about that, and she thinks the scooter was either blue or green."

"Well, that's something, I suppose but, without a description of the driver, it doesn't exactly move us forward," Jack said. "No, our best lead is the man Sandra was arguing with in the park. We need a name for him and a better understanding into the nature of Sandra's relationship to him. Let's see if Myra has any luck."

"I'm just closing up," the man behind the counter said as Myra Banks walked into the pavilion.

"Brian Porter?" she said.

"That's right."

"And you own the pavilion?"

"For my sins." Porter was a reed of a man with angular cheekbones and a protruding Adam's apple.

She walked up to the counter. "Do you recognise this girl?" she said without preamble, holding Sandra's photo out for him to see.

Porter took the picture from her and held it at arms length to study it. "I've seen her in here once or twice," he said. "Why? What's she done?"

Myra ignored the question. "Was she in here a week ago last Thursday?"

He closed his eyes and was silent for a moment. "That was the day I took my dog to the vet," he said. "We had to close early."

"But did she come in that day?"

"Oh, yes. I thought it odd because she usually came in on Tuesdays. I suppose it was because she was meeting Tim so she changed her usual day."

"Tim?"

"Tim Fellowes, captain of our bowls team."

"I see," Myra said.

"They shared a pot of tea out there on the veranda." He pointed to a covered terrace that ran across the front of the pavilion. "It didn't seem to be a happy meeting."

"In what way?"

"They appeared to be arguing."

"Have you any idea what they were arguing about?"

Porter snorted. "Are you suggesting I eavesdrop on my patron's conversations?"

"No, not at all," Myra said quickly. "But arguments? Raised voices? Sound travels."

"Well, it didn't travel to these ears," he said. "But it went on for a while. They finished their tea and took the argument down to the bench by the tennis courts."

"Do you know how long it went on for?"

"I couldn't say. It was lunchtime. It gets a bit frantic in here, lunchtimes in August. A lot of people from the offices and shops come in for their lunch breaks."

"Do you know Tim Fellowes well?"

"I was a member of the bowls team for a short while in '55, but I wasn't really good enough, so I stood aside to let a more competent player take my place. Know your strengths, but be aware of your weaknesses, and I was very aware of mine."

"Can you describe him?"

"An excellent bowls player and a superb captain. A master tactician."

"Physically?"

Porter smiled. "I can do better then that." He came out from behind the counter and walked across to a framed photograph hanging from the wall. He reached up and unhooked it from the screw securing it.

"Here you are," he said, handing Myra the photograph.

There was a small brass plaque affixed to the frame that bore the legend, *Winner of the All Herts Lawn Bowls Cup. 1957.*

"We won that last year, mind, I wasn't playing then so I'm not in the photograph."

"But Tim Fellowes is?"

Porter leaned over and pointed to a tall, good-looking man standing in the centre of a motley group of what looked like white flannel-wearing pensioners. "That's Tim. Our leading light."

Myra studied the photograph. Tim Fellowes did bear a striking resemblance to Ray Milland. She smiled.

"Do you know where I can contact him?" she said.

"I don't know where he lives, if that's what you mean, but he has an office in town. *Povey and Fellowes.* They're solicitors."

"I've heard of them," Myra said. "They're in the High Street aren't they?"

"That's right, although you won't catch him there now." Porter looked up pointedly at the clock on the wall. It said five past five.

"May I take this photograph?" Myra said.

Porter looked doubtful.

"We'll let you have it back."

"I'll need a receipt."

"Of course," she said, and took her notebook from the pocket of her tunic.

"We have a name and a photograph of our friend in the park," Myra said when she arrived back at the station.

"Really?" Jack said. "Good work, Myra."

"His name is Tim Fellowes. He's…"

"The solicitor?" Eddie Fuller said.

"Yes," Myra said. "Do you know him?"

"Only by reputation," Fuller said. "A real slippery one is our Tim."

Jack was rubbing his chin. "Yes, I know him, and you're right,

93

Sergeant. He's a bit of a smooth customer. What on earth would he be doing, arguing in public with Sandra Duncan? I would have put them in totally different worlds."

"Excuse me, sir." Andy Brewer was suddenly at Jack's elbow.

"What is it, Andy?"

"A body's been discovered, sir. That of a young woman. Down on the golf course, in one of the bunkers."

"Bloody hell!" Jack muttered under his breath. "Come on," he called to the room. "Let's get down there."

"All of us, sir?" Lesser said.

"Yes, Frank," Jack said. "Unless you think that wrestling 'Judo' Al Hayes at the Edmonton Granada is more important than the murder of a young girl?"

Frank Lesser's face had drained of colour. He turned to Walsh. "How the hell did he know that?" he said *soto voce.*

"Who knows? Walsh replied in a whisper. "But he didn't get it from me. Come on."

Two gleaming, black Wolseleys, bells ringing, tore through the golf club's gates and pulled to a halt outside the clubhouse, drawing curious stares from the half dozen or so golfers milling around their vehicles in the gravelled car park.

Before Jack could get out of his car, a grizzled-looking man in corduroy work trousers and a tatty tweed jacket emerged from the clubhouse and stood waiting at the foot of the steps.

"Arnold Masson, Head Green Keeper,' he said as Jack approached.

"Were you the one who found the body?" he said.

The old man shook his head. "Nah, that was Wilf, one of my lads."

"And where is Wilf now?"

"He was taken poorly," Masson said. "With the shock probably. So I sent him home."

"I'll need to speak with him," Jack said. "So give my Sergeant here his address before we leave. Now, can you take me to see the body?"

Masson licked his lips and nodded his head, mopping his brow with a grubby handkerchief. "This has properly shaken me up," he said as he led them across the links. "I've worked here for over forty years and I've never had anything like this happen."

They reached the second tee and Masson stopped walking. "It's in that sand trap down there," he said, pointing to a bunker a hundred yards away. "I'll stay here if you don't mind. I've seen enough for one day."

Jack glanced behind him and saw Barry Fenwick, doctor's bag in hand, trotting across the grass towards them.

"Another one, Jack?" he said as he approached.

"It certainly looks like it," Jack said grimly, stopping Fenwick before he dropped down into the bunker. "Wait here a minute, Barry. Tell me what you see."

"I see a dead girl lying in a sand trap," Fenwick said impatiently.

"Look at the sand," Jack said.

"There's nothing to see," Fenwick said.

"Exactly. Where are the footprints?"

"I don't see any."

"That's because there aren't any," Jack said. "Whoever dumped her here was careful not to leave any."

"Well, I'm afraid I can't be so careful. I have a job to do," Fenwick said, and dropped down into the bunker.

"He could have stood on the grass and rolled her down the slope," Lesser said.

Jack shook his head. "Look at the way she's laying. On her back, arms crossing her chest. She's been arranged like that. Almost posed for the benefit of whoever found her. We need to talk to the boy who made the discovery, and see if he interfered with the scene at all."

"He lives in Wilshaw Road, just the other side of the course," Fuller said. "I can go and see him now."

"Yes, do that," Jack said. "I'll meet you back at the station." He climbed down into the bunker and crouched down beside Fenwick. "Initial thoughts, Barry?"

There was a flash as Walsh started photographing the scene.

"Get one showing how the body was arranged," Jack said. He and Fenwick got to their feet and stood back so Walsh could get a clear shot of the body.

"My initial thoughts are that whoever killed Frances Anderton was also responsible for the death of this girl too. "Ligature marks on the wrists and on the throat. Eyes and mouth crudely sewn shut and wax poured into the ears."

"Yes," Jack said. "That's what I was afraid of."

15

WEDNESDAY

"Adam, it's me."

"Fiona? Why are you phoning me at work? We had an agreement," Adam Channing said.

"Yes, well, things have changed. Frances has been killed. Murdered."

"Good God! Are *you* all right?"

"Yes…no…I don't know. The thing is, the police have been here and they know about you, about us."

Fiona listened to the silence on the other end of the line. "Adam? Adam?"

"When did it happen?" he said at last.

"They think it was some time on Sunday. The thing is, Adam, I think they're going to want to question you."

"They have me down as a suspect?"

"They're going to want to question everyone who knew her."

"But I didn't know her."

"But you *did* meet her, at the end of term party."

"That was months ago and, sorry to say this about your sister, Fiona, but she hardly registered."

"Yes, I can understand that. Nevertheless…"

"Did you give them my address?"

"No, but they know you're a lecturer at the LSE."

"Well, that's a relief At least I won't have PC Plod turning up at the house upsetting Gwen."

"Is that your only concern, Adam?"

Silence again.

Eventually he spoke. "What other concerns would I have?"

"Well, being a suspect in a murder case for one thing," Fiona said.

"You say she was killed on Sunday?"

"That's right."

"Well, on Saturday, Sunday and Monday I was up at Falkirk in Scotland at a conference. Gwen's sister came down to stay with her while I was away. So as long as they come to the college to interview me, I can't see it presenting much of a problem, can you?"

Fiona let out her breath in a thin stream. She hadn't been aware she was holding it. Screwing a cigarette into her holder, she lit it and sucked in the smoke. "I need to see you," she said, and noticed that the hand holding the cigarette was shaking.

"Of course," he said easily. "I want to see you too."

"No, Adam, I *need* to see you." Hot tears were running down her cheeks. Hearing that Adam had an alibi for when Frances was killed was such a relief. She hadn't believed for a second that he might have something to do with her sister's murder, but Detective Chief Inspector Callum had started the wheels of doubt whirring in her mind, and she'd needed to hear it from Adam's own lips that he wasn't involved.

"Can we meet?" she said.

"I have a lecture to prepare tonight."

"Please, Adam," she said, aware she was sounding desperate and hating herself for it.

"Okay, but not until the weekend. Saturday evening," he said. "Our usual place. Eight o' clock?"

"Thank you," she said. "And, Adam, I'm sorry, but I feel so useless. It's the shock I expect."

"Yes, of course. There's no need to apologise. I understand. It must be awful for you and your parents. Your poor sister."

The line went dead. She hung up the phone and went into the morning room.

Her mother was lying full out on the chesterfield, a damp cloth covering her eyes. "Who were you on the phone to?" she said as Fiona entered the room.

"No one…just a friend."

"Why isn't your father in yet? How he could just go to work, as if nothing has happened."

"It's probably for the best, keeping occupied." Fiona said. "I'm sure he'll be home soon."

Jessica took the cloth from eyes that were red and sore from constant crying. She sat up, wringing the cloth in her hands, ignoring the water dripping onto the shag-pile. "Frances has gone, Fiona," she said.

Fiona sat down next to her mother and wrapped an arm around her shoulders

"Someone's taken our baby from us," Jessica said, and began to sob.

Fiona pulled her close. *Yes*, she thought. *But at least that someone wasn't my Adam.*

The house on Wilshaw Road was a neat two up two down that sat in the middle of a terrace of almost identical homes, nestled in the centre of an estate of new-builds, the uniformity of which was slowly, but inexorably, draining the character from this part of Hatfield.

He rang the doorbell and waited. Finally the door was opened by a grey haired man who looked to be in his late sixties or early seventies. He was wearing a beige cardigan and baggy jeans, patched at the knees.

"Hello," Fuller said and introduced himself. "I was looking for your son."

"I haven't got a son," the man said.

"Wilf?" Fuller said.

"Yeah, that's me."

"Sorry," Fuller said. "Arnold Masson said you were one of his lads."

"That's right. He calls all of us *his lads*."

"I was expecting someone younger."

"Obviously. Are you here about the body?"

Fuller nodded.

"Then you'd better come in."

Adam Channing leaned back in his office chair and tapped a pencil against his teeth. Fiona's call was not totally unexpected, he was just surprised she had waited until Wednesday to make it. He picked up the telephone receiver and dialled a number.

"Hello?" a cultured voice on the other end of the line said.

"I've been told to expect a visit from the police concerning the Anderton girl?"

"Are you surprised, Adam? You sound surprised. Surely, this

was what we were expecting."

"No, I'm not surprised."

"Then you know what to say. Your trip to Scotland will prove very fortuitous."

"Yes, I know."

"Then stay calm. It should play out just as we planned."

"I *am* being calm," Channing said. "I'm just bringing you up to date."

"Have you called Tim yet?"

"No. He's still in Zurich."

"Ah yes, until tomorrow. Well, there's no point wasting a long-distance call to tell him something we were expecting. I'll telephone him when he gets back to his office tomorrow and let him know. By rights he'll be getting a visit from them too in the next few days about the Duncan girl. He made sure he was seen talking to her."

"Do you think it's going well," Channing said.

"Like clockwork," the urbane voice said and hung up.

Channing put the phone down. "Like clockwork," Channing said to himself. *The bastard!*

Rosie Callum piled the last of the loaves into a wooden tray, and picked up another to load the cakes, when there was a tap at the window. She looked up into the smiling face of a young man with short, curly hair. "Are you closed?" he mouthed at her.

Rosie shook her head and pointed to the door. A few seconds later the bell above the door jangled as he pushed his way inside the baker's.

"I thought I was too late," he said as he entered the shop. "Do you have any sausage rolls?"

"I have a couple left," she said. "Are they for your tea?" she said, and mentally kicked herself for asking such an inane question. He would think she was a bit dim and that was the last thing she wanted. The young man was one of her regular customers. She knew his name was David and that he worked at the insurance offices along the street, but that was all she knew about him, apart from the fact that he had kind, brown eyes and a slightly lopsided smile that made her knees go weak.

"I'll take them then," he said, and watched her as she put the sausage rolls into a paper bag and secured the top by flipping it over and twisting the corners deftly.

"You did that like an expert," he said.

"Years of practice," she said.

"You don't look old enough to have mastered such an ancient art," he said.

"You'd be surprised," Rosie said. "I'm sixteen. That will be a shilling."

He pulled a handful of change from the pocket of his trousers and sorted through it, finding two sixpenny bits. He handed them to her and she gave him the bag. "Anything else I can do for you?" she said.

"Do you like films?"

"What kind of films?"

"The kind you watch, at the cinema."

"Yes," she said. "I like films, and I like the cinema, though I don't go that often."

"Would you like to go, with me? *High Society* is playing at the *Metropole*. Frank Sinatra, Grace Kelly. It's a musical."

"I like musicals."

"So will you come?" he said. "Please say yes, because I really want to see it, and I hate going to the pictures by myself."

She felt herself blushing. "When did you have in mind?" she said.

"How about tonight? There's a show at eight thirty. I could pick you up and we could drive into town."

"You have a car?" It was unusual for someone of his age to own a car.

"It's my dad's, but he lets me use it on special occasions."

"And taking me to the pictures is a special occasion?"

"Oh, yes, very special."

She felt her cheeks start to glow as the blush increased. She imagined she looked as red as the cherries on the iced buns she sold.

"Well, as it's a special occasion, I'd better say yes."

"I was hoping you would. My name's David by the way.

David Neville. My friends call me Davy."

"Rose Callum," she said. "Rosie."

"Well then, Rosie, I'll pick you up at seven thirty. Where do you live?"

She told him.

"I know it," he said. "Until tonight then."

"Until tonight."

She waited until he had left the shop and then went to the door and locked it, flipping the sign from OPEN to CLOSED.

"Have you locked up?" a voice called from the back of the shop.

"I've just done it." Rosie stuck her head around the door of the back room. Mrs. Painter, the owner of the bakery was sitting at the staff table, her head buried in the *Daily Mirror* crossword, a cup of coffee gradually growing cold at her elbow.

She looked up at Rosie. "You'd best be off then," she said. "Make yourself look beautiful for tonight."

"You heard?"

"He seems like a nice enough lad," Mrs. Painter said.

"I'm sorry. I didn't mean to…"

Mrs. Painter looked at her over her half-rimmed reading glasses and adjusted her ample bosom, which strained against the white nylon of her overall. "We were all young once, Rosie. Even me."

"Can you drop me off at home?" Jack said to Walsh who was driving. The mood in the car was sombre. No one felt much like talking.

The last thing Fenwick had said to them was hanging over the car like a cloud. "It looks like she's been interfered with."

They reached Jack's house and he climbed out of the Wolseley. "We'll pick this up tomorrow," he said. "I've had enough for one day."

As he was walking up the path to the front door, Rosie breezed in through the gate. She ran up to him and kissed his cheek. "Hello, Dad."

"Hello, yourself. You seem cheerful. Had a good day?"

"The best," Rosie said, grinning.

Jack turned the key in the lock and let them into the house.

A harsh chemical smell hit them as soon as they entered. "What on earth is that smell?" he said, and then saw Annie's friend, Avril, and understood. Hairdressers used all manner of concoctions these days. Avril was in the hallway, shrugging herself into a tangerine duster coat.

"Are you off?" Jack asked her.

"Mission completed, Mr. Callum. My work here is finished," Avril said with a smile, and threw him a mock salute.

Jack looked at her quizzically.

"They're in the kitchen," Avril said. "Go and look."

Jack squeezed past her and walked into the kitchen. Annie was sitting at the kitchen table, sharing a pot of tea with a young woman with dark, cropped hair. Jack stared at the young woman for a full thirty seconds before he realised he was staring at his eldest daughter.

"Joanie?" he said.

Joan ran her fingers through her newly shorn hair and smiled. "Yes, Dad, it's me. Do you like it?"

"Very Audrey Hepburn," he said. "Did you mean to go that short?"

"Avril said that all the peroxide had damaged her hair permanently..." Annie said.

"So I decided to go for broke and got her to chop it all off and colour it," Joan finished for her. "Do you approve?"

Jack shook his head tiredly. "Is there any more tea in that pot?"

"I'll get you a mug," Annie said.

"Well?" Joan said. "I'm waiting."

Jack smiled. "It looks lovely," he said. "Very...fetching."

"Fetching?"

"Very attractive. It suits you," Jack said. "More than the blonde did anyway."

"He said, damning me with faint praise," Joan said. "When did Dad become such an old fuddy duddy, Mum?"

"He's your father, Joanie. He's always been that way," Annie said.

"Hey," Jack said.

"Well, I think it looks gorgeous," Rosie said as she entered the kitchen. "I've been thinking lately about getting mine cut."

"Ooh, Rosie, you should do. I would really suit you with those cheekbones of yours."

"Steady, Joanie," Jack said. "I haven't got used to your haircut yet, without you organising a mass shearing in my house."

"Tell him, Mum, that it's nineteen fifty eight. Lots of girls are wearing their hair like this these days."

"Leave me out of this," Annie said as she poured Jack's tea.

"Very wise," Jack said.

"But then," Annie said to her eldest, "seeing yours could persuade me to do something different with mine."

Jack raised his eyes skywards. "You see, Joanie. You're back not more than forty eight hours and already you're starting a revolution."

"Liver for dinner," Annie said. "Why don't you go and clean up, Jack, and we can all sit down to a civilized meal?"

"Amen to that," Jack said.

"Can I use the bathroom first, Dad? Only I'm going to the cinema tonight and I need to get myself ready. I'm being picked up at half past seven."

"Picked up?" Joan said. "You've got a date."

Rosie said nothing but blushed furiously.

"You *have* got a date." Joan got to her feet and ran across to Rosie, grabbing her arm and propelling her out through the door. "Come with me, little sis. I'll help you with your make up."

Their feet clattered on the stairs as they ran up to the bathroom.

Jack sipped his tea. "I think I'll take my tea and go and listen to the radio in the living room."

"Sorry," Annie said. "Eric's in there doing his homework. Stay with me in here and tell me about your day."

Jack stared at her and gave a brief shake of his head.

"Was it that bad?" Annie said.

"Worse."

Annie moved away from the sink and came up behind him, wrapping her arms around his waist. "Sorry you've come back

104

to a madhouse. I didn't think Avril would take as long as she did."

"It doesn't matter," Jack said. "She did a fine job. And I don't mind."

"You don't mind what?"

"If you want to cut your hair. I won't mind."

Annie came around and looked at him guardedly. "You're being serious," she said.

"It's not important in the grand scheme of things. It's only hair. It will grow back."

Annie sat down on the kitchen chair next to him, taking his hand and staring at him intently. "You *have* had a bad day haven't you?"

"It was pretty grim," he said. "We found another dead girl. Dumped on the golf course this time."

Annie's grip on his hand tightened. "Oh no, Jack," she said.

16

WEDNESDAY

Some time later Joan came back downstairs. She found Jack and Annie in the living room.

"What do you think of your youngest daughter now?" she said pulling Rosie into the room behind her as if presenting her at court.

Rosie was wearing make up – too much, Jack thought – and her hair had been styled into a sophisticated side sweep.

"You're not going out like that," Jack said flatly.

"Jack?" Annie said.

"Dad!" from both the girls.

"Go back up upstairs, Rosie and wipe that stuff of your face and put on something more suitable. You're sixteen not twenty-six."

Annie got to her feet. "Jack, I really don't think it's necessary…"

"Annie," Jack said severely. "There's a monster out there killing girls of Rosie's age, and you're prepared to let her go out of this house dressed like a common prostitute."

Rosie burst into tears and ran from the room. Annie looked at her husband incredulously. "Jack, how could you?"

"I could because I care about our daughter's safety."

"You're over-reacting," Annie said.

"Maybe I am," Jack said, folding his arms. "But I'm still not allowing Rosie to go out."

"But she's so excited, Jack. I think it's the boy she's been mooning over for weeks."

"I don't care," Jack said. "She stays in tonight…and every night until we catch him."

Annie glared at him furiously, and then turned and stormed out of the room, following her daughter up the stairs.

Jack sat, arms folded and legs crossed, staring into the empty grate of the fireplace.

Joan wheeled on her father. "My running away taught you

nothing, did it?" she said.

"It taught me that I have to keep my family safe," Jack said.

"So what do you want to do? Wrap us all in cotton wool until you've slain all the monsters? Well, for your information, Dad, there are always monsters out there – believe me I know. I've met my fair share of them. But you can't protect us from them all, no matter how much you want to. Rosie's growing up, and treating her like a valuable piece of Dresden china is not going to help her grow into a woman who can take on the world and come out on top."

"Like you, you mean?" Jack said, unable to mask the bitterness in his voice.

Joan came across and sat at his feet. "I made mistakes, Dad, and I'm big enough to admit it. But you can't keep Rosie locked in a gilded cage and then be surprised if she does the same as me."

Jack continued to stare into the grate. "But this boy who's taking her to the pictures, we know nothing about him. For all I know he could be Jack the Ripper."

"And he could be a perfectly respectable young man who sees your daughter for the beautiful and intelligent young woman she is," Joan said. "If you carry on like this, you'll end up driving her away. The time I was away was the worst period of my life."

"Mine too," Jack said.

"Well, I don't want that for you, or for Rosie. Meet this boy – Rosie tells me his name's David, and he works for an insurance company in town – meet him and get the measure of him. You assess people all the time as part of your job. If you think he poses a threat to her, then keep her home and I'll back you all the way, but if not, let her go out tonight. Give her the chance to be the young woman she yearns to be."

Jack sat back in his chair and closed his eyes. "Daughters," he said tiredly. "Who'd have them? Eric never gives me these problems."

"Give him time, Dad."

Jack reached out and stroked her hair. "And when did you acquire this great wisdom?" he said.

"It's the way you and mum brought me up," Joan said.

'I suppose I should go and apologise."

"It wouldn't do any harm."

"Sometimes I can be a bloody fool," he said.

Joan nodded. "It's why we love you," she said.

Jack knocked on Rosie's door. Annie opened it, still glaring at him furiously. "May I speak with her?" Jack said.

"Not if you're still going to be pig-headed and rude," Annie said.

"It's all right, Mum," Joan said from the top of the stairs. "Let him talk to her."

Annie looked at her eldest daughter uncertainly. Joan gave a small nod of her head and Annie took a step out onto the landing, leaving the doorway clear. Jack walked into the room and closed the door behind him.

On the bed, Rosie sat, her knees drawn up to her chin, mascara trails streaking her cheeks.

"May I sit down?" Jack said.

Rosie regarded him cautiously, sniffed tearfully and gave a slight shrug of her shoulders. Jack sat down on the bed.

"Your mum was right," he said. "I was over-reacting."

Rosie remained silent and waited for him to continue.

"In my job I see all manner of terrible things," he said. "I did today, and the day before yesterday, and these things terrify me. For all my training in dealing with these awful events, of handling the tragedy and loss, nothing prepares you or makes you immune to the fear that one day these things could happen to your own family. Does that make sense?"

Rosie nodded and sniffed back the tears again.

"Can I meet this boy before he takes you out?"

A small spark of hope glimmered in Rosie's eyes. "I can invite him in tonight before we go, so you and mum can meet him."

"Do you think we'd pass muster?"

"Mum would, you I'm not so sure of," she said, smiling wanly.

"Am I that much of a dragon?" Jack said.

"You're pretty scary," Rosie said. "But I think David will like you."

"So that's his name? David?"

"David Neville, he sells insurance."

"Well, that's a respectable occupation."

"And he's driving me to the cinema in his dad's car."

"So his father obviously trusts him."

"Oh, Dad, you'll really like him. He has the kindest eyes."

Jack stood up and walked to the door. "Am I forgiven?"

Rosie gave a rueful smile and nodded.

"Then you'd better repair your make up before he arrives. You look like a panda. I'll send Joanie in. She can help fix it."

Joan was standing outside the door. "I think she needs help with her make up," he said, holding the door open for her.

Joan reached up and pecked him on the cheek. "As father's go," she said. "You're not so bad."

"As daughters go, you're not so bad yourself," he said, and watched as she went across to the bed and hugged her sister, and then he turned and walked slowly down the stairs, ready to build bridges with Annie. He could really do without days like these.

David Neville parked the Ford Anglia outside the Callum's house, got out of the car and walked up the garden path to the front door. He rang the doorbell and waited.

The woman who answered was probably in her forties, with shoulder length light brown hair. She was also extremely attractive.

"Hello," she said. "You must be David. I'm Rose's mother. She'll be down in a minute. Please come in."

She opened the door wide, and stood aside for him to enter.

"We're in here," she said, opening another door and ushering him inside.

Neville walked into the room and was confronted by three people, none of them Rosie. There was a boy, a teenager, younger than Rosie, a young woman with short dark hair and vivacious eyes, and finally a man dressed in a dark red sweater covering a shirt and tie and wearing grey slacks. He was standing by the fireplace, leaning casually against a wooden mantelpiece bedecked with framed family photographs. He stepped forward and stuck out his hand. "Jack Callum," he said.

"I'm Rose's father."

Neville took the proffered hand and shook it. "David Neville," he said, impressing himself with the firmness of his own handshake. His father had instilled in him that first impressions were vitally important. 'You can tell a lot about a man from the way he shakes your hand.' *Thanks, Dad. Lesson learned.*

"So, David, how did you meet my daughter?" Jack said.

Neville realised the handshake trick worked both ways. As Jack's eyes bore into his he realised that Rosie's father was no fool. He was weighing him up to see if he was a suitable candidate to be his daughter's companion for the evening.

"We met at the baker's," he said. "I buy my lunch there."

"And what film are you taking my daughter to see?"

"*High Society*, sir," Neville said.

"Ah, Bing Crosby," Jack said approvingly. "A *real* singer."

"And Louis Armstrong," Neville added.

"Indeed. Have you seen it before?"

Neville shook his head. "It's the first time they've shown it at the *Metropole*."

"Well, I'm sure you'll enjoy it. When did you pass your driving test?"

The sudden change of tack didn't put Neville off his stride. "Two years ago." sir."

"Two years? How old are you?"

"Nineteen."

"Jack," Annie said. "Stop interrogating the poor boy." She turned to Neville. "You'll have to forgive my husband, David. Sometimes he forgets he's not at work."

Neville's eyes widened slightly. "At work?"

"My husband's a policeman."

Jack watched the boy's Adam's apple bob as he swallowed. "Is that a problem to you, David," he said.

Neville gathered himself. "No, not at all, sir. My dad was in the police too, when he was in the army. Military police of course."

"He was a Red Cap then."

Neville smiled and nodded. "And never lets me forget it," he said, almost under his breath.

"The Red Caps do a difficult job," Jack said. "I know. I'm ex-army myself."

Conversation dried as the living room door opened and Rosie stood in the doorway. "I'm ready," she said.

Like a fish escaping the hook Neville hurried to the door. "Rosie. You look...radiant," he said.

A crimson flush rushed to Rosie's cheek. "Thank you," she said diffidently. "You look very nice too."

"Well, go on, get along with you," Annie said, clapping her hands and shooing them to the door. "You don't want to miss the start of the film."

"We'll be all right, Mum. There's *Pathé News* and *Pearl and Dean* on first."

"And what's coming next week," Neville added.

"Then you won't have to break any speed limits to get there, will you?"

"No, sir," Neville said.

"Back no later than eleven. Rosie has work tomorrow," Jack said.

"Jack," Annie said as they heard the front door close and a car's engine cough into life. "You probably scared the life out of the poor boy,"

"Personally, I was waiting for the questions on the Highway Code," Eric said. "That would have been fun."

"Was I really that bad?" Jack said.

"As inquisitions go, I think he got off pretty lightly," Joan said.

Jack smiled darkly, went across to the radiogram and switched it on.

"And you won't come to bed until Rosie is safely tucked up in hers, will you?" Annie said.

"Not a chance," Jack said, and sat down in the chair to listen to the news.

The mellow tones of Alberto Semprini's piano, playing on the radio, was rudely interrupted by the harsh ringing of the doorbell. Jack looked up at the clock on the mantel. 10.55. *Well, the boy was as good as his word*, Jack thought and went to let his daughter in.

Rosie was standing on the doorstep, facing the street. She waved as the Ford Anglia pulled away from the kerb,

"Did you have a nice evening?" Jack said.

Rosie turned and came into the house. "Wonderful," she said with a swoon in her voice. "It was so romantic. And Grace Kelly is *so* beautiful."

"Are you seeing him again?"

"I think so. He's going to come into the baker's tomorrow," Rosie said. At the bottom of the stairs she paused. "Did you like him, Dad?"

"Your mum does, and Joan. Eric is still deciding."

"But did *you* like him?"

"I think he seems like a nice lad," Jack said.

"But you don't think he's good enough for me."

"I didn't say that."

"You didn't have to. It's in your voice."

Jack wrapped his arms around his daughter and pulled her close. "Listen, Princess. I don't think any boy you bring home will ever be good enough for you, but that's a father's prerogative. It's my God given right to disapprove of the choices you make."

"But that's so unfair," Rosie said.

"That doesn't mean I'm always going to be right. I said that I think David is a nice enough lad, okay? Be satisfied with that for now."

Rosie looked at him sternly. "For now," she said. "But I assure you, once you get to know him better, you'll approve of him."

"Then I wait to be convinced. Now, off to bed with you. It's late. You have work tomorrow."

Rosie kissed him on the cheek. "Night, Dad," she said, and trotted up the stairs humming to herself.

Jack recognised the tune. He'd taken Annie up to London to see *High Society* when it first opened in the West End, and they had come back home on the train, both of them humming the same tune. He could still picture the scene from the film vividly. Bing Crosby reclining in an open boat pretending to play the concertina, while Grace Kelly lay with her head in his lap as they sang a duet. The song? *True Love.*

Daughters, Jack thought for the second time that day. *Who'd have them?*

17

THURSDAY AUGUST 14th 1958

Gavin Southland made a final flourish with his hog bristle brush, trailing a long gash of vermillion *Liquitex* acrylic paint down the canvas, and stepped back from the easel to admire his work.

"It's probably one of your best yet," said a voice behind him.

Southland turned away from the painting slowly. Tim Fellowes stood in the doorway of the studio, staring at the painting, a look of mild distaste on his face.

Yes," Southland said. "I'm reasonably satisfied with it, though I'm not sure I got the hair colour right. I think the girl's hair was more ginger, a notoriously difficult shade to capture. Have you just got back?"

"My flight landed two hours ago. I came straight here."

"Have you eaten? I can prepare breakfast for you."

"I ate at the airport, although the Heathrow facilities aren't exactly five star, they can't do much to ruin a cup of tea and toast. Did you have any problems with Sandra?"

Southland laid down his brush on the brush rest. "I've already started the preliminary sketches."

"I wasn't talking about your painting. I was referring to the disposal," Fellowes said.

"Ah, that. I'm assured that it went well. She was found on the golf course yesterday." Southland smiled. "In a sand trap."

"Risky. He might have been seen."

"You worry too much, Tim. He was very careful. He stole one of the golf carts from the clubhouse to transport her across the course and set her down just so, as per my instructions, and returned the cart before it was missed."

Fellowes stared at his old university friend. He was becoming increasingly disturbed by Southland's reckless streak. "You took a chance," he said.

"A calculated risk. Art never progresses unless you're willing to take chances," Southland said. He turned back to the canvas and picked up his brush again. "I think I'm going to try the hair again. I'm really not happy with the colour."

Fellowes went across to the cabinet in the corner and poured a small measure of whisky from a crystal decanter into a cut glass tumbler, knocked the alcohol back in a single gulp and shook his head. "The golf course? Really?"

"Imagine the image, Tim, the young virgin lying there, peaceful, serene, framed by all that pure, golden sand. It's almost Pre-Raphaelite in its composition, and I told him to be careful not to leave any marks in the sand. I wanted it to be perfect."

Fellowes walked back to the door. "I'd better get on," he said. "I just wanted to make sure there were no hitches."

Southland limped across from the easel and joined him at the door. "It's all going exactly as I expected, Tim," he said, resting his hand on Fellowes' shoulder. "All we have to do is to keep our nerve and stick to our plan. The police will be chasing their tails for weeks."

"Well, that was the original idea, wasn't it?" Fellowes said. "If you need me I'll be in the office for the rest of the day."

He walked to his car, popped an extra strong peppermint into his mouth to kill the smell of the scotch on his breath, and drove into town. His mind was turning over possibilities. He needed a way out of this, but solutions were proving elusive. He'd have to talk to Adam Channing. He knew Channing felt the same as he did, but they were trapped in Southland's game and Gavin Southland had made it clear that they were his rules and Fellowes and Channing would have to abide by them. If not, the consequences for the two men would be devastating. He wished now he had never met Gavin Southland, but the clock couldn't be turned back.

"How did you get on yesterday?" Jack asked as he climbed into Fuller's car.

Fuller smiled. "Masson's idea of a lad needs redefining," he said.

"Not a youngster then," Jack said.

"Wilfred Ellis is older that Masson himself," Fuller said.

"Did he see anything?"

"Apart from a golf cart trundling across the links sometime yesterday afternoon, not a lot."

"I was wondering how they would be able to transport a body across the course without carrying it. A golf cart would be the sensible solution," Jack said.

"But he'd be taking a hell of a risk that he'd be seen."

"Who would take notice of a golf cart on the links? Most golfers are too wrapped up in their own game to worry what other players are doing."

"He's getting bold," Fuller said.

"Bold or reckless," Jack said. "One or the other. I don't suppose Ellis saw who was driving it?"

Fuller shook his head. "He didn't notice."

"No, of course not. We couldn't be *that* lucky. We'll have to check out the course and see who was scheduled to play that day. They might have seen something."

"Do you want me to go?"

"Yes, and take Myra with you. She did good work yesterday."

"You like her, don't you?" Fuller said.

"I think she has the makings of a damned fine detective. She's tenacious, and has the ability to think on her feet. We could do with more like her on the team."

There was a tap on the door and Brewer walked into the office. He handed Jack a manila envelope. "This just came in from the lab. It's the forensic report on Frances Anderton."

"Thanks, Andy," Jack said, tore open the flap, took the thin sheaf of paper from the envelope and started leafing through the pages. "Her eyes and lips were sewn with back silk embroidery thread," he said, almost to himself as he read.

"Significant?" Fuller said, getting to his feet.

"It might be. Why use silk thread when polyester or cotton would do the job just as well?"

Fuller shrugged. "Search me."

"I'll go into town and have a chat with Tim Fellowes after I've broken the news to the Duncans. When I rang first thing, his secretary said she was expecting him to be in the office by about ten. He should be there by the time I arrive."

Tim Fellowes walked into the office and hung his fedora on the hat stand. His secretary, Doris Worthington, came out from behind her desk. "Hello, Tim, the old man's been asking for you," she said.

Fellowes frowned. Cyril Povey was starting to become the bane of his life. When Povey had offered him the junior partnership in the firm Fellowes had been somewhat reluctant to accept the offer. He'd enjoyed working for himself – he liked the freedom and autonomy the position afforded him, but rising business rates and the increasing cost of renting his centre-of-town office, had made it untenable for him to continue working on his own. Povey's offer of a junior partnership had bailed him out of an increasingly sticky financial situation.

But, the old man was no fool. He knew that taking on a junior partner enabled him to offload the bread and butter work, the house conveyancing, petty lawsuits and minor criminal cases, leaving himself to pick up the remainder of clients – the high-end and more lucrative side of the business, as well as allowing him more time to spend on the golf course.

Fellowes rapped on Povey's door.

"Come in."

He pushed open the office door.

"Ah, Tim, you're back. Did you have a good trip?"

Cyril Povey's wizened frame was dwarfed by the size of the antique walnut-veneered desk he sat behind.

Staring at him over the rimless half-moon spectacles he affected, the old man looked like some kind of grey, burrowing creature, just exposed to the sunlight.

"Not too bad. I got all the contracts signed as agreed," Fellowes said.

"I still don't know why you had to fly off to Switzerland just to get a couple of signatures when the whole transaction could have been handled just as well by post."

"Lassister was delighted I went to see him and talk through some of the clauses. Besides I paid for the trip out of my own pocket, so the cost to the firm was no more than the price of two day's work, and I can soon make that up."

Povey looked at him steadily for a long moment before shrugging. "I suppose so. In my day it wasn't so easy to hop on a plane and fly off to all these exotic places."

"I would hardly describe Switzerland as exotic. In fact Lassiter's chalet is quite modest, and very conservatively appointed. The most ostentatious part of it is the view over the lake, and you can get much the same effect up in Cumbria."

"It makes you wonder why he chooses to live out there," Povey said dismissively.

"Their tax laws favour a man in Alfred Lassiter's position."

Povey barked a laugh. "Position! I knew Freddie Lassiter when he was running around the streets with the backside hanging out of his trousers and his brother's cast-off shoes on his feet. He made his fortune when he married Virginia Allsop, and only then because her father died and landed his entire estate on his daughter. Grant Allsop was a very shrewd businessman and as rich as *Croesus*."

"You sound bitter," Fellowes said

"Probably because I am. Ginny Allsop was the love of my life. We were engaged until Lassiter made his move on her. She was dazzled by his roguish good looks and his easy way with the ladies. He made this particular provincial solicitor look very ordinary indeed."

"At least you kept him as a client. His business brought in two thousand pounds last year alone."

Povey looked at him bleakly. "What price a broken heart, eh, Tim?"

"She's fat now, if that's any consolation to you, and she has varicose veins."

Povey looked past him dreamily at the mantelpiece over a small cast iron fireplace in the corner of the office. There was a single, silver-framed photograph in the centre of if, of a young woman with vibrant eyes set in a porcelain face under a shock of unruly curls.

"But she was a beauty then," the old man said.

The intercom on the desk buzzed.

Povey reached across the desk and pressed a button. "What is it, Doris?"

Doris's voice crackled through the speaker. "Is Tim in there with you?"

"Yes, he is."

"Then you can tell him that he has a visitor?"

"Does his visitor have a name, Doris?"

"It's Detective Chief Inspector Callum from Welwyn and Hatfield police station."

Povey released the button on the intercom. "DCI Callum to see you, Tim," he said. "Is it concerning a case?"

"Not that I'm aware of," Fellowes said. "Callum, I don't think I've ever dealt with him before."

"Oh, you'd remember if you had. Like a dog with a bone that one. I've watched sure fire acquittals end up in the cells of Dartmoor and Pentonville. Once he has his teeth into someone, he rarely lets go. And although I'm loath to say it, he's rarely wrong. He has a copper's nose, and can sniff out wrongdoers at a dozen paces."

"I'd better watch my step then," Fellowes said with an easy smile. He got to his feet and walked from the room.

In the outer office he saw a tall, well-built man of about forty-five, wearing a dark suit, leaning casually against Doris's desk. As Fellowes stepped out of Povey's room, the man pushed himself away from the desk and took a step towards him, his hand extended.

"DCI Callum?" Fellowes said, taking the proffered hand. "What can I do for you?"

"May we speak privately?" Jack said.

"Of course. Come through to my office. Hold my calls, Doris," he said to the secretary, and led Jack through to another room.

"Please, take a seat," Fellowes said as he went behind a mahogany desk and made himself comfortable in a luxuriously upholstered leather office chair. Jack sat down in the chair's poor relation opposite him.

"Now, how can I help?" Fellowes said as Jack settled his large frame uncomfortably into the chair.

"Sandra Duncan," Jack said without preamble. "Is that name familiar to you?"

"It is indeed," Fellowes said. "Miss Duncan is a client of mine. I trust she's done nothing to warrant a police investigation."

"I'm afraid Miss Duncan is dead, Mr. Fellowes."

18

THURSDAY

"Dead? Good God! I was only speaking with her the other week. Was it some kind of accident?"

"Miss Duncan has been murdered, Mr. Fellowes."

"Murdered? Good God!" Fellowes said again. "By whom?"

"That is what we are attempting to find out." Jack was watching Fellowes closely, particularly his eyes. So far they were registering shock that looked pretty genuine.

"The poor girl," Fellowes said. "Who in their right mind would want to kill such an inoffensive creature as Sandra Duncan? I didn't know her well, Chief Inspector, but I would have thought that she wouldn't say boo to a goose, let alone upset anyone enough for them to want to murder her. Her poor parents. Do they know yet?"

"I've just come from seeing them," Jack said. "They haven't taken the news well."

"Who can blame them? I understand they were very devoted to their daughter."

"Indeed," Jack said. "As for your previous point, as to who Miss Duncan would upset, I have a number of witnesses who saw you arguing with her in the park three weeks ago today. That would be the 24th of July. Could you tell me what that argument was about?"

A troubled look crossed Fellowes' face. "I'd like to Chief Inspector, but I'm afraid that comes under the rules of client privilege and I'm ethically bound by that to hold my tongue."

"Yes, I understand that, but in these circumstances…"

"I would need a written waiver from Miss Duncan's next of kin before I could possibly make any disclosure of the matter Miss Duncan and I were discussing."

Jack leaned back in the chair. It was too small for him and he could imagine himself becoming wedged in it. He sat forward again. "But you don't deny you were arguing."

"I think arguing is too strong a term for it. A heated debate maybe?"

"And is it customary to hold onto somebody's sleeve to restrain them during a *heated debate*?"

"I resent the implication that I was restraining Miss Duncan in any way," Fellowes said indignantly.

"Really," Jack said. "How would you describe the action then, sir?"

"I laid my hand on her arm, certainly, but it was to calm her. The debate, as I said, had become rather heated."

"And you're not prepared to tell me what the…*heated* debate, was about?"

"If I receive written permission from…"

"Yes, her next of kin. I understand that. What I don't understand though, sir, is why you should be conducting, what sounds like, a very serious business meeting in a very public park, especially when you have a perfectly good office here."

"Happenstance," Fellowes said.

"I'm not sure I follow," Jack said. "Happenstance? Is that a legal term that I'm unfamiliar with?"

"It means coincidence, Chief Inspector."

"I know what it means, Mr. Fellowes. You're saying that meeting Sandra Duncan in the park and engaging her in a heated debate was just a coincidence. Am I right?"

"Yes…and no. I mean, I met her in the park by chance, and she engaged *me* in a debate."

"I understand that you started your discussion in the pavilion over a cup of tea, and then took it down to the bench by the tennis courts. Is this a correct summation of how the meeting went?"

"More or less"

"Well is it more, or is it less?"

Fellowes leaned back in his chair. It was wide enough to fit the man's slim athletic frame. *No chance of him getting stuck*, Jack thought.

"Let me take you through the sequence of events, as they happened."

"I'd be very grateful," Jack said.

"I had a light morning – only a couple of appointments – and when I'd dealt with them I took a stroll down to the park, to the bowling green to be precise, to get in an hour's practice. The club has a tournament coming up at the beginning of September and I want to be match fit. Anyway, I finished my practice and went along to the pavilion for a drink, a cup of tea, and there was Miss Duncan. She appeared to be taking her lunch out on the veranda. She invited me to join her, saying that she had a few questions she wanted to ask me. I didn't mind – I thought it would save her the inconvenience of making an appointment and trekking into town to visit me here."

"Very magnanimous of you, I'm sure. How would you best describe your relationship with Miss Duncan?"

"I wouldn't describe it as a relationship," Fellowes said. "Well, not in that way."

"What way would that be, sir?"

"You're making it sound as if we were a couple caught in a lovers spat."

"I don't think I am, sir, but if you've drawn that inference then I'm sorry. I'm just a simple copper trying to make sense of two people meeting in the park, having a blazing row, with the young lady rushing away from the scene of the argument in tears, and you're telling me that it was strictly business. Forgive me if I sound a little sceptical."

Fellowes frowned. "All right," he said. "Going against my ethics, I'll give you the gist of what our conversation was about. Perhaps that will put your mind at rest."

"It will trouble me to see you break your ethical code, not much, if I'm honest, but it will be a great help to me to hear what actually happened that day."

"If you've done any kind of digging into Sandra's life, you will have realized that she was not the most personable of young women – no boyfriends, didn't mix well with others."

"That's the impression I've been given so far."

"Well, all of that is absolutely true. So much so that she had decided to leave the country and start again somewhere else – France I believe."

Jack nodded and let Fellowes continue.

"She had opposition to her plan, from her parents, who were

of the opinion that their daughter, should she follow the plan, would be on a downward slope to depravity and debauchery."

"What, *by going to France*?"

"The Duncan's lead what can only described as a very sheltered life, heavily influenced by their Christian beliefs and the teachings of their church. Arthur Duncan threatened that if Sandra made good her promise to go abroad, he would cut her off without a brass farthing, and she asked me if he was able to do that. When I said he was perfectly within his rights to do so, she got very upset, railing against her parents, saying they had no right to interfere with her life, and that they were determined to see her miserable for the rest of her days."

"A slight over-reaction, I would have said."

"Yes, and I agree with you. But Sandra was adamant that the world, myself included, was conspiring against her to stop her living her dream. She was very upset, hence the tears and me trying to calm her."

"Did you have any contact with her after the incident in the park?"

Fellowes shook his head. "No, nothing. I haven't heard a word from Mr. and Mrs. Duncan either, thank Heavens. I'm afraid their type of evangelical bigotry leaves me a little cold."

"They were only trying to protect their daughter's virtue," Jack said.

"And look where that got them – their precious daughter lying dead on a mortuary slab. Well, I suppose they can give her a good Christian burial, if nothing else."

"A bit harsh, sir," Jack said. "Not a believer yourself then?"

"If I can't see it, smell it or touch it, then I find it hard to accept it. And to ruin a young woman's life over what is basically a superstition, I find nothing short of criminal. Sandra was a sweet girl and had a lot to offer the world. Her death is a tragedy."

Jack was watching Fellowes closely. He was very aware that 'Miss Duncan' had become 'Sandra' the more impassioned the solicitor became. He wasn't convinced that their relationship was *strictly business*, no matter what Fellowes said.

"Well, I think I've taken up enough of your time, Mr. Fellowes," he said, pushing himself out of the restricting chair and getting to his feet.

"I'm glad I could be of some help," Fellowes said.

Jack walked to the door. "And just out of interest, sir, can you account for your whereabouts over the last seventy two hours?"

"Zurich," Fellowes said. "That's in Switzerland. I flew out Monday evening and got the first flight back this morning. You can see my passport if you like," he said, reaching into the inside pocket of is jacket.

"Would you mind?" Jack said, holding out his hand.

Fellowes handed him the dark blue booklet and Jack flicked it open.

"Stamped at both ends of the journey," Fellowes said. "As you can see."

"I didn't know the Immigration Branch was always that thorough."

"I always insist of getting it stamped. It's an *aide-memoire*. Helps me remember my whereabouts at any given time."

"Well, it certainly does that," Jack handed the passport back to him. "Thank you again for your time," he said and left the office.

19

THURSDAY

"I'm sorry to trouble you again so soon," Jack said as Arthur Duncan answered the door. "May I come in for a moment?"

Duncan stared at him uncomprehendingly.

"This will only take a moment."

Duncan continued to stare. The man looked emotionally shattered. His eyes were red from crying and his face was pale. He looked as if he had aged ten years since Jack spoke with him just an hour ago to inform him of his daughter's death.

"Mr. Duncan?" Jack reached out and laid a hand on the man's arm.

Duncan reacted as if he had been stung. "Yes…yes, come in, but please keep your voice down. Allison is resting upstairs."

Jack followed him into the house and into the living room.

"Please, sit down," Duncan said, indicating a chair by the fireplace, and then flopped down onto the sofa. He leaned forward and scrubbed his face with his hands. "It feels like this day will never end," he said and looked directly at Jack. "Do you have children, Chief Inspector?"

"Yes," Jack said. "Three."

"Then you must realise what I'm feeling."

"I can barely imagine," Jack said.

"How do Allison and I get past this? Parents should never outlive their children. It isn't natural. It isn't God's way." Tears were dribbling from Duncan's eyes again. He dabbed at them with a sodden handkerchief.

Jack cleared his throat. "This is probably not the time to mention this, Mr. Duncan, but I have to in order to investigate your daughter's death. Was there any conflict between yourself and your daughter in the past few months?"

Duncan took a breath and slowly nodded his head.

"About her moving abroad?"

Duncan buried his face in his hands once more. "I didn't want her to leave us," he said. "I would never have gone through with it. I loved Sandra more than life itself. I just couldn't bear the thought of her going away...the thought that I might never see my little girl again..."

"You threatened to cut her out of your will?" Jack said as gently as he could.

Duncan squeezed his eyes shut and nodded. "But it was just to make her think about what she was intending to do. I never meant to actually carry it through."

"Get out." Allison Duncan stood in the doorway. She'd thrown a housecoat over her clothes, her hair was awry, and there was anger in her red-ringed eyes. "Haven't you spread enough misery for one day?" she said to Jack, "without coming back here and accusing my husband."

Jack got to his feet. "I wasn't accusing your husband of anything, Mrs. Duncan. I was simply asking..."

"Shut up!" Allison said. "I heard what you were asking him. And he was right. He needed to show that little hussy what would happen if she travelled down such a sinful path."

"Mrs. Duncan..."

"Shut up and get out of this house!"

"Allison," Duncan said from the sofa.

"And you can be quiet as well," she snapped. "If you had been more of a man and taken more of a role in your daughter's upbringing, shown her God's way, the true path, none of this would have happened. She wouldn't have grown up thinking she was above His teachings, that she could make her way through life without His love."

"I'd better go," Jack said.

"Yes, and don't come back. We have nothing more to say to you and your kind." Allison moved out of the doorway. Jack could feel her gaze boring into his back as he walked down the hallway, and out through the front door. He pulled the door closed behind him, went back to the car, and sat behind the wheel shaking his head.

Sometimes he hated this job.

He started the car and drove back to the station.

"There's room on top," the conductor said as Simon Nelson

stepped onto the bus. Simon glanced passed him to the crowded interior of the vehicle. Every seat seemed to be taken, and there were even a couple of passengers standing in the aisle. Shrugging his school satchel from his shoulder he started to climb the stairs as the bus moved away from the stop and out into the traffic.

He reached the top deck. It was nearly empty up here. The rear seats were occupied, but apart from a lone passenger sitting at the front of the bus, all the other seats were vacant. It was his lucky day.

He moved down to the middle of the bus, dropped his satchel onto a double seat and slid in next to it. Opening the satchel he took out an exercise book and, using the back of the satchel as a makeshift desk, attempted again to solve the maths problem that had given him such problems at school.

Simon was fifteen and a conscientious pupil, not that he considered himself a swot, but he wanted to make sure he obtained good grades in his lessons. He knew he would need good exam results if he ever wanted to fulfil his ambition of a job at *British Aerospace*, just half a mile from his home. He'd inherited a love of flight and of flying from his father, who had been a *Mosquito* pilot during the war, and then gone on to work in the Research Department at the factory until his death seven years ago. Encouraged by the memory of his father, Simon had geared his schooling towards that ultimate goal, and he was determined that a stupid mathematics problem would not derail him.

He didn't look up from the page as someone sat down in the seat next to him

"You like all that school stuff, do you?"

Simon glanced around at the speaker, another boy, a few years older than himself, who wore his black hair in an elaborate Brylcreemed quiff, had tight black drainpipe trousers and a purple, Edwardian styled drape jacket. On his feet was a pair of black suede shoes with thick crepe soles. The boy had a bad case of acne and smelt of cigarettes.

He leaned across and plucked the book out from under Simon's nose and handed it to one his two friends who were standing in the bus's aisle, and who were similarly dressed and looked every bit as menacing as the acne boy himself.

Simon recognised them for what they were – Teddy boys, gangs of whom were the scourge of many a town. Talk of them circulated around the playground at school –lurid tales of their clashes with the police, and of fights with bicycle chains and flick knives, of innocent people set upon for no sane reason. Simon looked about him frantically, looking for a means of escape and finding none.

"What's your name," the boy sitting next to him said.

Simon gulped and mumbled a response.

"I didn't catch that."

"Simon. Simon Nelson."

The elder boy smiled at him. "Well, Simon Nelson, today's your lucky day."

"Is it?" Simon said uncertainly.

The boy turned his acne towards the others. "It's his lucky day, isn't it, lads?"

The two Teddy boys in the aisle smiled evilly. "If you say so, Billy," the taller of the two said. His jacket was bright red, and his blond hair was similarly greased and styled. When he smiled he displayed a set of uneven, tobacco-stained teeth.

Billy draped an arm across Simon's shoulder, leaned into him and lowered his voice. "The reason it's your lucky day, Simon, is that I've decided that I'm going to let you get off our bus."

"Really?" Simon said hopefully.

"Yep," Billy said. "I'll even let you get off under your own steam, just walk off like any other passenger."

"Thank you," Simon said, gathering his satchel to his chest and trying to stand.

Billy clamped a bony hand across his leg and held him in his seat. "But," he said. "For granting you this huge favour, I think I deserve a reward. I deserve a reward, right lads?

In the aisle the other two Teddy boys nodded.

"Definitely," the blond one said,

"Indubitably," said the other.

"What do you want?" Simon said. Rivers of sweat were pouring down his back and, conversely, his mouth was as dry as a desert.

"Well, that watch will do for a start," Billy said. "Gold is it?"

Simon nodded. The wristwatch had been a gift from his parents last Christmas.

"And whatever money you have in your pocket."

"But I don't have any," Simon said, fumbling to unbuckle the strap of his watch.

The boy next to him shifted slightly. There was a small click and something sharp pressed into the side of Simon's neck.

"You're not going to disappoint me, Simon, are you?"

"But it's true. I only have my bus fare, nothing more," Simon said. He was close to tears, and desperately praying to hear the sound of the bus conductor's feet coming up the stairs, but it was a forlorn hope.

Billy reached for the watch. "Well, I'll take that...for starters...ow! Get off!"

The person sitting at the front of the bus had moved quickly along the vehicle towards the gang. He'd grabbed Billy's wrist and was twisting it back on itself, forcing the boy to open his fingers and drop the flick knife he'd been holding.

Simon looked up uncomprehendingly at his saviour, a young man, possibly in his late teens or early twenties, well built and tall enough that he had to duck his head slightly to avoid it banging against the roof of the bus.

From him Simon looked to the Teddy boys in the aisle. Both of them were watching the scene unfold with pale faces and genuinely frightened eyes. The blond one hesitantly reached into his pocket

"If that hand comes out holding a knife," the young man said, "I'll use it to gut you."

The Teddy boy withdrew his hand from his pocket and held it up to show it was empty.

The young man dragged Billy to his feet and propelled him down the aisle. Billy made a vain attempt to regain his balance, grabbing at the seats to try to catch himself but failed, ending up in a heap on the floor.

"Now, get off the bus, all of you, before I lose my temper," the young man growled at them.

The two Teddy boys hauled Billy to his feet and hurried down the stairs as the bus pulled into the next bus stop. Before it had fully stopped they leapt from the platform and tore off down the road.

The young man sat down in the seat next to Simon. "Are you okay?"

Simon nodded. "Yes. Thank you."

"I can't abide cowards, and that's all they are," the young man said. "Peter Lamb," he said, and stuck out his hand. With the other he scooped up Simon's maths book from the floor and handed it back to him.

Simon took the book from him and shook Peter Lamb's hand. Now he was sitting next to him he realised that Lamb wasn't as old as he'd first thought. He didn't look that much older than he was himself. He looked down and saw Billy's flick knife sitting in his lap, where the older boy had dropped it. Using his thumb and forefinger he picked it up and handed it to Lamb

Lamb took it, muttered, "Nasty", and dropped it into his pocket.

Simon stared out through the window and gave a small groan as he realised that he didn't recognise where he was. "I've missed my stop," he said.

"We'll get off at the next one and I'll walk you back," Lamb said.

"You don't have to walk me back," Simon said. "I'll be all right, really."

"Nonsense," Lamb said. "Besides, I didn't see where the yobs went. Can't have you running into them again. You might not be so lucky next time."

As the bus pulled into the next stop, Lamb stepped from the bus and put his hand out to help Simon alight. Rather self-consciously Simon took the proffered hand, and stepped down onto the pavement. He looked about him, but didn't have any idea where he was.

Lamb noticed the concern of the younger boy's face. "Where do you live?" he said.

"Myrtle Grove," Simon said. "Do you know it?"

Lamb nodded and smiled. "Myrtle Grove? Off of Campion

131

Way? I know it. This way."

They walked along a tree-lined avenue to a junction, and turned right onto another street with lime trees spaced out on each side at regular intervals. After several more turns and more anonymous streets Simon said, "Are you sure this is the way, only I don't recognise anything yet?"

"This is *my* way," Lamb said. "I know all of the shortcuts around here."

After another turn Simon found he was walking down another unfamiliar street, along the side of a high privet hedge. The hedge finally finished at a set of iron gates, and Lamb surprised him by turning into the gateway and pushing one of the iron gates open. "I have to make a call. An old friend of mine."

20

THURSDAY

Simon glanced at his watch. If he hadn't missed his stop he'd be home by now.

"It will only take five minutes."

Simon hesitated.

"Come on."

Simon gave an uncertain smile and followed Lamb through the gates onto a gravelled drive belonging to a very large detached house, fashioned from red brick, with black-painted, cast iron gutters and drainpipes, and high sash windows, cloaked on the inside with thick grubby-looking curtains. As they approached a heavy-looking, green-painted front door, Simon hung back.

Lamb glanced back at him. "Come on," he said again. "He doesn't bite." He stuck his thumb on a ceramic bell push and pressed. From somewhere deep within the house, a bell sounded shrilly.

The man who answered the door was shorter than Lamb and a lot older. He had on a paint-streaked cotton smock over a pair of baggy woollen trousers. On his feet he wore a pair of brown leather sandals. He looked to be in his late thirties, early forties. There was grey in his black hair at the temples, and silver streaks ran through the neatly trimmed goatee beard he affected.

"Peter," he said to Lamb, but was looking Simon up and down. "What a pleasant surprise. Do come in."

"Hello, Gavin. I've brought a friend. I hope that's all right."

"It's absolutely fine, dear boy. What's his name?" he said, continuing to stare at Simon.

"This is Simon," Lamb said. "He had a nasty run in with a gang of Teddy boys on the bus on his way home from school."

"And now you're escorting him home?"

Lamb nodded.

"Lucky for you that Peter was on hand," Gavin Southland said, addressing Simon directly.

Simon remembered the smell of Brylcreem and cigarettes, and the prick of the knife at his throat. He shuddered. "Yes, it was very lucky."

"Come through," Southland said, and led them into the house, down a long passageway. Simon noticed that he walked with a pronounced limp.

Paintings hung from the walls at irregular intervals. Even to Simon's uneducated eye, they didn't look very good. The passageway ended at a door. Southland pushed it open and stood to one side.

They entered a large densely furnished room with more paintings cluttering the walls. The room was lit by sunlight that seeped in through a wide set of French doors that gave onto a wild, unkempt garden. It was the only light in the room as the windows were draped with heavy brocade curtains. The curtains made the room feel closed in, almost claustrophobic.

"Take a seat," Southland said. "I'll fetch some drinks. "Beer for you, Peter?"

"Fine."

"Can I tempt you with a peppermint cordial, Simon?"

"That would be very kind, sir," Simon said. He didn't really want a drink. He wanted to go home, but didn't want to appear rude or ungrateful in any way.

"He likes you," Lamb as Southland left the room to fetch the drinks.

"Does he?" Simon said uncertainly.

"He doesn't break out the peppermint cordial for just anybody."

"Are you two related?" Simon said.

"Gavin and I? Good heavens, no," Lamb said with a chuckle. "Gavin's an artist. I model for him sometimes. Oils and acrylics mostly, but sometimes he'll just sketch me in charcoal."

Simon didn't really know what to say. Lamb had a fairly fleshy face, not in the slightest bit handsome.

Lamb noticed Simon staring at him and laughed. "I know what you're thinking – I'm not exactly Dirk Bogarde in the looks department."

"I'm sorry, I didn't…"

"No, you're right. Gavin's not interested in my face. I'm a life model. Do you know what that means?"

Simon shook his head.

"He's interested in the human body." He pointed at a large painting of a naked figure that hung on the wall above the fireplace. "That's me," he said. In the picture Lamb was sitting on a high-back chair, legs discreetly crossed, face turned away from the artist. If Lamb hadn't said it was a depiction of him, Simon wouldn't have made the connection. It really wasn't very good.

"Don't you find it embarrassing, posing in the nude?"

Lamb shook his head. "I did, at first, but not now, besides the money I make for a few hours sitting there with my clothes off more than compensates. You should consider doing it yourself, if he asks you, and I think he might. I saw how he was appraising you when we first arrived. Gavin has a very good eye for such things."

"I have a very good eye for what things?" Southland said as he limped back into the room carrying a tray of drinks.

"I was telling Simon here, that you can always spot a potential life model."

"That I can," Southland said. "That I can. Would you be interested in doing a spot of modelling, Simon?"

Simon felt the blood rush to his cheeks as he blushed furiously. "No!" He almost shouted it. "I mean, I couldn't possibly…"

"That's a shame," Southland said, and handed him a tumbler of clear liquid. As Simon raised the glass to his lips the astringent smell of peppermint assaulted his nostrils. He had never had peppermint cordial before and was unprepared for how strong and *minty* it was. Tentatively he took a sip, wincing slightly as the sweet liquid warmed his throat. He coughed.

Southland laughed. "I haven't made it too strong for you, have I?"

Simon shook his head. "No," he lied. "It's fine. Very nice."

"That's good," Southland said and turned to Lamb. "Now, Peter, to what do I owe the honour of this visit?"

"We were just was passing, and I just thought I'd call in and

135

pick up the money you owe me."

Southland sipped from his own glass. "Great heavens, you're right. I still owe you for that last sitting. Peter, forgive me, I forgot that I hadn't paid you. I'm mortified."

Lamb smiled easily. "I knew you were good for it, but I going out tonight and could use the cash."

"Of course, of course." He set his glass down on a small occasional table. "Wait here. I'll just fetch my wallet," he said, "Don't be shy," he said to Simon. "Drink up. I have plenty more where that came from,"

Simon smiled and took another gulp of the sickly drink.

Jack glanced up as Myra walked into the office. "Is Sergeant Fuller not with you?"

"He went straight to the canteen. We missed lunch."

"Didn't *you* want something?"

Myra shook her head. "I've got to watch my waistline," she said.

"How did you get on at the golf course?"

"It was pretty much a waste of time. No one had a round booked that day. We checked out the golf cart but there was nothing in the way of fingerprints. He either wiped it down or wore gloves. Either way he left us no clues."

"And no one else saw him take it and drive halfway across the links?"

"I think he's bloody lucky, excuse my French," Myra said.

"Either that, or he knows the golf course well enough to know that he wouldn't be observed."

Myra sat down at the desk. "So do you think we're looking for a golfer, someone who uses the course a lot?"

"We could be," Jack said. "What I *do* think is that we're not having an awful lot of luck with this case. Our killer seems to be invisible."

"We'll catch him, sir. He has to make a mistake sooner or later."

"Let's just hope it's sooner, before he gets the chance to kill again." He stood up from the desk and went across to the notice board and stared at the photos of Frances Anderton and Sandra

Duncan. Myra came up beside him.

"Why these two girls, Myra?" Jack said. "Where's the link?"

Myra stared at the photographs and considered Jack's questions. "They're different ages, from different social classes, and totally different in looks." She shrugged. "It beats me."

"Then forget about looking at the differences. What did the two girls have in common?"

Myra pondered this for a moment. "Well, neither of the girls was very worldly wise. Frances was very young and, by all accounts, quite naïve, and Sandra came from a very sheltered background, dominated by the church and her parents, and, by all accounts, a wallflower."

"As you say, neither of them were worldly wise, but both of them, I suspect, could be sweet talked by, say, an older, smooth-talking man. Tim Fellowes is a bit of a smooth talker. I wouldn't have thought he'd find it difficult to charm Sandra Duncan, and Frances Anderton came into contact with her sister's boyfriend, Adam Channing, a college lecturer who, again, is quite a bit older, and is obviously a smooth enough operator to ensnare Fiona Anderton who, believe me, is nobody's fool. Both men seem to have a penchant for much younger women."

"But you said that Channing didn't fit the description of our park keeper."

"Yes, and Fellowes claims that his relationship with Sandra was strictly business, even though I find it unlikely that a solicitor would have an argument with a client on a bench in a public park. But he was out of the country when Sandra Duncan went missing."

"So that rules them out," Myra said. She wasn't sure where her boss was going with this train of thought. The conversation she'd had with Eddie Fuller today had been surprisingly illuminating in regards to Jack Callum. She had found out for the first time that Callum's eldest daughter, Joan, had eloped with a much older man a few years ago but had recently returned to the family home when her marriage ended. She wondered how much that event was colouring his thinking in regards to this case. It was obvious from his reactions so far that the abduction of the two girls was resonating very strongly with him, and the thought of a young girl being seduced by an older man was anathema to him. She wasn't sure it was a productive line of enquiry.

"Have you spoken to Professor Channing?" Myra said.

"I called the LSE a little while ago. Apparently he's off today, looking after his sick wife, but he's expected back tomorrow, so I'm going up to London to speak with him."

Simon sipped his cordial and tried to listen to the conversation between Lamb and Southland but their words were blurring into each other and he couldn't follow it.

Somewhere, in the back of his mind, a small voice was whispering to him that he should be getting home but, somehow, the imperative to get up and go, to leave this house, seemed to have disappeared. The armchair he was sitting in seemed wonderfully comfortable and he found his eyelids fluttering. It was taking all his willpower to keep them open. The inside of his mouth was coated thickly with peppermint, but he was aware of another taste there – sharper, slightly medicinal. He didn't like it.

Finally he struggled out of the armchair and got to his feet and stood there, swaying slightly. "I should be..." he began, as the furniture in the room seemed to undulate. "I shou..." he started again, but his knees buckled and he sank to the floor, his eyes closing.

As he lay there on the rug they flickered open briefly and he was aware of Peter Lamb standing over him and looking down.

"Take him upstairs and put him in one of the bedrooms," he heard Southland say from somewhere a long way away, and then Lamb was reaching down and scooping him up in his arms. Simon felt himself lifted, but his eyelids were impossibly heavy and they slowly shut, plunging him into darkness.

21

THURSDAY

"Goodnight, Rosie. See you in the morning," Mrs. Painter said as she shut the door and locked it behind them.

"Yes, see you," Rosie said. "Bright and early." She set off briskly along the High Street. She wanted to call in at the newsagents before they closed, to pick up a fashion magazine. She needed some fresh ideas about the type of clothes she should be wearing. This morning, on her way to the baker's she had caught sight of herself in the window of the chemist next door and been alarmed at how frightful she looked in her blue pinafore-styled dress and her awful *little girl* plaits. *"You look like an overgrown schoolgirl,"* she chided herself. How any boy, least of all David, could take her seriously was a mystery to her.

The return of Joanie into her life had made her take stock of her own appearance. Her sister dressed more elegantly than she did. The clothes Joanie wore were not that expensive, but they fitted perfectly, enhancing her womanly charms, and her chic new haircut only served to make Rosie feel even more inadequate. She wasn't brave enough to get her own hair cut that short, but at least she could get rid of the plaits and start wearing clothes better suited to a young woman her age.

Mr. Shadbolt was already pulling down the dark blue window blinds when she reached the shop but the door of the newsagent's was still open and she slipped inside.

The magazines were displayed on a rack affixed to the wall.

"I'm just closing up," Shadbolt called from the window.

"I'll only be a moment," she said.

"Oh, it's you, Rosie. Sorry, I thought it was a customer. Take your time."

She pulled out a magazine, took it over to the counter and handed it to Shadbolt. He was a small, barrel of a man with a crinkled face and woolly grey hair. He adjusted his round, wire-framed glasses on the bridge of his nose and regarded the magazine in his hands. "*Vanity Fair*, Rosie?" he said, a sense of wonder in his voice. "It seems like only yesterday that you were coming in here for your copy of *School Friend*."

"Time flies, Mr. Shadbolt."

The old man chuckled. "It certainly does. That will be one and six, please."

"Thank you," Rosie said, opening her purse and taking out a half a crown to pay him.

"And tell your dad, when you see him, that this month's copy of *Practical Householder* has a feature on landscape gardening that he'll find interesting."

"I'll be sure to mention it, thanks," Rosie said, took her change and left the shop.

"Hello, fancy bumping into you."

Rosie looked up in surprise at the grinning face of David Neville, and was suddenly more aware than ever of her ridiculous pinafore dress and her stupid plaited hair. She felt herself blushing.

"I wasn't expecting to see you," she stammered. "I was just on my way home."

"Would you like some company? I could use a walk," he said.

"That would be nice," she said, and fell into step beside him.

"I really enjoyed the film last night," he said as they walked.

"Me too," Rosie agreed. "Grace Kelly's so beautiful, so elegant. That wonderful dress she was wearing in the car with Frank Sinatra...made mine look like a potato sack."

"I thought you looked very nice."

Rosie's blush intensified. "Get away with you," she said.

"I mean it. You looked very pretty... beautiful in fact."

"Now I know you're lying. It's either that or you need glasses."

He tugged the magazine she was carrying out from under her arm and glanced at it.

"Very posh," he said. "If you start wearing clothes like that I'll have to get another job, just to have enough money to keep up with you."

"They're just the latest fashions," she said. "I could never afford clothes like that really."

"Then it seems a bit pointless buying the magazine," he said.

She looked at him sharply to see if he was mocking her, but he was smiling and there was no malice in his eyes. "You wouldn't understand. You're just a boy."

"Sure I understand," he said. "I buy magazines full of cars I could never hope to afford, not as an insurance clerk anyway. But there's nothing wrong with having the dream that one day, just one day, I might."

"Me too," she said. "One day I'd like to think I'll be wearing clothes direct from the Paris catwalks."

"And I'm sure that one day you will, if you set your mind to it."

"What makes you say that?"

"Because, from what I know of you, once you set your mind to something you'll achieve it."

"And you know that based on one trip to the cinema?"

"I'm a quick learner," he said. "But I think you'll have to come out with me again, just so I can be sure."

"I'd like that," she said.

"Tonight?"

She shook her head. "I'm washing my hair. What about Saturday?"

"That sounds good to me. Do you like dancing?"

"I love it."

"Well, I'll pick you up at seven. There's a jazz band playing at a club I know in Stevenage. They've got a dance floor."

"That sounds great," Rosie said enthusiastically.

"As long as you don't expect too much from me," he said. "I've just about mastered the quick step and waltz, but my foxtrot leaves a lot to be desired."

"I can foxtrot. I can teach you. If you're such a quick learner, you should pick it up in no time."

As her house came into view she said, "We're here."

"So, I suppose I'll be seeing you Saturday. Goodbye." Before she realized what was happening he leaned in and pecked her on the lips.

She took a step back. "Right," she said, trying to keep the shock and surprise from her voice. "Right... Saturday...yes.

See you then."

She watched him walk away and then walked up the garden path to the front door.

"Well you look like the cat that got all of the cream," Annie said as Rosie walked into the kitchen.

"Yes," Rosie said. "I think I just did."

"Shepherd's pie," Annie said, setting the deep Pyrex dish down on table. "Give me your plates. "You first, Dad."

Jack handed her his plate and watched as she ladled the lamb mince and creamy mashed potato into the centre of it, He hadn't eaten all day and the steam wafting up from the Pyrex dish was mouth watering. When she had finished serving the shepherd's pie she took the lids from the vegetable dishes and handed him a serving spoon. "There's broccoli and carrots from the garden, but the peas are frozen – we've used all the fresh ones."

"Frozen is fine," Jack said, helped himself to a spoonful of each and passed the serving spoon down the table to Eric. "You girls would know, where's the best place around here to buy embroidery thread?"

"Jennings, in town," Annie and Rosie said together.

"Is Archers in Hitchin still there?" Joan said. "That's the haberdasher's I used to use when I was making my own clothes. They had a better variety than Jennings."

"You're right," Annie said. "I always use Jennings because it's closer, but Archers is still there, and they were always very good for more specialized items. Why do you want to know, Dad?"

"I'm thinking of taking up a hobby," Jack said with a smile.

"You're not," Eric said dismissively.

"Can't you see me sitting here in the evening making cushion covers and samplers?"

"Frankly, no," Annie said smiling. "If you're that keen on working with a needle and thread I have a pile of darning I can give you."

"It's for a case I'm working on," Jack said, put a forkful of shepherd's pie and vegetables into his mouth and the subject was dropped.

"Dad," Eric said. "Can you lend me ten bob?"

"Is this about that guitar?"

"Well, I've saved a pound already, and Eddie wants thirty shillings for the guitar."

"So what's wrong with waiting until you've saved the rest?"

"But that will take ages, and I want to learn to play now."

"Let me think on it," Jack said. "You realise it will mean no pocket money until you've paid me back?"

"I've thought of that," Eric said.

"I'm sure you have," Jack said.

"Dad," Rosie said. "David wants to take me to a dance on Saturday night. Can I go?"

Annie butted in. "Oh, for Heaven's sake, you two. Let your father eat his dinner without pestering him."

Jack smiled at her. "All answers will be given once I've eaten this delicious meal that your mother has made for us. Joanie, do you have anything you want to add to the list?"

"Only the bed," Joan said.

"Yes, yes. Your mother and I are going to Bennets at the weekend to see if we can pick one up."

"You see, he answered *her*," Eric said, disgruntled.

'Eric!" Annie said, her voice rising. "Eat your dinner. I don't want to hear another word from you until you've cleared your plate."

"Thank you, Mother," Jack said. "This really is quite delicious, you know? Of course, it's the home grown vegetables that make it."

"Cheek," Annie said, and gave him a playful tap on the ankle with the toe of her shoe.

"Ouch!" Jack said. "Careful, woman, you'll cripple me."

"You big baby. I hardly touched you," Annie said with a grin.

"What's this dance David wants to take you to," Jack said to Rosie. They were sitting in the living room waiting for the radiogram to warm up. Annie and Joan were in the kitchen washing up, and Eric was lying on his stomach on the rug reading a comic.

"I think it's a jazz club in Stevenage," Rosie said.

"So it's not a dance?"

"They have a dance floor. Really, Dad, I don't know any more than that, but it's a chance to go out, on a *Saturday night*. Chances like that don't come along every day."

"Then of course you should go," Jack said.

"You mean it?"

"I said it didn't I?"

Rosie launched herself out of her chair and wrapped her arms around his neck. "Thank you," she said, and kissed his cheek.

"The one proviso is that you're back here by eleven."

Her hold on his neck loosened.

"But, Dad, it's Saturday night."

"Okay. We'll make it twelve, but it's straight in when you get home. No spending half an hour on the door step saying goodnight to him."

"What kind of girl do you take me for?" she said with a smile.

"A very pretty, sixteen year old girl in the first flush of a romantic relationship. I remember your mother when she was your age, and I remember what I was like, so it's home and straight in, okay?"

"What about the ten bob?" Eric said from his prone position on the rug.

"I'm still thinking about it."

"That's not fair," Eric said.

"Press me on it again and I'll say no," Jack said.

Eric glowered at him.

"And another look like that and I'll say no as well. Now go and see if your mother needs any help in the kitchen."

Rosie waited until her brother had left the room. "Thanks, Dad. I won't disappoint you," she said.

"I hope not," Jack said.

22

FRIDAY AUGUST 15th 1958

"What's this," Fuller said as Jack got into the car and handed him two notes – one green and one brown.

"Thirty shillings. That's right isn't it? For the guitar?"

"Yes," Fuller said. "But I thought Eric was buying it himself."

"He is, but he's still saving up and if he doesn't have the damned thing soon he's going to drive me round the bend. Last night he asked me to lend him the ten shillings he was short. I didn't say yes or no. This morning I came down to breakfast to find a letter from him propped up against the teapot, asking the same thing, but this time going into some detail about his desire to learn to play and make a name for himself in the music business."

"So you're indulging him."

"No," Jack said. "I'm giving him the chance to prove himself."

Fuller looked sceptical.

"You'll understand when you have children, Sergeant."

"If you say so, guv."

"Can you bring it round tonight? I'd like him to get started as soon as possible."

"Sure thing," Fuller said. "When do you want me to begin the lessons?"

"As soon as you like. I'll pay you for your time. How does five bob an hour sound?"

"It's too much. Much too much. I'll happily teach him, gratis."

"That's good of you. Drop me off at the train station. I'm going up to the LSE to interview Adam Channing."

"Is there anything specific you want me to do while you're gone?"

"I want you to go to Jennings in town and Archers in Hitchin, haberdashers. See if anyone has bought a quantity of black silk embroidery thread and needles recently. The needles will be curved. He couldn't have sewn the eyes and mouth shut any other way without doing more damage to the surrounding tissue."

"You've given this some thought," Fuller said.

"Morning, noon and night," Jack said. "I'm even dreaming about it."

Jack walked through the high grey-stone arch of the London School of Economics and presented himself at the reception desk.

The woman behind the desk looked to be in her fifties. She was wearing a green knitted twin set, and had a pair of half-rimmed spectacles perched on the bridge of a protuberant nose. "May I help you?" she said.

"Professor Adam Channing. I understand he's a lecturer here," Jack said.

"He does, but I'm not sure if he's in today."

Jack pulled his warrant card from his pocket and presented it for her to see. "Can you check?"

"Yes, of course." She squinted at the card. "Detective Chief Inspector."

A few moments later he was climbing stairs and negotiating a seemingly endless maze of grey-painted corridors. Eventually he reached a door that had Channing's brass nameplate affixed to it. He rapped on the door and entered.

Adam Channing was sitting at a desk that was groaning under the weight of textbooks and untidy piles of paper.

"Excuse me," Channing said, not looking up. "Marking," he said, pointing with his pen at the bundles of paper. Jack watched him. Channing certainly didn't look like a middle-aged Lothario. He was quite thin with hair that was too long, curly and grey. His cheeks were sunken, and there was a day's growth of stubble on his chin. Jack wondered what a pretty girl like Fiona, who could almost have her pick of eligible bachelors, would see in a man like this, but then he'd thought the same about Joanie when she first brought Ivan to the house. Ivan was certainly no oil painting with his dark belligerent eyes that stared out from hollow sockets, and flat Eastern European features, but Joanie said he had charisma. Perhaps the same was true about Channing. Jack had given up trying to understand the workings of teenage girls' minds.

He waited for a few more minutes before clearing his throat, loudly.

Finally Channing looked up, his eyes registering surprise as he saw Jack sitting opposite him. "I'm terribly sorry. I was expecting it to be a student," he said affably.

Jack introduced himself.

"How do you think I can help you, Chief Inspector?"

"I'm looking into the abduction and murder of Frances Anderton," Jack said.

A troubled look swam over Channing's face. "Yes. Fiona told me. A dreadful business, truly dreadful. I must admit I was expecting a visit from the police before this."

"Really?" Jack said. "Why would that be?"

"I was given to understand that you were talking to everyone who had some kind of contact with Frances."

"We are. I would have come yesterday but you weren't here. You were at home caring for your sick wife," Jack added pointedly.

Channing sighed, and pulled a briar pipe from his jacket pocket, filled it with tobacco from a leather pouch, tamping it down before striking a Swan Vesta on the desktop, lighting it and taking long puffs to get it burning.

"I'm sorry if you find this tiresome, sir," Jack said as he watched Channing blow out a cloud of blue-grey smoke through pursed lips.

"I'm willing to help in any way I can, Chief Inspector," he said, dropping the spent match into a metal ashtray on the desk. "But it's your provincial attitude I find tiresome."

Jack ignored the criticism. He did not approve of Channing cheating on his sick wife with Fiona Anderton. It was something he couldn't hide, and he really didn't give a damn whether Channing found it tiresome or not. "Tell me about the evening you met Frances Anderton," he said.

"It was the end of term party. I was surprised to see her there. She was very young, underage. There was a bar, you see, but

147

Fiona must have found a way to smuggle her in."

"And, in the time she was at the party, did you engage her in conversation."

"Only to pass the time of day. To be quite honest with you, Chief Inspector, she barely registered. Frances was a timid little creature. She sat at our table drinking *Tizer* through a straw, watching what was going on around her but not really engaging. I wondered why Fiona had brought her along."

"When did you last have contact with Fiona Anderton?"

"I spoke to her on the phone on Wednesday. That's when she told me about Frances."

"It must have come a quite a shock."

"I was upset for Fiona and her parents but, as I said, I barely knew the girl."

"And can you account for your whereabouts last weekend?"

"Surely you don't consider me a suspect, Chief Inspector," Channing said with a smile. Jack didn't like that smile. There was a trace of mockery there.

"At the present time I'm not ruling anyone out."

"Commendable," Channing said. "Leave no stone unturned. But I'm afraid you'll have to cross me off your list of possible suspects. From Saturday until Monday I was up in Scotland, at a seminar in Falkirk to be precise."

"And someone can corroborate that?"

"I should think the staff at the Prince Edward Hotel can confirm my presence there, as well as the twenty of so attendees of the seminar."

"What was it about, this seminar?"

"Comparative politics."

"Interesting?"

"Oh, very," Channing said enthusiastically. "One of the items on the agenda was a discussion of the book Robert A Dahl published a couple of years ago: *A Preface to Democratic Theory*. Professor Alan Probert came over especially from Yale University in America to talk about it. Fascinating stuff."

"Riveting, I should imagine," Jack said. "But then I'm just a provincial copper, so what would I know?"

"Quite," Channing said, a slight smirk on his face.

148

"Well, thank you for your time, Professor Channing. If I think of anything else can I find you here? No more trips to Scotland booked?"

"I have a clear diary as far as I know," Channing said. "So I should be here."

Jack left the London School of Economics with the uneasy feeling that Channing was playing a game with him. There was nothing specific the professor had said to lead him to such a conclusion, just a general air of condescension that Jack found slightly annoying. The sister of Channing's lover had been murdered and yet the good professor didn't appear to give two hoots about it. He hadn't even asked about the circumstances of Frances's murder. Of course, Fiona could have given him all the grisly details that she knew, but still…

He wasn't going to cross Channing off his list of suspects, despite the alibi that had him four hundred miles away at the time of Frances's death. There was something about the professor that required further investigation.

"Nothing from Jennings," Fuller said when Jack got back to the station. "But someone bought a quantity of embroidery thread from Archers several weeks ago."

"Black?"

"All the colours of the rainbow apparently."

"Black isn't in the rainbow," Jack said.

"Oh, they bought black as well."

"Curved needles?"

Fuller shook his head. "Just the thread."

"Do Archers have a record of the sale? Who was it that bought it? A name and address?"

"I'm afraid not. The shop assistant at Archers remembers the sale though. It was bought by a man and he paid cash."

"Of course he did," Jack said heavily. "And I take it the shop assistant failed to get a description."

"A man, in his forties, with dark brown, thinning hair starting to go grey at the temples, who wore a thin goatee beard and walked with a limp," Fuller said.

"Who is this assistant, Sergeant? Does she want a job? That's the best description I've heard all week."

"Susan Clark. She's worked at Archers for fifteen years, so it's unlikely she's looking to change her employment."

"Oh, well. Never mind," Jack said. "Good work."

"And the Chief Superintendent wants to see you in his office."

"Terrific," Jack said with heavy irony.

"What did Channing say," Lane said. "Is he a viable suspect?"

"He has an alibi for last weekend. Apparently he was up in Scotland. I've got Frank Lesser checking it out," Jack said.

"So was it really necessary to go all the way up to London to interview him? Couldn't you have obtained the same information over the telephone?"

"I'm sure I could," Jack said. "But you can't get the measure of a man from a telephone conversation."

"Well, now you've met him face to face, what do you think?"

"I didn't like him," Jack said.

"I don't like a lot of people, Jack. It doesn't mean they're all killers."

"Granted, but there was something off about Channing."

"Off?"

Jack shrugged. "Nothing I can really put my finger on. But it was enough for me not to dismiss him from our enquiries just yet."

"I heard that Joan, your eldest, has come back home," Lane said, switching tack.

The change of subject caught Jack off balance. "Sorry?"

"Joan's come home," Lane said.

"Yes," Jack said. "Yes, she has," He was staring at his superior, wondering what the man was implying.

"Try to keep objective, Jack," Lane said. "With Channing, I mean. I know we want to solve this case, but we mustn't allow our personal feelings to influence our judgement."

"No, sir," Jack said, biting back a retort. "I won't."

"Splendid," Lane said. "That's all right then. Let me have the chit for your travel expenses today before you leave tonight."

"Yes, sir," Jack said and walked out of the office.

THREE MONKEYS

23

FRIDAY

"Myra, take yourself off to the library and get me everything you can find on Professor Adam Channing. He's currently a lecturer at the LSE."

"Employment record? Stuff like that?"

"Everything," Jack said. "I want to know what makes him tick. And while you're there, compile a dossier on Tim Fellowes."

"You're looking into both of them?" Fuller said.

"I am."

"Why?"

"Similar types," Jack said.

"You mean they're both middle-aged men with alibis for the days of the murders," Fuller said.

"There's that, and the fact that they both seem to enjoy the company of younger women."

"There's no crime against that," Lesser said.

"No, Frank, you're right. There's no crime against it. Did Channing's alibi check out, by the way?"

"Cast iron," Lesser said.

"Yes, I thought it might," Jack said.

"Dead ends then," Fuller said.

"So it would seem."

"Then why are you wasting Myra's time checking them out?"

Jack stood up and went across to the notice board and stood staring at it. "I don't know," he said. "There's just something about both of them that doesn't hang right. Call it a copper's intuition if you like."

"Or a bloody waste of time," Lesser said under his breath. Jack heard him but let it go. He couldn't blame his officers, or even Lane, for their level of scepticism, and maybe they were right to doubt his instincts. Maybe Joanie's return had exposed feelings he'd tried hard to bury and brought them to the surface, to be raked over once more. He stared at the photographs of

Frances and Sandra and saw Rosie and Joanie looking back at him. He shook his head to clear the vision away. "I'll be in my office," he said, and walked from the room.

As he was walking through the door he nearly collided with Andy Brewer. "There's a lady downstairs in reception. She claims her son didn't come home from school yesterday."

"Her *son*?" Jack said.

Brewer nodded.

"Well. That makes a change," Jack said.

"When did you last see your son, Mrs. Nelson?" Jack said as he showed a tearful Sonia Nelson into his office. "Please take a seat." He held a chair away from his desk, waited for her to sit and then went and sat down himself.

Sonia Nelson dabbed at her eyes with a handkerchief. "I suppose it was at breakfast yesterday morning," she said.

"So when did you realize he hadn't come home?"

"This morning, when I took him his cup of tea. He wasn't in his bed."

"Not yesterday afternoon, after school?"

"I have to work in the evenings, since my husband died."

"I'm sorry," Jack said. "Have you been on your own long?"

"Seven years this November. He died the day after bonfire night 1951."

"I see," Jack said. Sonia Nelson was an attractive thirty-something woman who had honey blonde hair and wore too much make-up. Her tears had made her mascara run, leaving two sooty black streaks down her rouged cheeks.

"Has this ever happened before?" Jack said. "Simon not coming home."

Sonia shook her head vehemently. "No, never. That's why I thought I should come straight to you."

"Well, you did the right thing."

Sonia made a frantic lunge across the desktop and grabbed Jack's sleeve. "You have to find him, Mr. Callum. He's all I've got left."

Jack gave her a reassuring smile and disengaged her fingers from his shirtsleeve. "We'll certainly make every effort to locate your son, Mrs. Nelson."

After another tearful thirty minutes he had learned everything he needed to know about Simon Nelson, and had a seven by five school photograph of him taken in the March of that year.

"I wondered if he had gone to the factory after school. He does that sometimes."

"Sorry? Factory?"

"*British Aerospace*. He'll go there and stand outside the fence, watching the planes take off and land. Obsessed he is. Just like his father. Fred was a fighter pilot during the war, and once it had finished he went to work there. His obsession for planes rubbed off on Simon."

"But he wasn't there, not this time."

"No. He's obsessed by them but not to the extent of staying out all night."

"Okay," Jack said. "We'll start looking for him then. Thank you for coming in." Jack got to his feet and walked her to the door. "And try not to worry," he said. "I'm sure he'll turn up. He's probably off on some adventure somewhere. I know what teenage boys are like."

"Do you have a son? Mr. Callum?"

"Yes. My Eric's about your boy's age. His latest nine-day-wonder is guitars and skiffle music."

"Then you know what it's like," Sonia said.

"I do indeed," Jack said, and walked with her into the reception area.

"Hello, Sonia. Starting a bit early today, aren't we?" DC Harry Grant said. He was leaning against the reception desk.

A startled look appeared on Sonia Nelson's face but she recovered herself when she saw who was speaking.

"Oh, it's you, Harry," she said. "It's Simon. He didn't come home last night," she said, giving Grant a wan smile.

"Don't you worry, Sonia. I'm sure he'll turn up. If not, you're talking to the right man."

Jack escorted Sonia out through the door and came back inside.

"So how do you know Sonia Nelson?" Jack said to Grant who was still leaning up against the desk.

"Who Sexy Sonia? I've pulled her in more times than I can remember."

"Pulled her in? Arrested, you mean?"

"Sonia's one of our regulars, sir. She's on the game. Has been since her husband, Fred, died a few years back."

"I've never seen her before," Brewer said from behind the desk.

"No, Sarge. She works nights, when you're at home tucked up in bed and drinking your *Ovaltine* with your missus," Grant said.

"Haven't you got any work to do, Constable?" Jack said. "Instead of standing here gossiping like an old woman."

"Yes, sir," Grant said, and headed off to the squad room.

Jack followed him into the room and pinned Simon Nelson's photograph to the notice board. "Right, gather round," he said to those in the room. "We have another missing child – a boy this time. His name is Simon Nelson, fifteen and a pupil at Birchwood Secondary. His mother hasn't seen him since yesterday morning, and she's worried sick."

"His mother's Sonia Nelson," Grant added.

"Sexy Sonia?" Fuller said from his seat.

"The same," Grant said.

"That's enough, Constable." Jack said.

"*Mrs. Nelson* is *very* worried about her missing boy, so let's pull out all the stops and try to find him. In the light of recent events, I don't have to impress upon you that speed is of the essence."

"You don't think it's the same person who took the two girls, do you?" Fuller said.

"I'll admit it's a bit of a change of pace, but I'm not ruling anything out just yet," Jack said grimly.

"How do you know Sonia Nelson?" Jack said to Fuller when they were out of earshot of the others. "No, don't answer that. I'm not sure I want to know. Anyway, I'm going home shortly. We'll start again in the morning. Is Myra back from the library yet?"

"She's on her way. I'll send her up to your office when she gets back."

155

"Good. And don't forget about the guitar."

"I'll pop round about half past seven," Fuller said.

"That will be fine. It will give Eric a chance to finish his homework before you start distracting him."

"An undervalued resource," Myra Banks said.

"Pardon?" Jack said.

"The public library. It's an undervalued resource. It's amazing what you can discover once you start scrolling through the microfiche files."

"Take a seat, Myra, and tell me what you found out," Jack said.

"You asked me to look into Adam Channing and Timothy Fellowes," Myra said. "Would it surprise you to know that they went the same university?"

"At the same time?"

"Channing was a year ahead of Fellowes but they shared two years."

"Which University was this?" Jack said.

"Norwich."

"What courses?"

"Channing was studying for a degree in political science and Fellowes took an undergraduate course in criminal justice."

"What are the chances of them crossing paths while they were there?" Jack said.

"Highly likely if they were living in the same halls of residence," Myra said. "And then there's the Student's Union. If they were both members of that then it's unlikely that they wouldn't bump into each other from time to time."

Jack leaned back in his seat. "Was there much else?" he said.

Myra held up her notebook. "I nearly filled this," she said. "I'll type it up before I go tonight and let you have it in the morning. Sergeant Fuller said there's another missing child. A boy this time?"

Jack nodded.

"Do you think this disappearance is linked to Frances and Sandra?"

"Time will tell," Jack said.

"If he turns up dead, you mean?"

"Yes."

Myra shook her head and got to her feet. "I'd better go and type up my notes," she said and walked to the door. She paused with her hand on the doorknob and looked back at him. "I haven't been with the force that long, sir, but this kind of case…it's not normal is it?"

He held her gaze. "No, Myra, thankfully not."

"But we *will* catch him, sir, won't we?"

"Yes," Jack said. "We'll catch him…eventually."

The shudder was involuntary. Myra Banks gathered herself, twisted the doorknob and let herself out of the office.

Jack stood up and slipped on his coat. Home and sanity were beckoning.

"Before you go, Jack, can you just pop into my office?" Lane stopped him on the stairs.

Jack followed him along the corridor. The office still smelled of fresh paint. Sitting at the desk was a man he didn't recognise, about his age,. Lane went and sat down.

"Jack, this is Detective Chief Superintendent Fisher from Scotland Yard. I want you to hand over to him all our files on the Anderton and Duncan cases, and I hear we have another one."

"Simon Nelson, yes. He went missing yesterday," Jack said.

"Then perhaps I can have those as well," Fisher said, addressing Jack directly.

Jack turned to Lane. "Would you mind telling me what all this is about?" he said.

"It's about our lack of progress in solving these cases, Jack."

Jack felt his temper rising. "But it's only been…" Lane cut him off. "I know, Jack, you feel aggrieved, but this hasn't come from me."

"Then where *has* it come from?"

"Orders from on high, Jack. The Chief Constable feels we're not making sufficient progress in apprehending this killer and has asked Scotland Yard, specifically, DCS Fisher and his team, to step in to assist us."

Fisher cleared his throat. "If I may interrupt you there, Chief Superintendent, our brief is not to assist, but to take over the investigation," He looked at Jack, a slight sneer on his lips. "From you, Chief Inspector," he said to Jack, "I'll expect nothing less than one hundred per cent co-operation. The sooner we can catch this bugger the better."

In the meantime, Jack," Lane said, "you've got a bundle of open cases sitting on your desk. Get results on some of those and the Chief Constable might start looking favourably on you again."

Jack stared at the pair of them, unsure who was annoying him more. Fisher with his expensive-looking suit, highly polished brogues and condescending manner, or Lane, whose easy acquiescence to the Chief Constable's demands spoke volumes about the man's basic weakness of character – a trait Jack had always known was there, but had rarely witnessed. He hadn't been neglecting the other cases, but a robbery at a local off-license tended to pale into insignificance compared to these murders, and he'd been happy to delegate them to junior members of the team

"Will that be all, sir?" Jack said to Lane tightly.

"For now, Jack," Lane said.

"If you can organise those files for me, post haste," Fisher said.

Jack nodded sharply, turned on his heel and strode from the office, before the urge to punch the Scotland Yard man in the face became unstoppable.

He reached the squad room, still seething, told his officers what was happening and ordered them to get the files ready to hand over. He silenced their protests with a wave of his hand.

"Any problems you have with these instructions then I invite you to take them up with Chief Superintendent Lane. It's now out of my hands. Frank, how are we doing with the off-license case?"

"It's in hand, sir," Lesser said.

"Well move it from the back burner to the front and turn up the heat. Let's see if we can crack it. And Eddie, where are we with the post office robberies?"

"I have a few leads," Fuller said.

"Good. Firm them up."

Jack went across to Myra Banks who was busy typing up her notes. "When you've finished transposing your notebook, Myra, perhaps you'll see to it that I get my copy first."

"Will do, sir," she said, looking up at him. "I take it you're not just going to roll over and take this," she said quietly.

"The hell I will," Jack growled.

"That's what I thought, sir" Myra said. "Could I drop your copy off at your house tonight, sir?"

Jack smiled at her. "If it's not putting you out, Myra."

"No problem, sir. No problem at all."

24

FRIDAY

"Well, you've got a face like thunder," Annie said as Jack walked in through the door. "Bad day?"

"They've taken the case away from me. Apparently I'm not making speedy enough progress on it?"

"Oh no, Jack. Who're *they*?"

"Lane and the Chief Constable. They've assigned some bod and a task force from Scotland Yard to handle it instead."

"Can they do that?"

"They just have," Jack said grimly, went across to the sideboard and poured a large Glenfiddich, knocking it back in a single gulp.

"I'm sorry, Jack," Annie said. "This case has been giving you sleepless nights. They can't fault your dedication. It just seems so unfair."

"Whether it's fair or not doesn't really come into it, neither does my insomnia. The Chief Constable wouldn't have taken this decision lightly. I suspect pressure has been brought to bear."

"Pressure? From whom?"

"Warren Anderton is the first name that springs to mind. He's an important man in the area and a brother Freemason to the Chief Constable."

"Really?"

"That's my best guess, but I don't think it's really that wide of the mark."

Annie shook her head. "You men and your silly secret societies," she said.

"Hey, don't lump me in with them," Jack said. "I never joined the Masons."

"Only because they've never invited you."

"No. It's because I'm not really their type," Jack said. "I don't go in for funny handshakes and arcane rituals."

"Thank Heavens," Annie said. "Dinner won't be long. Go and

get cleaned up before we sit down."

"Good idea. Oh, and Myra Banks is dropping by later, to bring me some files. And Eddie's going to pop in at about half past seven with…" He glanced around to see if they could be overheard and lowered his voice to be on the safe side. "…with what we were discussing this morning."

"Then I'd better make sure Eric has his homework finished." She smiled at him. "And Bennets in town is having a sale all this week, so we can go in tomorrow afternoon to look for a bed for Joanie's room."

Jack sliced through the lamb chop and had just popped the morsel of the succulent meat into his mouth when the doorbell rang. "That'll be Myra," he said, and got up from the table.

Myra Banks smiled as he opened the door, then saw the napkin tucked into his collar to protect his shirt and the smile faltered. "Sorry, sir. I didn't mean to disturb your dinner."

He waved away the apology and took a manila folder from her. "That's not a problem, Myra. This is much more important."

"Well, you've got the first copy. The boys from Scotland Yard won't get it until tomorrow," she said, smiling conspiratorially.

"I didn't mean to put you in a compromising position, Myra."

"Yes, I realise that," she said. "But, I mean, sir, it's a bloody cheek. We do all the legwork and they step in and claim all the glory. Everyone on the team feels the same."

"The least we can hope for is that there *is* some glory to claim. Was there any news on the Nelson boy before you left?"

"DS Lesser was leading that strand of the investigation, sir, but Scotland Yard are handling it now, so I haven't heard if they've got any further with it."

"Ah well, I'll check tomorrow when I get in. Thanks for popping this round, Myra. I want to have a chat with you on Monday about the possibility of you working for the CID permanently."

"I'd like that, sir," she said.

"I think you'd be a good fit."

"Thank you," she said. "Well, I won't keep you from your

meal any longer." She started to walk down the path. Halfway down she paused and turned back to him before he could shut the door. "Just one more thing, sir. Superintendent Fisher and his men have moved into your office."

Jack raised his eyes skywards. "Yes, Myra. Of course they have."

"Of all the bloody cheek!" Jack said as he returned to the dining room and resumed his dinner.

"Language, Dad," Annie said.

"Sorry," Jack said. "But Scotland Yard have moved into my office. *My office!* Is nothing sacred?"

Annie gave a small shake of her head. "More potatoes?" she said.

A slight smile played on his lips as he marvelled at the ease with which his wife could defuse a tense situation. "Yes," he said. "Why not?"

They were washing up when there was a tap at the back door.

"Hello, Eddie," Jack said.

His sergeant was standing on the back doorstep, a black canvas guitar case in hand. "I came around the back because I wasn't sure if Eric knew I was bringing this round?" Fuller said

"You did the right thing," Jack said. "I haven't told him yet."

"We want it to be a surprise," Annie said from the sink. "Do come in, Eddie. Cuppa?"

"Please, Mrs. C." Fuller said and stepped inside.

"Sit yourself down," Annie said, and turned on the gas ring under the kettle to boil the water again.

Jack dried the last plate with a tea towel and joined Fuller at the table.

"What do you think about Scotland Yard getting involved?" Fuller said to his boss.

"No shop talk," Annie said as she spooned more tea into the pot and added the boiling water.

"Sorry, Annie," Jack said. "Actually, I'm spitting nails," he said quietly to Fuller.

"I thought you might be," Fuller said, equally quietly.

Annie brought the tea tray across, set it down on the table and sat down with them, effectively ending their murmured conversation.

"Do you want to go and call him, Jack?" she said as she poured the steaming tea into the china teacups.

Jack walked to the door and stuck his head out into the hall.

"Eric! Have you finished your homework?" he called.

"Just done, Dad," Eric's voice floated back from the living room.

"Then come into the kitchen."

Moments later Eric walked out into the hallway, his sisters following close behind. "What do you want?" Eric said.

"There someone here to see you," Jack said, and went back into the kitchen.

"Hello, Eddie," Eric said as he walked into the room. "What are you doing…"

The question died on his lips as he spotted the guitar case leaning up against one of the kitchen chairs. His eyes widened and he turned to Jack.

"Really?"

"You can go without your pocket money until you've paid me back, and you can thank Eddie for bringing it round."

Eric's gaze shifted back to the guitar case. "Thanks, Eddie. Can I see it?"

Fuller grinned, lifted the guitar case and started to unzip it.

As he pulled the guitar from the case he said, "It's a little dusty and could probably use a new set of strings, but it plays fine." He handed the guitar to Eric, smiling at the stunned expression on the boy's face.

"It's the most beautiful thing I've ever seen," Eric said, and drew his finger across the strings. "Are you sure, Eddie?"

Fuller nodded. "It's nearly in tune. Here. Let me," he said taking the guitar from Eric and making a slight adjustment to the machine heads. He strummed the guitar. "That's better. How would Sunday morning suit you, for your first lesson?"

Eric took the instrument back from him and nodded his head enthusiastically.

"It's a date then," Fuller said. "Sunday at eleven."

"Thanks, Eddie," Annie said.

"My pleasure, Mrs. C.," Fuller said. "You'll be listening to him on the wireless one day."

"Dream on," Rosie said from the doorway.

"I'm being serious," Fuller said. "You've heard that Tommy Steele. He's hardly *Segovia* but, with three chords and a wiggle of his hips, the girls go crazy."

"Yes, but he's *Tommy Steele*," Rosie said. "A little bit out of Eric's league, I think."

"Hey," Eric said.

"Take no notice of her, Eric," Joan said. "He's got nothing you haven't got."

"You see, Eddie," Jack said, "The guitar's not been in the house five minutes and already World War three's erupting."

"My cue to leave, I think," Fuller said, getting up from the table and walking to the door. "Thanks for the tea, Mrs. C. I'll pick you up in the morning, guv."

"When we get to the station, we'll probably find we've been moved out into the car park," Jack said with a grim smile.

"Many a true word spoken in jest," Fuller said, and let himself out.

Jack lay in the bed, Myra's file open and propped up on his knees. Annie lay beside him, her face buried in a Catherine Cookson novel. She yawned and closed the book. "Are you going to be much longer?" she said.

"I'm nearly done," he said. 'You can put your light out if you're tired."

"You know that never works. You'll still have yours on, and you know I can't sleep unless it's dark. What's so interesting anyway?"

He told her what Myra had found out at the library.

"Interesting," she said. "But what does it mean?"

Jack finished reading, closed the file and reached over to turn off his bedside lamp. "I'm not sure," he said. "Do you remember that Hitchcock film we went to see a couple of years back? *Strangers on a Train*?"

"I remember. Farley Granger and Robert Walker," Annie said.

"Do you remember how each of them killed the other's victim, to give themselves a perfect alibi?"

Annie nodded. "Surely you don't think that's what happened with those two girls," she said.

Jack shrugged. "It's an idea," he said.

"An idea out of a book – Patricia Highsmith wasn't it?"

"It could be," Jack said. "I only know the film. You're the one for detective fiction."

"Yes, but it's *fiction* all the same. People in their right minds don't go around committing murders using plots from crime novels."

"But what if they did?" Jack said. "You have two men and two murders. Adam Channing was up in Scotland the day of the murder of Frances Anderton, and the day Sandra Duncan was killed, the man spotted arguing with her in the park, Tim Fellowes, was in Switzerland. What if they killed each others intended victim, giving themselves perfect alibis in the process?"

Annie yawned again and sunk down under the sheets. "It's an intriguing prospect, Jack. But you're forgetting one thing?"

"Oh?"

"Motive. As I remember it, Farley Granger and Robert Taylor had strong reasons for wanting their victims dead. In your case you have a fourteen year old girl whose main interests seem to be reading books and going to church, and a young woman who wouldn't say boo to a goose, whose sole ambition in life seems to be a children's nanny. Hardly the types of people to drive middle-aged men to commit murder."

"Unless there was more to it than that."

"Such as?" Annie said. "You said that Sandra had been interfered with, but Frances wasn't touched in that way, so that's a major difference. Frances's father is a fairly prominent public figure and controls a wealthy company, but Sandra's dad is what… a minor civil servant? So that's another difference between the two cases. I think you're reaching, Jack, trying to make the facts suit the crimes. Both girls had their eyes and lips sewn shut, which suggests to me that you're looking for one man, a very sick man, but a sole operator."

It was Jack's turn to yawn. "You're probably right," he said, leaned over and kissed Annie on the cheek. "Goodnight," he said.

"Goodnight," she said. "And try to get some sleep tonight. You're getting bags under your eyes."

"I saw them when I was shaving. Bags under the bags, I thought. I'll try anyway," he said, and shut his eyes.

25

SATURDAY AUGUST 16th 1958

"Are you sure it's him?" Jack said into the telephone.

"The body fits the description," Andy Brewer said.

"Have you told Superintendent Fisher?"

"He's not in yet, sir and I'd thought you'd rather be the first to know."

"Good man," Jack said. "But make sure you tell him as soon as he gets there. I don't want anyone accused of messing up a Scotland Yard investigation. I'll be there shortly."

He went back to the kitchen and picked up his slice of toast. It was cold, the butter congealed.

"Shall I make you another?" Annie said.

Jack shook his head. "Don't trouble," he said. "I've got to get to work. Simon Nelson's turned up."

"Alive?" Annie said, and then read the look on her husband's face. "Oh," she said, and picked up her teacup.

"That makes it three deaths, in a week," Jack said. "I've never had anything like this before."

"Are you sure it's the work of the same killer?" Annie said, and sipped her tea.

"You were telling me last night that it was. This one has most of the hallmarks of the other two, so I suspect it is."

"Except that this time it was a boy who was taken and killed."

"Yes," Jack said. "That's what so bloody odd about it. Normally a killer such as this has a type he goes for. This latest one breaks all the rules." The doorbell rang. "That'll be Eddie," he said, and went to get his coat.

"They've found the Nelson boy," Jack said as they got in the car.

"Dead?"

"As before. This time he was left on the railway embankment, just along from the Digswell viaduct."

"An easier place to dump the body, I suppose," Fuller said.

"Certainly less public. The spot where he was found backs onto the allotments."

"Then perhaps he's learning something. Not taking any unnecessary risks."

"I don't know if that's a good thing or not," Jack said.

"Why's that?"

"Because it means he's evolving, becoming better at his craft," Jack said.

"Are there any other differences?"

"The eyes and lips are sewn up, and wax has been poured into his ears, so no difference there."

"Has he been…touched?"

"Sexually molested like Sandra Duncan, you mean?" Jack said.

"I suppose I do, yes," Fuller said, uncomfortable talking about it.

"I don't know, Eddie. It's too early to tell. I dare say Hepton will be able to tell us that once he's done the post mortem. The body's been taken to North Herts. I'll give them a call when we get in and find out what time it's been scheduled for, and then I'll go along and observe."

"Will Superintendent Fisher let you?" Fuller said.

"Just let him try and stop me," Jack said. "He may have taken over the investigation, but it's still my case, and I'm not having it hijacked without a fight."

Fuller grinned. "Well I know who I'd put my money on to win that one," he said.

"Thanks for the vote of confidence," Jack said.

Jack walked into Lane's office without knocking. "Thanks for the support yesterday, Henry. It's good to know you were looking out for me."

Lane shrank back in his seat, intimidated by Jack's presence in the room. "My hands were tied, Jack. What else could I do?"

"You could have thrown your weight behind your own men, for starters. We have a loyal team here with some excellent officers, both senior and junior, and then, with one word from on high, you pull the rug out from under their feet, mine included."

"I'm sorry, Jack, but pressure was being brought to bear."

"Pressure from Warren Anderton no doubt," Jack said.

"It's not for us to speculate, but it was *his* daughter who was killed."

"Then it's a pity he didn't behave more like a father on Saturday night, instead of driving his daughter out of the house, forcing her to stay overnight with friends. Guilt is what's leading him to put pressure on the Chief Constable. Nothing more, nothing less."

Lane stood up from the desk and walked to the window that looked out onto the car park. He stared out, watching a gleaming, black Wolseley pull in from the street. "Fisher and his men have arrived," he said, hoping to break the tension between them.

Normally he would never let a junior officer speak to him in that manner, but he knew Jack Callum's passion for the job, and respected the man's abilities. He knew Callum's nose had been put severely out of joint and could excuse him his anger. He had felt much the same yesterday after receiving the telephone call from the Chief Constable. Jack's assumption that it was Warren Anderton pressuring the Chief Constable was on the money. He knew the two men attended the same lodge, and was aware, after having dealings with them in the past, that together the Freemason brotherhood wielded enviable power in the town.

"Try to work with him, Jack. I know Brian Fisher – I was at Hendon with him – and I know he's got the reputation of being something of a martinet, but he's a pretty good copper for all that, he's had some good collars down in London. You never know, he might bring a fresh perspective to the investigation and get things moving forward."

"I wish I shared your confidence," Jack said. "But I just don't see how a London man can have a better perspective on a spate of, what are essentially, local killings, than a group of officers who know the area like the backs of their hands."

"Jack, as a favour to me," Lane said.

"As a favour to you, Henry, I'll continue to work on the case, and I won't get in Fisher's way."

"Thank you, Jack."

"But God help him if he gets in mine."

"It's good of you to see me, Sir Maurice," Jack said.

"It's not my usual *modus operandi*," Hepton said. "But, in the circumstances, I think we need to apprehend this creature, before he takes any more victims." Hepton looked to be in his fifties. He had a shock of unruly grey hair, a slim goatee beard and ferociously intelligent blue eyes that looked out on the world as if challenging it to a fight.

"You think we're looking for the same killer then?"

"I'd be very surprised if we weren't," Hepton said.

They were sitting in a small office leading off from the mortuary.

"Your reasons?" Jack said.

Hepton flipped open a thin file lying on the desk in front of him and began to scan the pages of handwritten notes.

"All fairly circumstantial, but all three bodies that have come to me in the past week have marked similarities. The sewing shut of the eyes and lips in all three cases was executed using the same type of silk thread."

"Embroidery thread, yes. I read the reports on Frances Anderton and Sandra Duncan."

A slight smile flickered across Hepton's lips. "Yes, good. It's gratifying to know that someone reads my reports. Usually, I don't get to hear about it until the case comes to court and some barrister or other is standing there quoting my words back at me. I like to think of myself as important resource for the investigation team, not just an old, dried up, 'expert' witness."

"I happen to think forensic pathology is an important factor in any murder investigation."

"Yes, yes, thank you for that. It's nice to hear it from the horse's mouth, so to speak. Anyway, to continue, the paraffin wax he used to fill the ears, all came from the same source. Household candles of the most common variety – the type you can buy in any ironmonger's store, even *Woolworths* sell them. All three victims were strangled using a waxed rope, a washing line or something of a similar gauge. Frances Anderton seems to have been subdued a short time before death with something like trichloromethane...you probably know it better as chloroform, and I make that assumption because of the slight redness around the girl's mouth. It was a bit difficult to see at first because of the damage caused to the lips by the sewing, but in her case, the assailant must have used a significant quantity of the stuff because there's a slight trace of redness around her nostrils as well.

"Awkward stuff chloroform, if you don't know what you're doing with it, and the hoary old trick, so beloved of writers of detective fiction, of holding a pad of chloroform over a victim's nose and mouth to knock them out, doesn't actually work very well. You'd have to hold it there for about five minutes for it to achieve total efficacy. Saying that, I think he did just that to the Anderton girl. She wouldn't have given in without a struggle, and that would explain the gash to her foot – kicking out as he tried to subdue her, her foot catching on something – but she was only a child, and slightly built, so he was either lucky or fairly strong. Chloroform would explain the redness around the nose and mouth, if he used it then as an anaesthetic to keep her subdued for longer."

"But what about Sandra Duncan?"

"Ah, you see, I think he realized the mistake he made with the first abduction, and moved on to injecting the girl with a narcotic. I'm still waiting for the blood analysis to come through, but I found a small puncture mark in the side of the girl's neck."

"And the boy, Simon Nelson?" Jack said.

"Different again. I checked the stomach contents and there was a significant amount of peppermint cordial in there. The cordial has a very strong flavour and could mask the taste of all manner of narcotics; again I'm waiting for the results of the chemical analysis."

"And yet you still see it being the same man, despite the different methods of subduing his victims," Jack said

"Oh, yes, going by the use of embroidery thread and paraffin wax, and the fact that they were all strangled using the same type of rope, I've no real doubt that we're dealing with the same perpetrator, but one who is evolving, learning from his past mistakes and refining his method. The fact that he has done all this in barely a week is worrying – very worrying indeed. You have to stop him, Chief Inspector, and I'll help in any way I can."

"Was there any evidence of sexual abuse?" Jack said.

"Nothing that I could see. No bruising to the genitals or anus, which you would expect to the see if the boy had been sodomized."

"Thank you, Sir Maurice. It's much appreciated, and thank you for your time."

Jack shook his hand and walked from the office, in time to see Fisher push his way through the double doors at the end of the corridor.

With a face like thunder Fisher stormed along the corridor towards him.

"Callum," Fisher said as he reached the office. "What the hell are you doing here?"

"He was here to see me," Hepton said emerging from the office. "What business is it of yours?"

Fisher introduced himself and glared at Jack but spoke to Hepton. "I'm here to get the results of the Nelson boy's post mortem, Professor Hepton."

Jack watched Hepton bridle. "Then you're going to have to wait for my report like everybody else…and it's *Sir Maurice* to you."

Fisher's eyes clouded with confusion, but within seconds the bluster was back. "I really must insist, *Sir* Maurice…"

"You can insist all you like, Superintendent, but it won't make me change my mind. Wait for my report." He turned abruptly, walked back into the office and closed the door behind him.

"I think you've offended him, sir," Jack said, trying not to smile.

Fisher's glare deepened. "I'll see you back at the station, Chief Inspector, and you'll damned well tell me what you two were talking about."

"Yes, sir," Jack said with studied contempt, saluted and walked from the mortuary.

"What the hell do you think you're playing at, Callum?" Fisher said.

For Jack it was a strange, almost surreal moment, sitting on the wrong side of his own desk, being read the riot act.

"I wanted an early start, sir."

"So you go behind my back and interview an important witness without the say so from me."

"With respect, sir, you weren't here, and I didn't think we had the time to waste waiting for you to arrive from London."

Fisher's eyes narrowed. "Be very careful, Chief Inspector. With the click of my fingers, I could have you back pounding the beat."

"I'm sure you could, sir.'

Fisher glared at him. "You're a cocky sod, aren't you, Callum?"

Jack said nothing.

"But Chief Superintendent Lane speaks very highly of you, and I've checked your arrest and conviction record. Quite impressive for someone working in a small catchment area, so, just this once, I'm willing to overlook your indiscretion. But I emphasize, *just this once*. You pull a stunt like that again and I'll have you back…"

"Pounding the beat, sir. Yes, I got that."

Fisher's glare intensified. "The chief superintendent said you have other cases pending, so you'd better go and attend to them."

"Yes, sir," Jack said, getting to his feet.

"Hold hard," Fisher said. "Before you get on, you can tell me exactly what Sir Maurice bloody Hepton, the pompous little prig, told you. And leave nothing out."

26

SATURDAY

The room was large and heaving with people, not what Rosie Callum was expecting at all. She had imagined a small intimate nightspot with tables and chairs, subdued lighting, and perhaps a small jazz band playing subtle melodies for couples to smooch to on the dance floor. Instead she felt as if they had gate crashed someone's loud and raucous wedding reception. All that was needed to complete the illusion was an inebriated bride wearing a meringue dress, tripping the light fantastic with an equally drunken uncle.

The lighting was bright and cigarette smoke hung heavy in the stale air, making her eyes smart. A long bar took up most of the end wall, and several young men were working behind it, dispensing drinks to a seemingly endless stream of other young men, dressed for an evening out in sharp, mohair suits, and highly polished shoes, with matching hair. The smell of their pungent, richly scented hair oil and aftershave mixed with the cigarette smoke hung like a miasma above their heads as they bought drinks to take back to their girlfriends, who sat in small groups at tables pushed against the two adjacent walls. Against the fourth wall was a low stage where a seven-strong band pulsed loudly with the hits of the day, together with some jazz standards.

In front of them was an area given over to a dance floor where a dozen more adventurous couples were practicing the steps they had learned from *Victor Sylvester's Dancing Club* shown on television the previous week.

"Archie Trott and his band," David Neville shouted above the din, as he guided Rosie across the dance floor to a vacant table in the corner. "They're one of my favourites. They're really good. Sit yourself down and I'll go and fetch the drinks. What would you like?"

"Do they sell *Coca Cola*?" Rosie said uncertainly.

"*Coca Cola*? On a Saturday night?" Neville said, a smile in his voice.

He'll think I'm just a kid, Rosie thought. "*Babycham*. I meant *Babycham*," she said quickly. *I'll just have the one*, she thought. *Dad will never find out*.

"*Babycham* it is. Wait here. I'll be back in a minute," he said, and then he was gone, pushing back through the dancers to get to the bar.

Rosie sat alone at the table, feeling self-conscious. She took a small powder compact from her patent leather handbag and flipped it open, checking her hair in the small, round mirror. She'd let Joanie loose on it tonight and her sister had managed to make her look sophisticated with just thirty minutes of teasing, and a liberal spray of hair lacquer. She closed the compact and watched Neville as he stood at the bar, a ten-shilling note gripped between his finger and thumb. He waved it occasionally to attract the attention of one of the barmen.

"Half of bitter and a *Babycham*," Neville said to the barman, glancing back at the table to see that Rosie was all right.

"Who's your girlfriend, Davy boy?"

Neville jerked around and found himself face to face with Derek Webster. Towering behind him was the intimidating form of Peter Lamb, his straight black hair brushed back from his face and pomaded flat, giving him a look reminiscent of Bela Lugosi. Both of them wore suits, which, if anything, made them appear more menacing.

"I haven't got a girlfriend," Neville said.

"So who's the *Babycham* for, your mother?" Lamb growled.

"I…"

"Don't deny it, Davy," Webster said. "The little tart you came in with? Who is she?"

"Rosie," Neville said. "But she's not my girlfriend. Not properly anyway."

"Well, take her drink back to the table and meet us in the gents' toilet when you're finished," Webster said and wheeled away, Lamb following close behind.

Feeling suddenly sick, Neville paid for the drinks and carried them back to the table. He put them down. "I have to go to the lav," he said. "I'll only be a minute."

Rosie looked up at him, concern in her eyes. "Who were they?" Rosie said.

"Just some chaps I know," Neville said.

"Friends?"

"Just some chaps."

"Are you all right?" Rosie said. "Only you look a bit green."

He managed a smile. "I'm fine," he said. "Something I ate, probably." He scurried off before she could respond. She watched him go, and then picked up her glass, sipping the *perry* cautiously, screwing up her nose as the bubbles tickled her nostrils. She checked her watch and turned her attention back to the dancers.

The gents' smelled of disinfectant, stale urine and the ubiquitous cigarette smoke. Webster and Lamb were waiting for him. Derek Webster had a comb in his hand and was standing in front of the mirror making some minor adjustments to his neatly-cut hair, while Peter Lamb was leaning against the sinks that lined one wall, using the toe of his winkle picker shoe to score lines and circles in the puddle of water at his feet.

"Ah, Davy," Webster said, staring at him from the mirror. "Good of you to join us."

"What do you want, Del?" Neville said.

"Have you told Gavin about the tart?" Lamb said.

Neville shook his head.

"Do you think that's wise?" Webster said, turning away from the mirror to face him.

"He doesn't need to know," Neville said.

Webster and Lamb exchanged looks.

"Oh, I think he does," Lamb said. "You know how the game works, Davy. We fetch them and turn them over to Gavin, and, when he's finished with them, we get rid of them and Gavin pays us. *That's* how it works."

"A perfect financial arrangement," Webster said.

"And we don't want you messing it up," Lamb said, moving away from the sinks threateningly.

Neville took a step backwards. "I'm not messing anything

up," he said. "I've played my part. I did the golf course."

"Yes, and you did it well," Lamb said. "A golf cart. Inspired. But you still need to tell Gavin about the tart."

"Her name's Rosie," Neville said petulantly.

"Yes, Rosie," Webster said. "He needs to know."

Neville shook his head. "Not this one. She's special."

"They're all *special*...to Gavin," Lamb said.

The door to the toilet opened and a young man walked in, unbuttoning his fly. He took one look at the three young men, his eyes focussing on the intimidating look on Peter Lamb's face, and hurriedly buttoned himself up, turned tail and walked out again.

Lamb went across to the door and leaned against it, holding it closed. "So are you going to tell him?" he said. "Or do you want us to do it for you?"

Panic flared in Neville's eyes. "Please, Pete. Don't tell him."

"So *you* will?" Lamb said.

Neville nodded. "Yes, I'll tell him. Just give me a few days."

Lamb crossed to him and wrapped his arm around Neville's shoulder. "I'll tell you what, Davy. Del and I are your friends, your mates. We'll let you have the weekend with her. That's the rest of today, and all day tomorrow – perhaps you can take her for a picnic in the park, or over the Common – something nice, just for the two of you. And then on Monday, before you go to work, you can go round to Gavin's and tell him all about Rosie. If you don't, I'll tell him myself. You never know, he might let you keep her."

"But he might not," Webster said, grinning sardonically.

Neville opened his mouth to protest but knew they wouldn't be listening to him, so he shut it again.

Lamb pulled open the door. "Run along," he said to Neville. "Have a nice evening. Enjoy the dancing."

Still feeling sick, Neville hurried from the toilet and went back to the table where Rosie sat sipping at her *Babycham*.

"Feeling better?" Rosie said on his return.

He stuck out his hand. "Let's dance," he said, and tugged her out of her seat.

He pulled her onto the dance floor, put his hand on her waist and led her in a lively quickstep to the strains of *This Can't Be Love*.

The quickstep finished and without a pause Archie Trott and his men launched into a slow waltz.

Neville was a fluid dancer and it took all of Rosie's concentration to keep up with him in the quickstep, but now she found herself able to relax. She leaned into him and he responded by leading her gracefully in the waltz.

"I'd like to see you tomorrow," he said, his lips pressing close to her ear.

"This evening's got a long way to go yet," she said.

"I know. But tomorrow I thought it would be nice to do something, just the two of us. A picnic maybe?"

Suddenly she felt like was dancing on air. "Yes," she said, as the music carried her away. "I think I'd like that."

"Nice evening, love?"

"Wonderful, mum," Rosie said as she walked into the living room. "We're going for a picnic tomorrow. Is everyone in bed?"

"Your dad's not long gone up," Annie said. "Joanie went up early to try out her new bed – your dad and I spent most of the evening sorting out the box room. I know it's only a single but it's still more comfortable than the put-you-up. And we sent Eric up to his room at about eight. We couldn't stand the tuneless strumming. I'll be glad when Eddie gets here tomorrow to show him how to play the damned thing properly. Now, what's all this about a picnic?"

Rosie sat down on the settee and crossed her legs underneath her. "He came out with it, just like that. We were dancing and he suddenly blurts out that he wants to spend the day with me tomorrow and would I like to go on a picnic."

"That's very nice," Annie said. "It sounds as if he's quite sweet on you."

"Oh, Mum, do you really think so?"

"Spending the day with you? Taking you on a picnic? Yes, it sounds to me as if he's smitten. Is he supplying the food?"

Rosie mouth dropped open. "Heavens! We didn't even discuss it. What am I going to do?"

"For one thing, you don't panic. There's stuff in the larder you can use. There's a fresh loaf, some ham off the bone, a pound of cheddar, and there's those sausage rolls you brought home for your dad's tea tomorrow."

'Won't he mind?"

"I'm sure he'll be most put out, but if you take them you'll be doing his waistline a favour, so it's for the greater good." Annie got to her feet. "Look, you turn in. You look tired – too much dancing I expect. I'll put on some eggs to boil. You can have a couple of those each."

Rosie got to her feet and hugged her mother. "Thanks," she said.

"You just make sure you have a lovely day tomorrow."

Rosie grinned, "Oh, I think I will," she said, and went off to bed.

Annie went out to the kitchen and took some eggs from the larder, filled a saucepan with water and set it to boil on the stove.

"Making tea?"

Annie spun around from the cooker. "Jack Callum! You gave me a start. I thought you were in bed."

"I was," Jack said. "I couldn't sleep."

"You're not still thinking about that case?"

"Afraid so."

"Sit down at the table then and I'll put the kettle on."

"I thought that's what you were doing."

She shook her head. "I'm boiling some eggs for Rosie. David is taking her on a picnic tomorrow."

Jack sat at the table. "Is he indeed? He sounds keen."

"Mustard," Annie said.

Jack raised his eyebrows.

"Don't look surprised," Annie said. "In case you haven't noticed, your little girl is growing into an extremely beautiful young woman. I'm just surprised that would-be suitors aren't queuing down the road for the chance to take her out."

"It will happen one day," Jack said glumly.

"Is it making you feel old?" Annie said, sitting down next to him, taking his hand in hers and squeezing it.

"*Life* is making me feel old, pet."

"Get away with you, you old grouch. I look at you and still see the handsome, virile young man I married."

Jack tugged her onto his lap and kissed her.

The whistle on the kettle began to trill.

She broke off the kiss. "Saved by the whistle…is that an expression?"

Jack smiled at her fondly. "Make the tea, woman," he said, letting her go.

"Perhaps we can take it up with us?" she said.

"What a deliciously decadent idea," he said. "Shall I bring the biscuits?"

She shook her head. "I have something just as sweet in mind…and, my way, we don't get crumbs in the bed."

As she poured water into the teapot he went across and nuzzled the back of her neck. "You're a temptress, Annie Callum."

"Yes," she said lightly. "I know."

27

SUNDAY 17th August 1958

"So that's A, D and G," Eddie Fuller said. "With those three chords you can play all manner of songs."

Eric perched on the edge of the armchair, the guitar resting on his knee, his fingers contorted to make the chord shapes, his tongue stuck resolutely between his teeth as he concentrated. He looked across at Fuller. "What songs?" he said.

Fuller smiled. "What about a song by one of your heroes. Lonnie Donegan? *The Rock Island Line*?"

"Yeah," Eric said. "I love that one. Will you show me how it goes?"

"You know Lonnie was the same age as you are now when he got his first guitar."

"Really?" Eric said.

Fuller nodded and smiled. "And he's done all right for himself, hasn't he?" Fuller said. "Now, hand me the guitar."

"He's improving," Annie said as she stood at the sink peeling potatoes, listening to the sounds coming from the other room.

"He hasn't got that good that quickly," Jack said. "That's Eddie playing."

"You mean we haven't got a child prodigy on our hands?"

"I think the hit parade's safe for another couple of years yet," Joan said, her hands buried in a mixing bowl as she rubbed butter, flour and sugar into the flour to make the crumble topping for their dessert. "Do you know where Rosie's gone for her picnic?"

"She was muttering something about the Common," Annie said. "So my guess is they'll go there."

"On a hot Sunday afternoon? She'll be mad if she does. The place will be packed."

Jack looked up from his newspaper. "Did mum tell you that Rosie took the sausage rolls that I had earmarked for my tea?" he said bleakly.

"Then she did your arteries a favour," Joan said.

"But not my stomach," Jack said. "I was looking forward to them."

The telephone in the hall started to ring.

"If that's work, you're not going in," Annie said.

"Don't worry. I'm not having another roast ruined." Jack said, and went to answer it.

"Andy, what can I do for you?"

"I just thought I'd let you know, sir, another envelope has arrived. Light blue like the last one, no stamp."

"Who is it addressed to?"

"The Chief Investigating Officer."

"Not Sonia Nelson?" Jack mused. "And when you say, it's arrived, when was this?"

"I found it here on the desk when I got in."

"So whoever delivered it simply walked into the station without being seen and left the envelope there."

"It certainly looks that way," Brewer said.

"He's a cheeky sod," Jack muttered. "Open it, Andy, and carefully take out what's inside. Try not to smudge any latent fingerprints."

There was silence on the other end of the line as Brewer did as he was requested.

"It's the same as before, sir – three monkeys, drawn in green ink. Are you coming to check it out?"

"Is Superintendent Fisher there?"

"It's his day off, sir."

"Not any more," Jack said. "Give him a call and get him there to investigate." *See how he likes a stone cold Sunday dinner*, Jack thought as he hung up the telephone. *Petty and childish, Jack – you won't go to Heaven*, he thought, and smiled to himself as he went back to the kitchen to finish reading the paper.

Fuller walked out into the kitchen. Annie hadn't moved from the sink. Now she was scrubbing carrots and listening to Eric, in the living room, still painfully practicing his chords.

"You're making progress, Eddie. It's a vast improvement on yesterday."

Fuller smiled. "What he lacks in talent. He makes up for in dogged persistence and determination."

"He takes after his father," Annie said. "Can I get you anything?"

"A glass of water would be grand," Fuller said. "Where's your husband?"

"Outside. You'll probably find him in the greenhouse." She ran some water into a glass and handed it to him. He chugged it back and set the empty glass down on the draining board, then opened the back door and stepped out into the garden.

The heat hit him as soon as he stepped outside. It was like stepping into an oven. He walked down the path to the large rectangular greenhouse at the end. Jack was inside, watering the tomato plants that lined one side of the greenhouse. They were heavy with fruit, large green tomatoes, some of them starting to ripen, a pale orange blush creeping over the skins.

"You have a good crop this year, sir," Fuller said.

"Jack, please, Eddie. It's the weekend." Jack tipped the watering can and sent a steady stream of water into the earth. "You don't garden, Eddie, do you?"

"My landlady wouldn't be very pleased if I did. It would probably help if my flat had a garden," Fuller said.

"Shame." Jack said. "It's very restful, as well as being productive, and it's therapeutic. I can lose myself out here. I find it focuses the mind."

"I can see that it would," Fuller said, leaning against the doorframe.

"Another letter arrived," Jack said. "Three monkeys again. This time left at the station."

"At the station? Not at Sonia's?"

Jack shook his head.

"Perhaps he doesn't know where she lives."

"That was my initial thought, but then Andy Brewer told me that it was addressed to *The Investigating Officer*. Strange, don't you think?"

"You're thinking that he's trying to send us a message?"

183

"That's exactly what I'm thinking," Jack said, and switched his attention to another plant.

"What do you think it means?"

"I think he's taunting us, Eddie, the same way that Jack the Ripper used to taunt Fred Abberline and his men, only more obliquely."

"From what I've read," Fuller said. "A killer does that because, deep down, he wants to get caught."

"Yes, I've read that too, but I'm not sure that's the case here. As I say, the message is oblique, so bloody oblique as to be obscure. No, I think he's challenging us. 'Look at me, you dim coppers, do think you can catch me?'" Jack turned off the hose he was using to keep the watering can topped up and watched the flow of water reduce to a steady drip.

"I wouldn't take it personally, Jack," Fuller said.

"I'm not," Jack said. "No, damn it, *I am*! This chap thinks he's smarter than me, thinks he's fireproof. Why? What makes him so sure I won't be able to catch him? He's killed three times in a week. That's a very short time frame for your average multiple killer. He's barely giving himself enough time to draw breath. It doesn't make sense. What's his motive? It doesn't fit any rationale that I've come across, or read about before. The killings may be sexually motivated, but that only applies to one of the victims. There's evidence that Sandra Duncan was molested, but no sign of anything like that with Frances Anderton or Simon Nelson."

"So can we write off sexual deviance as the motive?" Fuller said.

"We can certainly discard it as the primary motive," Jack said. "No, there's something else at work here – something I just can't put my finger on."

"Well, I suppose it's Scotland Yard's problem now," Fuller said.

Jack coiled the hose and hung it from a hook in the corner. "Yes, I suppose it is."

Fuller was watching his boss closely. He'd seen that look of steely determination on the face of Eric Callum just minutes before as he struggled with the finger shapes of the guitar chords. "But you're not going to let it go, are you, Jack?"

"Am I hell," Jack said. "Are you staying for a bite to eat, Eddie? Annie's cooking a leg of lamb. Apple crumble to follow."

"It's tempting, Jack, but I'm meeting Judy after her shift at the *Dog and Duck*. I thought we'd go for a walk this afternoon. She likes walking."

"She sounds like the healthy type," Jack said.

"She likes to keep her body in shape," Fuller said.

"As I'm sure you do,"

Fuller smiled. "I'm sure I don't know what you mean, Chief Inspector."

Jack dug in the pocket of his corduroy trousers and pulled out a handful of coins. "Five shillings," he said and handed Fuller two half a crowns.

"I told you, Eric can have the lessons for free," Fuller said refusing the coins.

"Then buy Judy an ice cream when you're out for your walk," Jack said. "I insist." He pressed the money into Fuller's hand. "And thanks. From what I heard, Eric's sounding a lot better than he did last night."

"Oh, he'll master it in the end. He likes a challenge...just like his father."

Dusk was beginning to settle over Hertfordshire when David Neville eased the car into the kerb, outside the Callum house.

"Thank you for a lovely day," Rosie said to him.

"You're very welcome," Neville said. "Thanks for bringing the food, though I feel quite bad, inviting you for a picnic and expecting you to bring your own."

"It wasn't a problem," she said. Her hand reached for the door handle but she didn't open the door. "Well," she said. "I suppose I should go inside."

"I suppose you should," Neville said, and slid his arm around her shoulders.

"Only I've got work tomorrow," she said.

"Yeah, me too," he said, leaning across and kissing her.

She had been waiting for him to do it all day but, when the

kiss came, it still took her by surprise, leaving her breathless.

The kiss ended and she glanced around at the house, imagining that her entire family would be watching from the windows, but there was no sign of anyone looking out at her.

"I suppose…" she started and he kissed her again, more intensely this time, covering her mouth with his, his tongue darting into her mouth and dancing with her own. She closed her eyes and let herself relax into it, enjoying the sensations caused by her first, real, adult kiss. She kissed back just as passionately, feeling a delicious thrill as his hand crept up inside the front of her blouse and cupped her breast.

"We shouldn't," she said, but hadn't the will to stop him.

It was only when the hand moved down to her thigh and crept under her skirt that alarm bells started ringing in her mind. As his fingers skimmed the lace of her underwear, she brought her own hand down and clamped her fingers over his wrist.

She tore her lips away from his. "No!" she said. "Not that. Not yet."

But he wasn't going to be denied. He wrenched her arm away and moved his hand further up her skirt.

Suddenly she was fighting him, twisting her face away to stop him kissing her, and smacking his arm. "I said no!" she said.

When he refused to stop, she brought her hand back and caught him a stinging blow across the cheek. "I'm not that type of girl, David Neville!"

He reacted to the blow with shock, falling back into his seat and sitting there, wide eyed, his breath coming in short gasps. Finally he found his voice. "I'm…I'm sorry," he stammered.

She was glaring at him. "You ruined it," she said, and reached for the door handle again, this time opening the door and kicking it open with her foot.

She stepped out of the car.

"Rosie, wait. I'm sorry I…"

She was standing outside the car, looking in at him, shaking her head. "Everything," she said. "You ruined everything." She slammed the car door and ran up the front garden path, fumbling in her purse for the front door key. As she slid the key into the lock, she heard the car's engine roar, followed by a squeal of rubber on tarmac as he sped off down the road.

Annie was standing in the hallway as Rosie burst in through the door.

"I thought I heard a car," Annie said. "Have you had a nice time?"

Without looking up, Rosie barrelled past her and ran up the stairs. There was the loud bang of her bedroom door being slammed shut followed by silence.

Joan came out into the hall and stared at the shocked expression on her mother's face. "Was that Rosie?"

Annie nodded dumbly.

"Where is she?"

Again Annie said nothing, just pointed up the stairs.

Joan frowned. "I'll go up and see if she's all right."

"She's very upset," Annie said, shaking her head. "I don't know what…"

"Leave it to me," Joan said, and trotted up the stairs.

Annie walked into the living room, ignored the questioning looks from Jack and Eric, went across to the sideboard and poured herself a sherry.

"Problems?" Jack said.

"The course of true love…" Annie said and knocked back the sherry.

28

SUNDAY

Joan tapped at the bedroom door. "Rosie? Are you all right in there? Can I come in?"

"Go away and leave me alone," Rosie replied tearfully.

Joan turned the doorknob and stepped into the room. Her sister was lying face down on the bed, her cheeks buried in the pillow.

Joan went across and perched on the edge of the bed, reached out and stroked Rosie's hair. "Do you want to talk about it?"

Rosie shook her head from side to side.

"Well if you do, I'm right here," Joan said. Rosie reached behind her and found Joan's hand. Fingers intertwining with her sister's she squeezed hard.

"Men, eh?" Joan said. "What would you do with them?"

Her face still buried in the pillow, Rosie nodded her head. "He ruined everything," she said, her voice muffled.

"Yes," Joan said, still stroking her sister's hair. "They make a habit of doing that. Do you want to tell me what he did," she said gently.

Rosie shook her head.

"Just between you and me," Joan said. "Mum and dad don't have to know."

Rosie turned around on the bed until she was facing her sister. "Promise you won't tell?"

"Cross my heart."

Rosie's gaze searched her sister's face, uncertain whether or not to believe her. She shut her eyes. "He tried to touch me," she said softly.

"Where?" Joan said. "Your titties?"

Rosie shook her head. "The other place," she said.

"You didn't let him touch you there, did you?" Joan said, concern making her forehead crease in a frown.

Rosie shook her head again.

Joan let out a sigh. "Well, that's all right then."

A sob broke in Rosie's throat. "It's not all right. It will never be all right," she wailed.

"You didn't let him touch you, so no harm done."

"You don't understand," Rosie said. "I made him stop…but I didn't want to. I wanted him to touch me."

Joan stared at her, and then leaned forward and took her in her arms. "Oh, you poor lamb," she said, and hugged her little sister tightly.

"So why all the histrionics?" Jack said as he climbed into bed beside Annie.

"Search me," Annie said, and picked up her book.

"Doesn't Joanie know?"

"I'm sure she does, but she's staying tight-lipped."

"If that boy's done anything to upset my Rosie I'll take his bloody head off."

Annie clicked her tongue and shook her head. "Sometimes, Jack, you're such a typical man. You can't solve everything with a left hook."

Jack let out a breath. He hadn't even been aware he was holding it. "Yes," he said. "You're right, as usual. Are you going to talk to her?"

"I looked in on her before I came up. She's sleeping like a baby. It will keep, but I do intend to find out why she was so upset. I made a mistake with Joanie all those years ago. I tried to keep all the problems buried, and look where that led. Now, let me read my book. I'm just about to find out who done it."

"Which is more than I am," Jack said, and switched off his bedside light.

The Old Sergeant public house was on PC Alistair Kirby's regular beat, and being Sunday evening it was usual for him to stop by to have a chat with the landlord and owner, Ted Fairly, to make sure everything was as it should be. In return for the consideration, Fairly would provide a bowl of mild ale for Satan and a tomato juice for Kirby.

As Kirby pushed open the partly glazed double doors, the pungent smell of beer struck him like a physical blow. Not being a drinker himself, Kirby wrinkled his nose but pressed on, his dog keeping faithful step beside him at his heel. Someone in the corner was pounding the pub's piano – a recognisable rendition of *Daisy, Daisy* – and the regular patrons were united in song.

"Everything in order tonight, Ted?" Kirby said above the noise of the singing as he reached the bar.

"It is now, Al," Fairly said and slid an earthenware bowl half-filled with mild ale across the bar to Kirby. "Mind, I thought we were going to have some trouble in here earlier. We had some of those Teddy boys in, behaving like the scum they are, but Ray and his friends soon sorted them out and sent them packing." He nodded towards three very well built men, propping up the other end of the bar and singing lustily.

"With a security detail like that you hardly need my visits," Kirby said, and set the bowl down on the floor for Satan to lap.

"It does no harm for the punters to see a uniform in here every now and then. It makes them feel safe. Your usual?"

"Please, Ted. I'm a little parched. It's still warm out there."

"And close too," Fairly said. "I wouldn't be surprised if we have a storm later."

"When I've finished my beat, hopefully," Kirby said. "I left my waterproofs back at the station."

"I can always lend you an umbrella," Fairly said.

"I think not," Kirby said with a smile. "But thanks all the same."

Kirby took his drink and made a circuit of the pub, nodding at familiar faces, pausing to watch a couple of the regulars playing dominos, and stopping at the oche to watch the pub's darts team as they went through their paces, practicing for an up and coming tournament match with a rival pub.

By the time he got back to the bar he had finished his drink. Satan's bowl was empty, and the dog was lying on the floor, eying the earthenware dish expectantly, as if waiting for a refill that it knew in its heart would not be forthcoming, but hoped it might.

Further along, Ray, one of the pub's unofficial protectors, was making his goodbyes to his cronies. "I'm off then, Ted," he called out across the bar.

Fairly threw him a salute. "See you tomorrow, Ray. And thanks for earlier."

Kirby set his empty glass down on the bar and watched Ray lurch unsteadily across the pub and elbow his way out through the doors.

"He's drunk," Kirby said.

"After ten pints you would be too," Fairly said.

Kirby reached down and picked up Satan's lead. "I'd better be off myself," he said. "Come on, boy. You've had enough for one night." He tugged on the lead and the dog got to its feet, still eyeing the empty bowl. "I'll pop in sometime in the week," he said to Fairly.

"See you, Al."

Kirby followed Ray's path across the pub and, as he went out into the street, a low rumble of thunder greeted him. He adjusted the cap on his head and looked up at the sky. There was no moon, but he got the impression of thick cloud above him. "Just what I need," he muttered as a fat raindrop splashed against his cheek.

Looking along the street he could see Ray weaving his way along, pausing at each lamppost and holding on to it as if he might topple over at any minute.

Kirby turned to follow him. It was the direction of his beat anyway and he was concerned that the man might step out into the road and under a car or bus at any moment. Not there was much chance of that happening. There wouldn't be a bus along for at least another hour, and there were few cars around at this time of night. In fact there was no one on the street except for Ray and Kirby with his dog. Which was why, when the shout came, it took him by surprise and made Ray stop in his tracks.

"Hey, Big Man! Not so tough now, are you? Without your mates to back you up!"

Three Teddy boys appeared in the road and started moving towards the inebriated Ray. "Now, look, fellas, I don't want any trouble, right."

"Wrong." The Teddy boy, who had a Brylcreemed quiff and was wearing the regulation drape jacket, tight drainpipe trousers and thick soled shoes, moved away from the group and stood directly in front of Ray, pressing him back into the lighted doorway of a shop. The Teddy boy reached into his pocket. From where Kirby was standing he heard the click and saw the shop lights glint on something metallic.

He reached down and unclipped the lead from the dog's collar. "Sic him, Satan."

The dog needed no further prompting. Like a greyhound out of the trap the dog tore across the distance separating them from the Teddy boys. Growling deeply and then barking loudly, the dog's sudden appearance made two of the Teddy boys turn tail and run, putting as much distance between themselves and the ferocious Alsatian as possible. The Teddy boy holding the flick knife did not fare so well. Before he realised what was happening, the dog had launched itself into the air and clamped its jaws shut on the wrist of the hand holding the knife.

Kirby was running, trying to keep pace with his dog, but was three steps behind as the dog did as it had been trained to do. By the time he reached the scene, the Teddy boy was on the ground, struggling pathetically to fend off the dog, and Ray was leaning against the door of the shop, vomiting noisily.

Kirby took out his torch and shone it into the tear-streaked face of the fallen Teddy boy. "Hello, Billy. Now what have I told you about playing with knives?"

Billy was writhing on the ground, trying to free his arm.

"I didn't mean anything by it, Mr Kirby. Honest," he said. "Get him off me…please!"

"Satan, leave!" Kirby barked, and the dog released its grip on Billy's wrist. Kirby leaned down and snapped a handcuff over it, attached the other cuff to his own wrist, and hauled Billy to his feet.

Ray had partly recovered and was leaning against the door, wiping his mouth with a khaki handkerchief. "Do you know this clown, Officer Kirby?"

"Let's just say that Billy and I are acquainted," Kirby said. "Now, I suggest you get off home. You'll have no more trouble tonight."

"But what about him? He attacked me," Ray said belligerently.

"Don't you worry yourself about him. Billy here is going to spend the night in a police cell. If you wish to press charges then be at the station first thing tomorrow and a member of CID will take your statement."

"But I've got to go to work tomorrow," Ray said.

"You're welcome to come back with us to the station now, if you like. I'm sure the duty officer will oblige."

Ray seemed to consider this for a moment, and then closed his eyes and started to sway again.

Kirby stepped back sharply to avoid the spray of vomit that spewed from Ray's mouth. Finally it stopped and Ray groaned as he dabbed at his lips again. "Best get home," he mumbled.

"You're probably right," Kirby said, picking up the flick knife and closing it. He clipped the lead back onto Satan's collar and tugged on the handcuff, stepping out of the doorway at a sharp pace and pulling Billy along behind him. Every few paces the Alsatian looked up at the handcuffed Teddy boy and growled.

"Don't let him go for me again," Billy pleaded as they walked back to the police station. Rain was now falling steadily from the sky, accompanied by rolls of thunder and the occasional flash of lightning.

"Don't worry, Billy. He had his dinner earlier. You were merely a snack."

"Bastard dog," Billy muttered, but remained docile on their journey back.

"Billy Flynn," Kirby said to the desk sergeant when they arrived back at the station. "Attempted assault with a deadly weapon," Kirby said. "He needs to spend the night in the cells until the Chief Super decides what to do with him?"

"Bread and water for him, Constable Kirby?" Desk Sergeant Alan Turner said with a slightly evil smile.

Kirby shook his head. "We don't want to spoil him, Sergeant."

Turner accepted custody of Billy. "No," he said. "That would never do."

29

MONDAY August 18th 1958

"Chief Inspector," Fisher said. "My office please."

Jack followed him upstairs and into the room that until a few days ago had been *his* office. An extra table had been brought in and two of Fisher's men were seated either end of it, both with files open in front of them as they read through witness statements.

"Inspector Lymon and Sergeant Greyling," Fisher said by way of introduction. "Two of my best men. Gentlemen," he said to them. "If we can have the room."

The two officers closed their files and trooped out of the office.

"Take a seat, Callum."

Jack pulled up a chair and sat down at the desk.

Fisher shrugged off his raincoat and hung it on the hat stand, then went around the desk and sat down in Jack's office chair. "Since I arrived here I've been reviewing your investigation," he said, glancing down at a sheet of paper lying on the blotter in front of him. "And I'm afraid I have to say that I'm not impressed."

Jack said nothing, waiting for Fisher to continue.

"Perhaps you can help me try to make some sense of your thinking," Fisher said. "These characters Fellowes and Channing, why haven't you eliminated them from your enquiries? Both men have cast iron alibis. Damn it, man, one of them was in Switzerland for Christ's sake, the other up in Scotland. So why are you wasting precious resources investigating men who weren't even in the country when the crimes were committed, and there's nothing to link them to the Nelson boy."

"But they know each other."

"*Possibly knew* each other, at university, what, twenty odd years ago? You're reaching, Chief Inspector. You have no concrete evidence connecting them to these murders."

"They each knew one of the victims," Jack said.

"Circumstantial," Fisher said. "As I said, you're reaching, trying to turn coincidence into evidence."

"I don't think so," Jack said.

"Well, that's your opinion," Fisher said. "My opinion is that you've been sending your men down blind alleys, investigating improbable, if not impossible suspects." Fisher picked up the piece of paper from the desk, screwed it into a ball and dropped it in the wastepaper basket. "Needless to say, I've eliminated them from *our* enquiries. Have you looked at the sexual motive for these crimes?"

"Yes," Jack said.

"But you haven't taken it anywhere."

"There isn't anywhere to take it yet," Jack said.

Fisher took a file from the small pile on his desk and flipped it open. "The pathologist's report on Sandra Duncan," he said. "Hepton thinks that sexual congress took place, post mortem."

"Yes, I read that, sir," Jack said.

"Then we're looking for a sexual deviant. Have you checked for similar cases of necrophilia in the files?"

Jack shook his head.

"No, I didn't think so. But no matter. I have my men working on that angle now. Which brings us to your rather far-fetched theory about the three monkeys."

"I think it's valid," Jack said. "You saw the letter that was left at the desk yesterday."

"Yes, and I did not appreciate your man Brewer contacting me at home on a Sunday to drag me down from London to look at a child's scribble."

"They're significant, sir," Jack said.

"So *you* say." Fisher said. "*I* think it's another blind alley – another avenue to send your team down that will eventually prove fruitless. You can't even be sure they're monkeys. They look more like the three bears to me. In other words, Chief Inspector, a bloody fairy story."

Jack stared down at the desk in front of him. Fisher was rubbishing his investigations, and nothing Jack could say was going to convince him otherwise.

"So I'm tearing up your investigation, Chief Inspector, metaphorically at least, and starting my team on other paths. I'm very disappointed that you've wasted a whole week on this and essentially got nowhere with it. And that is what I'll be telling the Chief Constable when I see him later on today."

Jack stared at Fisher steadily. "As is your prerogative, sir," he said. "Was there anything else?"

"Not at the moment," Fisher said. "But I will be calling on your team to do most of the legwork on our investigation. You will make them available to us."

"Of course," Jack said tightly.

"I must admit to be very disappointed, Chief Inspector," Fisher said. "I'd heard some good things about you before I came up here, but from what I've seen of your methodology so far, I haven't been impressed, not impressed at all."

"I'm sorry I've been such a disappointment, sir," Jack said.

"Disappointing me should be the least of your concerns, Chief Inspector. My report on this shambles will go on your record, and then officers more senior than me will look at it and take the appropriate action. If you're fortunate you'll receive a rap on the knuckles and nothing more. Your past record stands in your favour, so demotion, while it remains a possibility, seems unlikely, but there are no certainties in this life. That will be all."

Jack stood. "Very good, sir," he said, and turned and walked from the office.

In the corridor outside, Lymon and Greyling were standing sharing a whispered conversation. Without acknowledging them Jack walked past them and went down to the squad room where a small desk had been cleared for him. He felt the eyes of his team on him as he sat there, taking slow and steady breaths, trying to quell his temper, which was threatening to erupt.

At the adjacent desk Fuller was speaking with a scruffy-looking young man who wore a crumpled, mud-spattered, purple drape jacket, and tight black drainpipe trousers, scuffed at the knees. His unkempt hair made him look as though he had been dragged through a hedge both backwards and forwards several times.

"Name?" Fuller said.

"You know my name," Billy said.

"For the record."

"Flynn, Billy Flynn."

"And you realise you're being charged with possession of a deadly weapon, and the intention to use said weapon."

"I wasn't going to use it," Billy said. "I just wanted to shake him up a bit, that's all."

"And is that your defence?"

"It's as good as any. You lot will be stitching me up anyway."

"Do you deny being in possession of the weapon – a flick knife to be exact?"

Billy shrugged. Fuller made a note on his pad.

"You haven't asked to see a solicitor?" Fuller said.

"I don't know one, and, as I said, what's the point?"

"A duty solicitor can be appointed to you," Fuller said.

Billy said nothing. He was staring intently over Fuller's shoulder at the notice board where the photos of the murder victims were pinned.

"Have you anything to say? Any mitigating circumstances the might help your case?' Fuller said, his patience slowly eroding.

"I need my comb back," Billy said. "That prick down in the cells took it off me. Said I might harm myself with it."

"A comb?"

"Yeah, the bastard. What did he think I was going to do, comb myself to death?" Billy said, his voice rising. "I mean, look at the state of me. Bloody trousers are ruined. Mud and dog spit all over my jacket. I'll have to buy new ones – a week's wages right there. The least you can do is give me a comb so I can make myself look presentable."

A smile twitched at the corners of Fuller's mouth. "Okay, Billy, I'll get you a comb…but you need to give me something in return."

"What have you got in mind?"

"A full account of the events of last night, and an admission that you intended to use the knife to carve up Raymond Willows. What do you call it? Striping him?"

Billy leaned forward in his seat and shook his head. "Do you think I've just come in off a bleeding banana boat? You let me have a comb and I'll tell you about the boy."

"What boy?" Fuller said.

"The one in the photo there." Billy pointed at the notice board.

Fuller stared at him for a moment and then turned and looked across at Jack, who was listening in on the conversation and watching the scene play out. Some strange instinct was making the hairs on the back of his neck prickle. He went across to Fuller's desk and pulled up a chair. "Chief Inspector Callum," he said. "Billy, is it? What can you tell us about the boy in the photograph?"

"Comb?" Billy said.

"Let him have your comb, Sergeant."

"What?" Fuller said.

"Your comb. Mr. Flynn here wants to tidy himself up."

Fuller stared at Jack incredulously, then shook his head, produced his comb from his jacket pocket and handed it to Billy.

"Mirror?" Billy said.

"Don't push…"

"Fetch him a mirror, Sergeant."

Swearing under his breath, Fuller pushed himself to his feet and went off in search of a mirror.

"Right," Jack said. "What can you tell me about Simon Nelson?"

"Was that his name?" Billy said. "Only we were never introduced."

"That was his name, Billy. Simon Nelson, fifteen years old, strangled and dumped on the railway embankment between here and Welwyn."

Billy glanced round, looking to see if there was any sign of Fuller and the mirror. Then he turned back to Jack. "Okay, I'll tell you what I know," he said.

"So this young man on the bus who interrupted your chat with Simon, do you have a description of him?"

"I can do better than that. I'll tell you his name." Billy was almost triumphant. He had given the copper a largely sanitized account of what had happened on the bus on Thursday, and it looked like the fool was buying it. He had learned from experience that the rozzers were gullible, and would swallow any old toffee if you dressed it up in a language they understood, and gave them some facts they were eager to hear. That was why Billy had never had any use for solicitors. He relied upon his guile to get him out of trouble.

"So what is it?" Jack said, leaning forward slightly.

"Peter Lamb. He's a big bugger – literally," he added with a smile.

"How do you know this Lamb?"

"He went to my school. A couple of years above me."

"So did he recognise you on the bus?"

Billy shook his head, "Nah, I doubt it. I wasn't a Ted then, just a spotty kid in a school uniform, and Lamb was the school bully so I kept my head down and stayed out of his way. Anyway he was as thick as shit, like the rest of his mates."

"And the last time you saw him on Thursday he was talking to Simon on the bus?"

Billy smiled. "Yeah, chatting with him and acting all brotherly."

"Why are you smiling?" Jack said.

Billy chuckled. "Well, everyone at school knew that Lamb was a bender – queer as a coot. I'm sure that Simon there saw him as his knight in shining armour, his bloody saviour. Little did he know. I'll bet Lamb had other ideas in mind."

"Do you know where he lives?"

"Nah…but I know where he works – Hennessey's in town – the chemist's. He delivers for them, out there on his push bike, peddling like the clappers, taking pills and sanitary towels round to all the old bids that are too lazy to get off their fat arses and go and get them themselves." Billy looked smug.

Fuller returned with a shaving mirror on a stand from the officer's rest room and handed it to him. With a flourish Billy set the mirror down on the desk, adjusted it so he had a clear view of himself, and then wielded the comb and styled his hair back into its elaborate quiff.

"So is that it then?" he said to Jack. "Can I go now?"

Jack looked up at Fuller who was regarding Billy Flynn with ill-concealed contempt. "I take it Mr. Flynn's been read his rights."

"Yes, Chief Inspector," Fuller said, knowing full well where Jack was going with this and playing along.

"Then charge him and take him back down to the cells. While you're at it, get on the telephone to the duty solicitor and tell him we have a client for him."

Billy suddenly realised what was happening. "Hey! You can't do this. We had a deal."

Jack looked at him steadily. "Indeed we did, Billy, and we're very grateful for the information you've supplied us with. You in return have a comb and a mirror. I hope you and your quiff will be very happy together. Get him out of my sight, Sergeant."

"With pleasure," Fuller said, and hauled Billy to his feet, through the squad room and back down to the cells.

Jack sat down at his desk and called across to WPC Banks. "Myra, do you know Hennessey's in town, the chemist's?"

"Yes, sir," Myra called back.

"Then get your coat. You're coming with me."

30

MONDAY

In the offices of *Povey and Fellowes*, Doris Worthington looked up from her typewriter at the young man who had just walked into the office. "May I help you?" she said.

"I'd like to see Mr. Fellowes," David Neville said.

Doris opened a large, leather bound book and flicked through the pages. "Do you have an appointment with Mr. Fellowes?"

"No," Neville said, "but I'm sure he'll see me."

Doris looked sceptical. "Really? Take a seat over there and I'll check for you."

Neville went across to the seats lined up against the wall and sat down, watching the secretary as she pressed a button on the intercom and spoke quietly into it.

Neville heard Tim Fellowes' disembodied voice float from the intercom's speaker. "Send him in."

Doris looked across at Neville and, with her finger, indicated that he should go in to see Fellowes.

Fellowes met him at the door. "David, good to see you. Do come in."

Neville walked into the office and Fellowes closed the door behind him. Walking back to his desk he suddenly turned and brought his face to within inches of Neville's. "What the hell do you think you're doing coming here?" he hissed.

Neville backed away. "I needed to see you," he said, close to tears.

"What on earth for? Haven't you been paid?"

"Yes, I have… it's not that."

"What then?" Fellowes went behind his desk and sat down, the glare in his chocolate brown eyes never leaving Neville's face.

"I've met someone, a girl," Neville said.

"So?"

"I took her to a dance on Saturday and bumped into Peter and Derek. They said I should tell Gavin. Give him first refusal so to speak."

"And so you should," Fellowes said. "You boys entered into an agreement with us, David. We tell you about suitable candidates and you bring them to us, and when Gavin has finished with them, you dispose of them for us in a manner he chooses. In return you are all paid handsomely. Are you telling me you wish to renege on that agreement?"

Neville shook his head. "No, Tim. I don't want to back out of the agreement, but this girl...she's different. I think she's special. She could be *the one*."

Fellowes leaned back in his chair and yawned. "Oh, David, please. How old are you, twenty-one, twenty-two? And you're talking about this girl being *the one*? You sound pathetic, do you know that?"

"But Rosie's special," Neville said, wounded by Fellowes' words.

"Is that her name? Rosie? What make her so special?"

"She's sweet and kind, and very pretty."

"An ideal subject for Gavin in fact," Fellowes said.

Neville looked bereft. "Tim, please. Have a word with Gavin for me. Persuade him that Rosie's not suitable for what you want."

"Why should I?" Fellowes said coldly.

"Look, I've more than played my part in all this. I dumped the girl on the golf course for you. I took a huge risk following Gavin's instructions. It was all right for you. You were up in Scotland, away from it all. It would have been my neck in the noose if I'd been caught."

"Yes, and I'm am very grateful. But what you're asking... Look, I don't like this thing any more than you do. I had no idea you were friends with Peter Lamb, or that he'd ask you to get involved, but you came into it of your own free will."

"So did you," Neville fired back at him.

Fellowes looked at him steadily. "You really think that, don't you?"

"Well, didn't you?"

"You don't know the half of it," he said quietly.

Neville stared at him curiously. There seemed to be genuine

regret in Tim Fellowes' voice.

Fellowes suddenly got to his feet. "Look, here's what I'll do. I'll have a word with Gavin on your behalf. I'll make no promises. He has a very clear vision in all this, a clear goal in mind, so the chances are that he won't let you keep her. But I'll do my best to persuade him. Is that good enough for you? We still need you on the bowls team, and we don't want anything to get in the way of that."

Neville nodded his head and stood up. "Okay."

"Right then, cut along. I have work to do. Call me tonight and I'll let you have Gavin's decision."

"Thank you," Neville said, unable to look the older man in the eyes for fear of seeing the lie there. "I'll wait to hear from you."

"And, David?"

"Yes?"

"Don't you ever dare come here again. Understood?"

Neville nodded his head sharply and hurried from the office.

Fellowes sat down at the desk again, rubbed his eyes with the balls of his hands and then picked up the phone.

"Adam," he said as the receiver at the other end of the line was picked up. "We need to talk."

Hennessey's was set out like an old apothecary's shop with large mahogany multi-drawer cabinets, and rows of shelves holding jars and bottles of every shape, size and colour, that were mostly used now for display purposes, but some of the slightly worn hand-written labels told of a shop with a rich history, and reflected a time where ingredients such as camphor, arsenic and alum were the stock in trade of the contemporary apothecary.

"Shop!" Jack called as they entered. The bell above the door also announced their presence, but there was no sign of movement from behind the old glass-topped counter.

"Won't keep you a moment," a querulous voice called back.

Myra was walking slowly around the shop, stopping to look in the glass-fronted display cabinets. She was peering at a display of white bottles of Old Spice aftershave and grey oval tins of talcum powder.

"Are you choosing Christmas presents for your boyfriend?" Jack said, coming up behind her.

"My dad, more like. I can't imagine ever going out with a man who wore that. Too old fashioned."

"I wear it myself sometimes," Jack said.

"Yes, I know," Myra said. "No offence."

"None taken."

"Can I help you? Do you have a prescription?"

They turned as one to see a tall, cadaver-like man standing on the other side of the counter. He was smiling at them, which made him look rather ghoulish.

Jack produced his warrant card and showed it to the man. "And this is WPC Banks. We'd like to ask you some questions, if we may."

"Ernest Hennessey," the man said, sticking out his hand. "Ask away, Chief Inspector. My time is yours."

"That's very good of you," Jack said. "Actually we need to ask you about one of your employees."

Hennessey seemed taken aback. "Freda? You want to ask me about Freda? She's been with me for years. Not in any trouble I hope. It's her day off today, otherwise she would have been here to help you when you first came in."

"A young man?" Myra said. "Peter Lamb?"

"Peter?" Hennessey said.

"He works for you?" Myra said.

"Well, yes, I suppose he does...now and then. He helps with the deliveries mostly, and he's an absolute boon when it comes to stocktaking. Strangely enough, I've never thought of him as an employee. Just as someone who helps out. But I suppose, now you come to mention it, I do pay him for what he does, so that would make him an employee."

"Is he around?" Jack said patiently.

"What's today? Monday? Yes, Monday. So he won't be in until after lunch, and then he'll be taking out the deliveries."

"Do you have an address for him?"

Hennessey scratched his balding head. "Well, I suppose I must have, somewhere. You'd be better off talking to Freda about that sort of thing. She looks after all the paperwork – has a system – a complete mystery to me. But it's her…"

"Day off?" Jack said. "Yes, I gathered that. Is there any way you'd know where to find it?"

"I suppose I could try," Hennessey said. At that moment a stout woman in tweeds, dragging a yapping terrier on a lead, entered the shop, a prescription clutched in her hand.

"Mrs. Davenport," Hennessey said. "Is that your usual?"

"It's my sciatica, Ernest. Doctor Frost thinks he might have a handle on it, but I'm not convinced." She handed Hennessey the prescription.

He glanced at it. "Would you like to wait for it? It will be about fifteen minutes."

"Yes," Florence Davenport said. "I can wait."

"Mr. Hennessey," Jack said. "Peter Lamb's address?"

A flustered look clouded Hennessey's face. He looked at the prescription in his hand, then at Jack and back to the prescription and shrugged. "Just give me fifteen minutes," he said. "And I'll be with you."

"Give me strength," Jack mumbled darkly.

It was thirty minutes before Hennessey emerged with a slip of paper clutched in his hand. "Peter's address," he announced. "I knew it had to be somewhere."

Jack took it and read it. "Mill Road," he said to Myra. "Do you know it?"

She nodded. "Yes, I know it. It's one of the roads leading onto the council estate."

"You can drive then," Jack said. "I don't know it at all." He turned to Hennessey. "Do you have much call for chloroform?" he said. "Only I noticed you have a bottle of it on your shelves." He pointed to the top shelf of the cabinet where a number of bottles were slowly gathering a fine patina of dust.

Hennessey's gaze followed the direction of Jack's pointing finger.

"Ah, trichloromethane, no, not these days," he said. "I used to use it in some of the processes, years ago, but it's largely been superseded now by less volatile compounds. In those days I had to use a fume cabinet every time I used it in case I put myself to sleep – it will do that, you know, if you inhale it for long enough – but I don't suppose I've used the fume cabinet in over fifteen years."

"But you still keep the bottle on your shelves?" Jack said.

"For display only these days. If you look closely, there are a number of bottles up there that would have many a modern day pharmacist running for the hills, but I like to keep them, to remind myself of how things have changed since I first started in this business."

Jack nodded and smiled. "I still have my first set of handcuffs at home. Clunky things compared to today's stainless steel jobs. I suppose I keep them for the same reason."

"Peter's not in any kind of trouble, is he?" Hennessey said suddenly.

"Nothing for you to worry about. We just need to eliminate him from our enquiries," Jack said.

"That's a relief," Hennessey said. "Only he's very useful to have around. He knows all the addresses, and my customers know him and like him."

Myra took his arm and squeezed it reassuringly. "I'm sure there's nothing to get alarmed about," she said. "We just want to ask him a few questions, that's all."

"Good," Hennessey said. "That's very good to hear. It's so hard to find people you can rely on these days."

"Did you mean what you said in there, about him having nothing to worry about?" Myra said as they sat back in the car.

"No," Jack said bluntly.

"That's what I thought," Myra said.

"Consider this, Myra. Peter Lamb, as far as we know, was one of the last people to be seen with Simon Nelson, and we know from the forensic report that chloroform was used in the abduction of Frances Anderton. Not an easy thing to get your hands on I would have thought, and yet Lamb works in a place that has a bottle of the stuff just sitting on the shelf, and remember what Hennessey said about Lamb being useful at stocktaking time. He must have known the bottle was there. How easy would it have been to decant the stuff into another container and spirit it away? It's not as if Hennessey was going to check. You heard him yourself. He hasn't used it for years. And the other drugs used in the abductions – Hennessey's is a convenient source."

"You have a point," Myra said

"And another thing," Jack said, warming to his theme. "You saw the bottles on that top shelf. Dust on them going back for years, except for the bottle of chloroform. There was very little dust on that one, which suggests to me that someone has used that bottle quite recently."

"The art of detection isn't dead," Myra said with a smile.

"I hope not," Jack said. "Or the time I spent as a kid reading Sherlock Holmes stories was totally wasted. Drive on."

31

MONDAY

The house of Mill Road was in a state of disrepair, with peeling paintwork and brickwork that badly needed re-pointing. There was no doorbell so Jack rapped on the door with his fist. After what seemed like an age the door was opened by an elderly man wearing sunglasses, impeccably dressed in a white shirt, navy blue tie and grey slacks. His white hair was neatly cut and swept away from his face, but on his feet, incongruously, were a pair of maroon carpet slippers.

"Hello, can I help you?" he said, staring to Jack's left.

Jack introduced himself and Myra. "Mr Lamb, I'd like to speak with your son, if I may."

The man turned his head at the voice and Jack realised that he was blind. "My son's dead."

"Peter Lamb?" Jack said.

The man smiled. "You mean my *grandson*," he said.

"Right," Jack said. "May we see him? We have a few questions we'd like to ask him."

The man continued to smile. "I'd like to help you," he said. "But I'm afraid he's not here at the moment."

"I see," Jack said. "Will he be back any time soon?"

The old man shook his head. "I really couldn't say. It's Monday. He always goes out on a Monday. He could be back at any time. I'd ask you in to wait for him, but it could be a long one. Then again, he could be back in the next ten minutes."

"Perhaps we could do that, then – maybe for ten minutes or so? It would save us calling back."

"Of course," the old man said, and stood aside. "Go on through. The living room is at the end of the passage, on the right."

Jack and Myra walked into the house, wrinkling their noses at the smell of burnt toast.

"Forgive the smell," the old man said. "I made a bit of a balls up with the grill."

"Is it just you and your grandson that live here?" Myra said.

"It is now," the old man said as he followed them into the living room. "My wife passed five years ago. We've been alone since then."

"I'm sorry," Myra said.

Jack was looking around the room, noting the old, but comfortable looking armchair placed at the side of a tiled fireplace. Every flat surface seemed to be filled with photographs in all manner of frames, ranging from tarnished silver to cheap plastic *Woolworth's* specials.

Above the fireplace hung an oval mirror, and pinned to the walls were pictures, copies of old masters taken from magazines and books.

"Please take a seat," he said, waving airily in the direction of a couple of dining chairs pushed up against the wall.

An ancient Bakelite wireless stood atop an equally old oak sideboard. It was broadcasting music, but the volume was set so low that Jack had to strain his ears to hear what was being played. "Glenn Miller," he said when he finally identified the tune.

"The Joe Loss Orchestra, actually," the old man said. "But an easy mistake to make. *In the Mood.* It's Joe Loss's signature tune."

"Wasn't it Glenn Miller's as well?"

The old man laughed as he settled into his armchair. "You fell into the trap that so many people do. You assume that as Miller recorded the original, it was his signature tune, but it wasn't. That honour went to *Moonlight Serenade.* Is the wireless loud enough for you? Can you hear it?"

"It's a little quiet, but it's fine," Jack said.

The old man raised his wrist and ran his fingers over his watch. "A quarter to eleven," he said.

Jack looked at him in surprise and then it dawned on him that Lamb senior had no glass in his wristwatch and was tracing the minute and hour hand with the tips of his fingers.

"So you'll give him ten minutes. Is that enough time for a cup of tea?" the old man said.

"Oh, I think so," Jack said.

"I'll make it," Myra said, standing up.

"Would you, my dear? That would be very kind," the old man said. He turned back in Jack's direction. "Is she pretty?" he said. "She sounds pretty."

"Very pretty," Jack said.

Myra smiled, mouthed "Liar," silently at Jack, and went out to the kitchen.

"Yes, I thought so," the old man said.

"Do you take sugar?" Myra called from the kitchen.

"Two please," Lamb senior called back. "It's in a bowl in the cupboard above the sink."

"Do you know where everything is?" Jack asked him.

"Of course," the old man said. "I have to," he pointed to his dark glasses. "I know the contents of every cupboard, know what's on every shelf, and the position of every piece of furniture. It would be a disaster if I didn't. I'd be falling arse over tip every five minutes."

"When did you lose your sight?" Jack said.

"1944 at El Alamain. Bloody hand grenade. Shrapnel."

"You seem to cope very well."

"I get by. Having Peter here helps. He's my eyes more often than not."

"It must be a great comfort."

"When my son and daughter in law were killed in '47, the authorities wanted to take him away from me, to put him in some damned orphanage. They didn't think I was capable of looking after him. But I fought them like I fought the bloody Nazis, and won. Now, the irony is, he looks after me."

"You're very close," Jack said.

The old man nodded. "He's a good boy. Hasn't got much up top – never much of a scholar – but his heart is in the right place."

"The pictures on the walls. Are they for his benefit?"

"Well, they wouldn't be for mine, would they?" the old man said with a chuckle.

"No, I suppose not."

"Peter loves art. Sometimes he will sit and describe the pictures to me, and he describes them so well it's almost as if I can see them." He fell silent for a moment. "Come to think of it, that's where he could be right now."

"Where's that?" Jack said.

"He could be at Gavin's."

"Gavin's?"

"Gavin Southland. He's a local artist. Lives about ten minutes away. Has a big house on Ridge Road – a bloody mansion according to Peter. Fancies himself as a bit of a Bohemian, so Peter tells me."

"And you think your grandson may be there?" Jack said.

"More than likely, I would have thought. Peter sits for him now and then, for pin money. It supplements the pittance they pay him at Hennessey's. Bloody old miser, Ernest Hennessey is. Tight as a nun's…well, I won't say what. Suffice it to say, Ernest is frugal, always has been. So Peter's lucky to have a friend like Gavin who's willing to pay him just to sit there while he makes sketches of him. Supposedly they're very good, but I have to take Peter at his word on that one."

Myra came back into the room with a tray containing a teapot, cups, milk and sugar, and set it down on a small drop-leaf table. "Shall I be mother?" she said with a smile.

They stayed for another thirty minutes drinking tea with the old man, listening to his wartime anecdotes and being regaled with stories of his grandson's childhood.

"To listen to him you might believe that Peter Lamb can walk on water," Myra said as they got back to the car.

"For all we know, he can," Jack said.

"Well he certainly likes to look at himself. The walls of his bedroom are covered with sketches of himself. Charcoal, pencil – he certainly has some artistic talent."

"It's not him who has the talent," Jack said as Myra pulled away from the kerb. "He sits for a local artist. Lamb's just the model."

"Anyone I would know?" Myra said.

"You might," Jack said. "Does the name Gavin Southland mean anything to you?"

Myra looked thoughtful. "Gavin Southland," she mused. "It's

ringing a bell somewhere," she said. "I've definitely heard or seen…" She shook her head. "No. I can't place it. Back to the station?"

"Might as well," Jack said. "The old man thinks that his grandson may be at Southland's now. He has a place on Ridge Road, but that's a very long road and I don't fancy spending the rest of the day knocking on doors."

"We could stop at the library," Myra said, "and check the electoral roll."

"Good thinking," Jack said.

"There it is," Jack said as they sat at the table in the library. "Gavin Southland, 41 Ridge Road."

"Sssssh!" The bespectacled librarian at the desk hushed him.

"Come on, let's go and pay him a visit."

"Can we go back to the station first, sir? I just want to check something out. I think I remember where I've seen Southland's name before."

"I knew I'd seen it," Myra said, running her fingers down a list of names. "This is the list I printed out from the microfiche the other day. Gavin Southland was a student at Norwich University, at the same time as Adam Channing and Tim Fellowes."

Jack took the list from her and perused it, scratching his head.

"A coincidence, sir?" Myra said.

"I don't believe in them, Myra. I think we're onto something here. This could be the breakthrough we've been waiting for."

"Are you going to tell Superintendent Fisher about this?" Myra said.

"Yes, of course…once we've checked it out."

"So are we off to Ridge Road?"

"Presently," Jack said. "But first we're going to go and have another chat with Mr. Fellowes. Let's find out what else he's omitted to tell us."

'I don't wish to be speaking out of turn, sir," Myra said as they reached the car park. "But shouldn't Sergeant Fuller be accompanying you on this?"

"By rights, Myra, he should, but Chief Superintendent Lane has most of the squad tied up on the post office robberies, and the rest of them are investigating the off-license break in, which leaves me with you as my number two. Unless you have a burning desire to go back to uniform spending your days dealing with traffic offences and giving crime-prevention talks to the WI and other worthy bodies."

"I'd rather stick with you, sir,"

Jack smiled. "I thought you might say that, and it's good experience for you. Like I said to before, you have a nose for this kind of work. There are a lot of good coppers out there, Myra. Good detectives are a different breed."

"Thank you, sir. I'm very grateful."

"I'll remind you of that when you're pulling triple shifts and sitting in freezing cold cars surveilling suspects around the clock. It's not all glamour work."

"I'll bear that in mind, sir," she said.

"Is Mr. Fellowes expecting you, Detective Inspector?"

"No, but I'm sure he'll see me. I have a few more questions for him."

Doris Worthington looked put out. "Well, if you'll take a seat, I'll find out when he can fit you in."

"Detective Chief Inspector Callum," Fellowes said. "Two visits in the space of a week. To what do I owe the pleasure?" He looked to Myra. "And this would be?"

"Detective Constable Banks," Jack said, drawing a questioning look from Myra.

"Then won't you both take a seat?"

Jack sat at the desk. Myra pulled up a hard chair and sat down next to him. Jack pulled out his notebook. Flicking it open, he pretended to read from it. "Does the name Adam Channing mean anything to you, sir?"

Fellowes looked at him blankly. "Not at all, Chief Inspector. Should it?"

"You were at Norwich University at the same time," Myra

said.

"Was I indeed?" Fellowes said. "I suppose anything is possible. I think the intake that year ran to several hundred. I can't be expected to keep track of them all."

"What about the name Gavin Southland. Does that ring any bells?"

"Was he at the university as well?"

"Yes," Jack said. "He was."

"Well, I'm sure I could reel off two dozen names of my university pals, but they probably wouldn't mean anything to you," Fellowes said. "Look Chief Inspector, what is all this about? Only I'm a bit pushed for time at the moment," He made a show of looking at his watch. "My next appointment will be here in a little under five minutes."

"I'll be a quick as I can, sir," Jack said. "If, as you say you don't remember him, you won't be aware that Gavin Southland lives just fifteen minutes away from where we're sitting."

"Here, in Hatfield?" Fellowes said.

"Ridge Road to be precise."

"How extraordinary. They say it's a very small world. I guess that proves it. You'll have to give me his address before you leave. I'll look him up. It's never a bad thing to reconnect with people from the past."

"*Reconnect*, sir," Myra said. "An odd choice of words if, as you say, you didn't know him at university."

"A figure of speech, Constable, nothing more," Fellowes said easily.

"Were you aware that Sandra Duncan was sexually assaulted, probably after she was killed," Jack said, changing tack.

The smile dropped from Fellowes' lips and he blinked three times, rapidly. He recovered himself quickly. "No, I wasn't aware of that. How ghastly."

"Quite," Jack said.

"Then you have to find this person, quickly, before he can take another life," Fellowes said.

"I'm afraid it's too late for that, sir. Only this time the victim was a teenage boy."

Fellowes closed his eyes for a moment. "What was his

name?" he said.

"Simon Nelson. He was fifteen."

"Dreadful," Fellowes said, his voice being drowned out by the buzzing of the intercom. He reached across and pressed the button. "What is it, Doris?"

"The Penhaligons are here, Tim."

"I'll only be a few more seconds." He turned to Jack. "Was there anything else, Chief Inspector? As you can see…"

"You're a very busy man," Jack said. "No, I think that will be all for now." He got to his feet. Myra followed. "If you could wrack your brains, sir, and see if you can recall either Adam Channing or Gavin Southland and give me a call if you do."

"Certainly," Fellowes said and reached across the desk to shake Jack's hand.

"We'll see ourselves out," Jack said.

"If you don't mind me asking, sir, what was the point of that? He could be lying about not knowing Channing and Southland," Myra said as they walked to the car.

"Oh, I'm sure he was, Myra. The purpose of the visit was to drop the names in his lap and see how he reacted."

"And he denied knowing them."

"Yes, he did," Jack smiled. "Tell me, Myra, have you ever heard the phrase, '*As the tongue speaketh to the ear so the gesture speaketh to the eye*.'?'

"Can't say that I have, sir."

"Francis Bacon said that about King James the First in the early sixteen hundreds. He was referring to the king's ability to read people, to read their body language. So while Fellowes was denying knowing Channing and Southland, his body language was telling me something entirely different."

"I didn't see it, sir," Myra said.

"You would have done if you had known what to look for. Do you sometimes get an odd feeling from someone where you suspect they're lying to you?"

"Oh, yes, I've had that."

"Well, you're not imagining it, nor is there anything supernatural about it. Consciously or sub-consciously you're picking up signals from them, little things, the way they move their eyes, their posture, all sorts of little *tells* that alert you to the fact that they're not speaking the truth. It's something you really need to read up on. It will help you enormously when you transfer to CID permanently."

"About that, sir. In there you introduced me as Detective Constable."

"I'm aware of that, Myra." Jack said. "Well, it's only a matter of time isn't it?"

Myra smiled and opened the car door. "Yes, sir. Only a matter of time."

"When you next go to the library, see if they can get hold of a book called *The Language of Gestures* by William Wundt. You'll find it invaluable. I know I have over the years."

Jack climbed in beside her. "Ridge Road," he said. "Let's go and see if we can track down Peter Lamb."

32

MONDAY

In the sumptuous four-poster bed he was sharing with Gavin Southland, Peter Lamb froze as the doorbell sounded from downstairs. "Who's that?" he said, his voice rising in panic.

"Stay calm," Southland said, as he slid from the bed and covered his nakedness with an elaborately embroidered silk kimono. "It's probably the police."

"The police?" Lamb said, his voice rising still further.

"Relax," Southland said. "I've been expecting them. Tim telephoned me a little while ago. They'd just been to see him." Southland limped to the door. "Just stay here and don't make a sound."

"Hello," he said as he opened the door to Jack and Myra. "Can I help you?"

Jack flashed his warrant card and made the introductions. Myra was staring wide-eyed at Southland's attire. Southland noticed.

"I'm afraid you interrupted my siesta," he said. "I'm something of an early riser, and about now, approaching midday, I usually take myself off to bed for a couple of hours, to revitalize myself."

"I'm sorry to have disturbed you, sir," Jack said. "But we're looking for Peter Lamb. I understood from his grandfather that he might be here with you."

"Well, he's not," Southland said calmly. "But you are very welcome to come in and see for yourself."

"Not that I'm doubting your word, sir, but if we could just pop in for a moment or two. I have a few things that you yourself may be able to clear up for us."

"Please," Southland said, and ushered them inside.

They followed him down a wide passageway, through the house, finally into a large glass conservatory that seemed to cover the entire back of the house. A third of the floor space was taken up by large, ceramic flowerpots containing exotic-looking ferns and palms. At the far end of the conservatory was a freestanding auricular theatre, with serried ranks of spectacularly coloured and patterned primulas – a florist's dream. Shelves covered the house wall and these held some of the most unusual orchids that Jack had ever seen, their pots interspersed with knick-knacks collected over the years. Jack wandered over to them and picked up a small gold coin sitting on a small stand. He turned it over and over in his finger, noting the hole in its centre and writing around its edge.

Southland limped across to him and plucked it from his fingers, replacing it in its stand. "Excuse me," he said. "Acid from the sweat on ones' fingers can damage the metal."

"Yes, of course," Jack said. "Excuse me."

"Not a problem," Southland said with an easy smile.

It was stiflingly hot in the conservatory, the humid air being moved listlessly around the room by an underpowered ceiling fan, whose flat wooden blades rotated lazily and silently.

Jack pulled a handkerchief from his pocket and mopped his already perspiring brow. He felt as if he had just walked into the middle of a Tennessee Williams novel.

Southland noticed his discomfort. "Please excuse the heat, Chief Inspector, but I find it helps this." He slapped his game leg with his palm. "Polio, as a child," he said in answer to Jack's questioning look. "Summer is my friend. The winter not so much." He pointed to the easel standing in the middle of the floor, the work-in-progress covered demurely by a white sheet. On a small table standing next to it, were jars containing brushes, knives and a couple of well-used artist's palettes.

"I tend to work in here during the summer months. During the winter I have to retreat back to my studio inside the house."

"When did you last see Peter Lamb?" Jack asked.

"Earlier today as it happens. He came in to sit for me first thing this morning." He limped across to the painting on the easel and pulled back the sheet, and Jack and Myra were treated to a large painting of a nearly naked young man holding a decorously placed rugby ball. "That's Peter," Southland said. "One of my better pieces, though I say so myself."

Jack went around to the front of the easel and stared at the painting. "Would you say that it's an accurate likeness?"

Southland smiled. "I like to think so. I'm certainly no Rembrandt, but I think I do as well as I can with the tools God gave me."

"Do you have any idea where Mr. Lamb might be now?" Myra said, avoiding looking directly at the painting.

"Not really. He left here just before I went up to have my siesta. I understand he had some errands to run in town."

"That would be what, an hour ago?"

"Approximately," Southland said.

"Does the name Tim Fellowes mean anything to you?"

"Indeed it does," Southland said.

"Really?"

"We went to the same university. I heard he'd become a solicitor. Has a practice in town, I believe."

"So do you have regular contact with him?"

Southland laughed. "I don't have any contact with him at all, Chief Inspector. We travelled in different social circles at Norwich. We were never friends. When I heard he was a solicitor working out of Hatfield, I was at pains *not* to have any contact with him. I'm not a great believer in raising ghosts from the past. It always seems such a futile endeavour to me. Life is to be lived in the here and now, not in some imagined nostalgic idyll. That can only lead to disappointment and disillusionment."

"What about Adam Channing, another ex-alumnus of yours?"

"Ah, there you have me," Southland said. "The name means nothing, I'm afraid."

Jack mopped his brow again. "That's a shame. I thought there might be a connection."

"I'm afraid not. What's he done, this Channing character?"

"Nothing, as far as we know. We just need to eliminate him from our enquiries."

"Well, I'm sorry I can't help you."

"No matter," Jack said lightly. "If you see Peter Lamb before we can track him down, perhaps you can tell him that we'd like to speak with him?"

"Am I able to tell him what your interest is?"

Jack smiled. "That won't be necessary, sir. Just tell him to call me at his earliest convenience." He handed Southland one of his cards,

Southland took it, read it, and stowed it away in the voluminous pocket of his kimono.

"Thank you for you help, sir," Jack said.

"I'm afraid I haven't been much help at all," Southland said.

"I wouldn't say that, sir. A police investigation is rather like one of your paintings. You add to it stroke by stroke, detail by detail, until you have the complete picture sitting in front of you."

"An interesting analogy," Southland said. "But the two things are quite different, I assure you. I would think a police investigation is compiled of random facts coming together to make a credible whole. It doesn't allow for wild flights of imagination or the elements of self-expression, which is what art is all about."

"I think the actual truth would surprise you, sir," Jack said. "We'll see ourselves out, and thank you again."

"Was it the police?" Lamb said as Southland returned to the bedroom.

"Yes," Southland said, pulling back the sheets and sliding into the four-poster.

"What did they want?"

"You," Southland said flatly.

"Why me?" Lamb said, alarmed.

"I have no idea, but I think it may be wise to keep a low profile for a while, until we know."

"It was hotter than Hades in there," Myra said as they stepped outside and walked to the car. "I thought I was going to pass out at one stage."

"I was stationed in Burma during the war," Jack said, "and I thought I could take the heat, but that glass house wasn't pleasant. How he can work out there I'll never know."

"But was it a useful visit, sir?" Myra said.

Jack was miles away. "Eh?"

"Seeing Southland, sir. Was it useful?"

"Well it brought us no nearer to finding Lamb, and it failed to establish a connection between Southland and the others, but there *was* something."

"What, sir?"

"I don't know, Myra." He shook his head as if to dislodge the cobwebs shrouding his thoughts. "But something I either I saw or heard is niggling away at the back of my mind, and just as I feel I'm bringing it to the front to be identified, the damned thing slips away again. It's like trying to grab a handful of smoke."

"I'm sure it will come back to you, sir."

"I wish I had your faith in my thought processes, Myra, I really do."

Tim Fellowes sat in his car in Hatfield train station car park. As Adam Channing emerged from the entrance Fellowes reached across and opened the car door.

"It's good of you to drop everything and come up," he said as Channing slid into the seat beside him."

"It was only some marking," Channing said. "No, you were right to call me. Is Gavin at home?"

"Where else is he going to be? He rarely goes out," Fellowes said. "And we need to see him right away. He's out of control. Adam, and we're in this as deeply as he is himself. We've got to try to control him, slow him down somehow. The mad bastard is going to get us hung."

Fellowes started the car and drove out of the car park.

"Do you really think he messed with the girl like the police say?" Channing said.

"No, I don't," Fellowes said. "We know, Gavin's tastes don't run to the female of the species, neither do Lamb's. But, the police must know something. Why else would they say such a thing?" He changed gear and pulled off of the main road. Minutes later they were turning into Ridge Road.

Southland took a long time coming to the door. When he opened it he just stood there, looking at the two men in surprise. "Tim, Adam, what an unexpected pleasure. Come through."

221

He led them through to a large, comfortably furnished lounge. "Take a seat," Southland said. "Drinks. Whisky for you, Adam? And Tim, are still taking that God awful Russian firewater?"

"Vodka, on ice," Fellowes said.

Southland limped across to the small cabinet in the corner and then turned on them angrily. "Would you mind telling me what the Hell you're doing here?" he said as he poured the whisky and vodka, and a small amount of brandy into a snifter for himself.

Channing took the whisky from him, watched as Southland added two cubes of ice to Fellowes' vodka, and then spoke.

"The police told Tim that Sandra Duncan had been sexually assaulted, post mortem. Is this your great artistic statement?"

Southland blinked furiously, his brandy glass an inch away from his lips. He turned to Fellowes. "You didn't mention that when you called earlier to tell me they'd been to see you. That I was half-expecting, but this…"

"I wanted to speak with Adam first, before I said anything to you."

"You don't think that I'd touch her like that, do you?" Southland raised the glass to his lips and drained the brandy in one long swallow.

"We wanted to ask you directly, face to face," Channing said.

In a rare display of temper Southland hurled the empty glass at the wall where it smashed into a hundred shards. "What do you take me for?" he yelled at them.

"We were hoping you'd enlighten us."

"Jesus Christ, isn't it enough that my vision has been ruined, that my artistic statement has been defiled, without you two morons coming here to my house and accusing me of something so obscene?"

"That's what we thought," Fellowes said. "But we had to hear it from your own lips."

"Sex was never the objective," Southland said. "You know that, and now the police will think we're just the same as all those other perverts who rape and kill."

"Worse," Channing said. "They'll think we're necrophiliacs."

Southland poured himself another brandy. He looked down at

the hand holding the glass. It was shaking, badly. "It was David bloody Neville," he said. "It has to be him. He was tasked with getting rid of the body."

"He came to see me today," Fellowes said.

"Why?" Channing said.

"It seems he's fallen in love. He was all bleeding hearts and flowers. He

wants me to have a word with you, Gavin, to ask you not to use her in your plan."

"Can I have another vodka?" Fellowes said.

Still standing at the bar, Southland picked up the bottle and poured another measure into a glass, added two more ice cubes and handed it to Fellowes. "Adam?"

"I'm good," Channing said. Never much of a drinker, the first scotch was already making his head spin slightly and he was very aware that he needed to be thinking clearly.

The whole idea of using their intellect to outsmart the police had originally come from Southland, one boozy evening in the student bar. It was one of those idiotic challenges that had been nurtured over the years, but would be forgotten about once they had all graduated and gone on to find suitable careers.

During their time at Norwich University they would meet up once or twice a month and the challenge would rear its ugly head and, after perhaps the tenth time of discussing it, it had metamorphosed from being a student folly, a Quixotic fantasy, into a definite plan, a challenge to their egos. Southland was leading the charge. For reasons best known to himself he was pushing hard to turn the fantasy into reality, and Fellowes and Channing, always slightly in awe of the older man's intelligence and creative intellect, paid lip-service to it, thinking that, as usual, the idea would disappear like smoke up a chimney.

And so it had on leaving university. Until events engineered by Southland in the April of that year, took a much darker turn.

33

APRIL 1958

Both Tim Fellowes and Adam Channing had come a long way from their student personas, both excelling in their chosen fields. They had stayed in touch with each other over the years and now classed themselves as firm, if occasional, friends.

As for Gavin Southland, he had been consigned to a footnote in their personal histories, like so many of their school and university friends. They hadn't seen him for a number of years, so the invitation to dinner at the house in Hatfield, inherited from a great aunt who had always smiled on him in childhood, was as intriguing as it was unexpected.

"I don't know how he tracked us down," Fellowes said to Channing during the drive down the A1 to Hatfield. "I haven't heard from him for years."

"If I remember, Gavin was always very resourceful. I just wonder why," Channing said.

There was no answer to Channing's question when the men arrived at Southland's sprawling Victorian house, tucked away behind a high privet hedge on a tree-lined Hatfield avenue.

Southland met them at the door, greeted them effusively, and ushered them inside to a large dining room, with a table set for dinner with a white bone-china service and gold-plated cutlery. He was obviously going for opulence and had broadly succeeded, making Fellowes wonder about the size of the estate visited upon him by his late great aunt.

Their fellow dinner guests were a rather motley assortment of, as Channing described them, Bohemians or, as Fellowes preferred to think of them, arty types. There was a thin-faced man with a curling waxed moustache and arched, painted-in eyebrows who Southland introduced as Luther, an artist friend; a big-breasted woman who hid her ample frame beneath a voluminous purple paisley dress and her hair beneath a matching turban bedecked with a peacock feather, her eyes hidden behind impenetrable dark glasses. Her name was Veronica and was described to them as a sculptor, the equal of Barbara Hepworth.

Sitting next to Southland at the far end of the table was a youth, possibly eighteen or nineteen, with a fleshy, pasty face with black, swept back hair, and dark hooded eyes that regarded them incuriously. Their host introduced him simply as Peter, but offered no explanation of who the lad was, but judging from the way Southland fawned over him, the two men were left in little doubt about the nature of their relationship.

Despite their initial reservations the evening proved to a lively mix of serious conversations on various topics, ranging from the nature of high art, the philosophy of Bohemianism, the work and dubious lifestyle of artist and sculptor Eric Gill, to broader, more light-hearted subjects such as West End revues and risqué Soho cabaret acts. Everyone contributed to the conversations, except the mysterious Peter who sat silently throughout, watching the various speakers with ill-disguised contempt.

The food was plentiful, delicious and superbly cooked – apparently Peter was just as useful in the kitchen as he was in the bedroom, and wine flowed like water throughout, and it was just after midnight when Veronica – who proved herself to be a witty fount of the most ribald show business stories – "I used to be a dancer on the stage, my dears, before I picked up the pounds and decided I needed to do something with my hands instead of my feet." – announced that she was going to take Luther home, "Before I have to carry him out of here."

Luther, who was swaying slightly in his seat, regarded her gratefully, got unsteadily his feet and let himself be led out on the, almost motherly, arm of Veronica, to the car they had arrived in.

"They're a lovely couple," Southland said once he had seen them to the door and waved them off. "Been married to each other for nearly twenty years. Fuck whomever they like of course. True Bohemians."

"I suppose we should be getting off as well," Fellowes said.

"Nonsense," Southland said. "We still have lots to talk about." He turned to his companion. "Peter, fetch the absinthe from the

225

cabinet in my studio." To Fellowes and Channing he said, "Do you two remember the conversations we used to have at university?"

"Regarding what?" Channing said.

"Whether it is possible, using our combined intellects, to outwit the police and commit the perfect crime."

Both men sighed. "Not that old chestnut again, Gavin," Fellowes said.

"You really ought to put that one to bed," Channing agreed. "We're not students anymore. You think about that kind of stuff when you're that age but, as you join the real world and have to face the realities of marriage and holding down a job, you put away your pipe dreams…"

"And become middle-class bourgeois bores," Southland said.

"Steady on, Gavin," Fellowes said, leaping to their defence. "There's no need to be insulting."

But Southland would not be dissuaded. "Well, just look at you now, with your safe respectable jobs. Pillars of the community, both of you."

"We can't all be Bohemians, Gavin, kicking against the pricks, regardless of what other people think of you," Fellowes said.

"I'm an artist," Southland said. "I don't recognise conventional boundaries." He looked up as Lamb came back in the room holding a silver tray containing a bottle of the green liquid, a small bowl of sugar cubes, a jug of iced water and a silver absinthe spoon, pierced and fluted with a point at one end. "Perhaps this will jog your memories and let them float back in time to when we were free spirits, with the world at our feet," Southland said.

"I don't know," Fellowes said. "I think we've drunk enough. We should be going." He made to get to his feet, but Southland clamped a hand over his wrist and held him in his seat.

Channing was watching Southland's eyes. There was a slightly manic gleam in them, and Channing realised that the evening could very easily turn ugly. "Perhaps just the one, eh? How about it, Tim?" he said to his friend. "For old time's sake?"

Fellowes relaxed into his seat. With a sigh he said, "Okay, just one, and then we head home."

A smile spread over Southland's face. "Peter, do the honours." He turned to the others. "Peter here works in a pharmacy. He knows all about mixing things. Don't you, Peter?"

Lamb said nothing, but a smile spread over his face, his first all evening.

The next thing Adam Channing was aware of was the sunlight pouring through the window and the sound of birdsong rising to a crescendo. "What the hell," he said and moved his read, realising at once that he was not waking up in his own bed. Instead he was sprawled backwards on an over-stuffed and uncomfortable leather couch. With bleary eyes he looked across the room to where Tim Fellowes was folded into an armchair and dead to the world, snoring loudly.

With his whole body one long continuous ache, his head being the worst, Channing pushed himself off the couch and staggered across to where Fellowes was sleeping. Grabbing him roughly by the shoulder he shook his friend awake. "Come on, Tim. Wake up. It's morning."

"Eh? What?" Fellowes said thickly. He felt like he'd grown an extra tongue. "But how? I only had the one drink."

Channing shook his head. "I know. Me too. The absinthe must have been drugged. I think Gavin slipped us a Mickey Finn."

"Wha…why?"

Channing shook his head again, and felt his brain slopping about in his skull. Gingerly he sat down on the edge of the armchair and tried to gather his wits, trying to make some sense of what had happened to them.

"I thought I heard movement," Gavin Southland's voice boomed as he came into the room. Peter Lamb entered the lounge a pace behind Southland, his eyes watchful, his muscles tensed.

Southland was dressed in a silk kimono and he was holding the strangest looking camera the men had ever seen. As they watched he put it to his eye and said, "Smile."

The flash took them both by surprise, leaving them blinking

as they watched Southland do something with the back of the camera. "A friend of mine in America sent me this as a gift. It's a camera for taking instant photographs. He thought it might help me with my artwork…and he wasn't wrong." As he spoke he pulled something from the camera and stood, letting a small rectangular packet hang from his fingers. "Now, watch this," he said, took the packet over to them and held it out for them to see.

At first they didn't know what they were supposed to be watching, but gradually, as the seconds passed something started happening to the thin package. Soon they were staring at a photograph of the two of them, looking wide-eyed with surprise.

"Impressed?" Southland said, beaming at them.

They nodded.

"Yes, I thought you would be. We had fun in the night. Show them, Peter."

As Lamb walked towards them he produced a bundle of photographs from the pocket of his shirt and handed then to Fellowes, who started leafing through, all the while giving short gasps of shock at the graphic nature of the photographs.

"Let me see," Channing said.

Without a word, Fellowes handed them across to Channing, who did as he had done, looking at them one shot at a time.

"I am a true artist," Southland said. "Anyone looking at them would have no idea that you were both unconscious when these were being taken."

Fellowes glared up at Southland. "Why?"

"You were going to renege on our agreement," Southland said simply.

"We had no agreement," Channing said.

"That's not the way I see things. These photographs are my guarantee that you keep your word."

Channing came to a photograph of him nude on a bed, entwined in the arms of an equally naked Peter Lamb. With a sound of disgust he launched himself out of the chair, arm outstretched, his hand reaching for Southland, ready to rend and tear.

Lamb moved quickly, stepping between them and pushing Channing back down in his seat. "Bastard!" Channing shouted.

Fellowes took the photographs and started ripping them in half. Southland made no move to stop him. Instead he watched with an indulgent smile on his lips. "Tear away, Tim," he said. "They're just the tip of the iceberg. As I said, we had a busy night. There are many more where those came from. You're a solicitor. What is the maximum jail time for homosexuality these days?"

Fellowes looked up at him bleakly and shook his head. "What do you want?" he said.

"Ah," Southland said. "You're beginning to realise the extent of the jam you're in. The newspapers would crucify you if they got their hands on these. Heaven knows how your personal reputations would suffer."

"So, what do you want from us?" Channing said.

"I'm planning my master work. A triptych based on my long-held Buddhist beliefs, and for that I need models, preferably female, ideally young and beautiful, and I'm not being disingenuous when I suggest that neither Peter nor I are the answer to a maiden's prayer. You two, however, must come into contact with suitable models every day. All I want you to do to acquire their names and addresses. You can leave us to take care of the rest of the details."

"And you'd hire them as you would any other model," Fellowes said.

Lamb snorted with laughter – an unpleasant sound like a donkey braying.

"Yes," Southland said. "I can see why Peter's so amused." He shook his head. "No, Tim. I won't be paying them anything – nothing at all. You see, what I am planning satisfies my artistic needs, but also address the other question. Can I defeat the police, using only my intellect? I believe I can."

"You're mad," Channing said.

"Were you ever in any doubt of that?" Southland said.

34

MONDAY August 18th 1958

And now they were accomplices in two murders, no, three if DCI Callum was to be believed, and Channing was starting to feel sickly apprehensive about what may be in store for him in the future.

"Simon Nelson," Fellowes said suddenly to Southland.

"Eh?" Southland said.

"The policeman, Callum, who came to see me today," Fellowes said, "told me there had been another killing. A teenage boy called Simon Nelson. Was he another one of your bloody models?"

"Such a pretty boy." Southland said. "It was Peter, acting on his own initiative. He rescued this boy from being beaten up by a gang of Teddy boys and brought him here. Why he didn't take him home I'll never know, but he didn't, and once the boy was here…well…it was too good an opportunity to pass up. Think of it, what better way to throw the police off our scent than to give them a victim of a different gender?"

"Jesus, does this never end," Channing said.

"Why didn't you consult with us first?" Fellowes added. "Supposedly we're all in this together. We have as much to lose as you do. We've come a long way from gross indecency. We're looking at capital punishment if we're caught."

Southland looked aggrieved. "Do you think I wanted to go it alone with this one? I know, but there simply wasn't time to do anything about it. The boy was here. The odds of him keeping his mouth shut about it were minimal. I had to act and act fast. Though I do find it gratifying to see that you're now as invested in our success at beating the police as I am."

"You haven't given us much choice," Fellowes said bitterly.

Southland sipped his brandy. "No I didn't, did I? Still, needs must and all that."

"And you can say, hand on heart, that there was no sexual motivation for this one."

"Well, he was an extraordinarily pretty boy, Adam, but no. Sex didn't enter into it. It was purely an artistic decision."

"I'm beginning to doubt your wisdom in using Peter and his friends to help you," Fellowes said.

"And I'm beginning to tire of your hypocrisy. You knew David from the bowls club, Tim, and you were more than ready to vouch for him when Peter suggested him for the job, Southland said.

"And look where that led," Channing said, which earned him a stern look from Fellowes.

"The fact is, the boys have been important to the plan. Derek dumping the first girl's body in the park, disguising himself as a park keeper was a masterstroke. I hate to think how many man-hours the police wasted running down that particular blind alley. Peter's disposal of the boy on the railway embankment was handled efficiently and discreetly. Even my idea of dumping Sandra in a sand trap on the golf course was fairly inspired, and not without artistic merit, if David had followed my instructions to the letter."

"Instead he decided to have some fun with her, the sick bastard," Channing said. "You didn't see that coming, did you, Gavin?"

"No, I did not," Southland said, glaring at Channing. "No, David needs to be suitably punished, and you can leave that to me. I think it's wise if we don't see each other, for the foreseeable future anyway. We can communicate by telephone, but don't come here again...unless you're invited."

"Agreed," Fellowes and Channing said together, both relieved to bring this meeting to a close.

"Right. Now get out," Southland said. "I'll contact you if anything else urgent or unexpected crops up."

Southland accompanied them to the door, returned to the lounge and poured himself another brandy. He was furious and smarting from the humiliation of having his decisions questioned. "How dare they?" he said to the empty room. If they only knew what all this was taking out of him, knew what was driving him on. But it was something he'd buried so deeply within him, it was doubtful now he could talk about it even if he wanted to.

Callum, the policeman today, had that air of quiet authority and superiority that reminded him so much of his father. He too had been a policeman, who wore his uniform around the house as a badge of supremacy – a man to whom feelings of empathy and compassion were as alien as a foreign language. A domineering yet weak figure, whose response to finding that his son had polio was to run away and neglect his responsibilities, to take up with some little whore almost young enough to be his own daughter, and to leave his wife to care for and raise a desperately sick child. And as the years went by, and his sickness receded, leaving him crippled, Gavin Southland swore every day that one day he would have his revenge on his father and all men like him, who put order and discipline before care and nurture, and matters of the law before matters of the heart.

His thoughts turned to David Neville's betrayal. He had entrusted him with disposing of Sandra Duncan's body and doing it in such a way that it would become art – not just dumping it unceremoniously as they had with the first girl, but presenting it like a picture on canvas, a tableau, a still life. David's perverted lust had sullied that image and for that he had to pay.

Southland picked up the telephone and dialled a number.

"Derek, I need you to do something for me."

34

TUESDAY August 19th 1958

The summer rain had stopped, giving the pavements a just-scrubbed appearance, and making the whole world smell cleaner, fresher.

Rosie Callum was feeling fresher as well. The incident with David in the car on Sunday had disturbed her, more so than she had told her sister, and yesterday had been torturous as she tried to reconcile what she had felt when he'd kissed her and touched her breasts, with the moral guidelines that had been her roadmap throughout her life. Today, with the sun shining again, and the heat of passion washed away, she was feeling more capable of facing the day – able now to deal with the customers coming into the baker's without feeling that the shadow of guilt was hanging over her.

"Hey, Rosie? It is Rosie, isn't it?"

Rosie stopped in her tracks and looked around at the young man sitting on the motor scooter parked in the kerb.

"Do I know you?" she said.

"It's Derek Webster...from Saturday night at the dance. Davy's friend."

The recognition slowly came to her and she smiled. "Yes, of course. I didn't recognise you in casual clothes."

"I was hoping I might see you. Davy told me you worked along here."

"At *Painters*, yes. Why did you want to see me?" Rosie said.

"It's Davy who wants to see you," Webster said.

She frowned. "Why doesn't he ask me himself then?"

"You know Davy," Webster said.

"What does that mean exactly?"

Webster didn't answer, but smiled darkly.

"Is it about what happened on Sunday?" Rosie said.

"It could be. He didn't say. All he told me was it was important that he see you."

"Then he should be here to tell me himself."

"He would if he could, but he can't. That's why he asked me to pick you up and bring you to him."

"Where is he then?" Rosie said.

"Working," Webster said. "Visiting a house on the other side of town, talking insurance with the owners, otherwise he would definitely have come to see you himself."

"Well, it will have to wait until later. I have to get to work myself." She turned and made to resume her journey.

"Wait!" Webster said. "He's really upset about Sunday. He's desperate to talk to you. I've never seen him so cut up about something."

Rosie hesitated. "Was he *really* upset?"

"He seemed devastated. Look," Webster said. "I don't know what went on between you two, and I don't want to, but I'm just trying to help a mate out here. I don't want to let him down."

"How long will it take?" Rosie said, feeling her resolve start to crumble.

"We can be there in ten minutes. After that, I suppose, it's up to you two."

Rosie glanced at her watch. She still had twenty minutes until the baker's opened. Mrs. Painter wouldn't mind if she were a few minutes late.

"Okay," she said. "Take me to see him."

Webster smiled. "Hop on," he said.

Jack's report to Fisher had been met with the usual apathy. He was getting used to having his ideas dismissed out of hand by the Scotland Yard man, so much so that he was considering keeping his thoughts to himself in future.

"We've got someone in the frame for the post office jobs," Fuller said as he returned to the squad room.

"Anyone I know?" Jack said, feigning interest.

"Reggie Bull."

"Christ, that's a name from the past," Jack said. "I thought he was doing a five stretch in Wandsworth."

"He was," Fuller said. "Got out after three for good behaviour."

"They don't know him very well then, do they? A nasty piece

of work that one. The owner of the Co-op still walks with a limp after Reggie's firm turned them over and robbed them of their Christmas takings," Jack said.

"Yes, but the prosecution failed to make a case against him on that one."

"But not on the job he got sent down for. We got him in the end. That's why I'm surprised he's out so soon. And you like him for the post office jobs?"

"They've got his mucky little signature all over them," Fuller said.

"Well, good luck with that one," Jack said. "A slippery customer is our Mr. Bull."

"What about you? What are the gods from Scotland Yard letting you do, now you're effectively off the *Three Monkeys* case?"

"Frankly, Eddie, I may as well take up knitting for all the good I'm doing here."

"That's not so bad. They've forecast a harsh winter this year. You could knit yourself a Spurs scarf."

"With matching gloves and bobble hat," Jack said with a smile. "I'd be the envy of the terraces."

"That you would."

"And for your information, it's not the *Three Monkeys* case any more. Fisher thinks the pictures we've been getting are of the three bears, as in the fairy story."

"Fisher's off his chump," Fuller said. "According to Frank, who's been working very closely with them, they're getting nowhere."

"The clues are out there, Eddie, you just have to see them for what they are."

"And I suppose you do?" Fuller said.

Jack winked and tapped the side of his nose.

Fuller smiled. "You old...I knew you wouldn't let it alone. Knitting indeed."

"It's still my case, Eddie, whether Fisher likes it or not. If I turn anything up that I feel he needs to know then I'll tell him, but until I do..." He left the sentence hanging.

"You're the boss," Fuller said.

"Whisper it quietly, Eddie. At least until we're rid of them."

"Where are we going?" Rosie shouted over the noise of the scooter's engine.

"We'll be there soon," Webster called back as he steered them onto Ridge Road.

"We'd better be."

They were on a street that Rosie didn't recognize. There were rows of large detached houses on either side, hiding behind brick walls and barred gates. They were passing one now, tucked in behind a high privet hedge. Halfway along Webster pulled in through some wrought iron gates, steered the scooter across a gravel forecourt, and brought it to a stop outside a large Victorian house. He pulled the scooter up onto its rest and stepped off, smoothing the creases out of his grey slacks.

Rosie climbed from the bike and made a forlorn attempt to tidy her windswept hair. "Are we here?" she said. "Is David inside?"

Webster ignored her and started walking towards the front door, fishing in his pocket and producing his key ring.

"The owners let you have a key?" Rosie said, not really making sense of what was happening.

Webster stuck the key in the lock and Rosie grabbed his arm. "I don't think we should," she said.

Webster shook her off. "I really don't get what Davy sees in you, you silly little bitch," he said, and pulled back his fist.

Before she could react, he swung the fist, connecting with her cheek. For a moment the world spun and lights danced before her eyes, and then the pain rushed at her like an express train. Her legs buckled and she pitched forward, unconscious, into his arms.

"Mrs. Callum? It's Barbara Painter. I wondered if Rosie is going to come in today."

"But she left here over an hour ago. She should be with you by now."

"Yes, that's what I thought, but one of my regular breakfast customers has just come in and told me she'd seen Rosie take off down the street on the back of a motor bike."

Annie felt a small hole open up in the pit of her stomach. "Was it a motor bike or motor scooter?"

"Does it matter?"

"It's very important. Mrs. Painter. A bike or a scooter?"

Annie sensed the woman cover the mouthpiece with her hand and heard the muted question called out across the shop.

"Phoebe, was it a bike or a scooter?"

The answer was indistinct.

"It was a scooter," Mrs. Painter said when she came back on the line.

And the hole became a chasm.

"So will she be in?"

"I...I...I'm not sure," Annie said. "I'll call you as soon as I know."

She disconnected and rung Jack at the station.

"Annie, it's not like you to call me at work."

"It's Rosie, Jack. I think she's been taken."

"Rosie? What?" Jack said.

"She's been taken. Mrs. Painter just called me. Rosie hasn't turned up for work, and one of the customers saw her being ridden away on the back of a motor scooter. Jack, what shall I do?"

"Annie, calm down. You could be jumping to all the wrong conclusions here. For all we know, David might ride a motor scooter. They're very popular with the kids these days."

"But David drives a car."

"It was his dad's car he used to take Rosie out. For all we know he uses a scooter to get to work."

Annie scratched her head, trying to remember if Rosie had ever mentioned it. She came up with nothing.

"You're probably right," she said. "I'm overreacting. I just heard the word scooter and immediately thought of what you told me about Sandra Duncan. I shouldn't have called. I'm just being stupid."

"No, you're not," Jack said, trying to calm his wife. "I would have probably thought the same. Did Mrs. Painter say what colour the scooter was?"

"No," Annie said. "I'll call her back."

"No, you won't," Jack said. "*I'll* call her. You can go and make yourself a cup of hot sweet tea, and calm down. When I hear anything at all I'll ring you. And don't worry. Rosie's not stupid. She knows better than to go off with strangers."

Jack reassuring words were beginning to soothe her frayed nerves. "I'm sorry, Jack. I've heard you trying to calm down anxious parents over the telephone and I've always thought, 'get a grip', and here I am doing the self same thing. Just call me when you hear anything."

"I will. Promise."

Annie put down the telephone and went out to the kitchen to boil the kettle.

"Problems?" Joan said as Annie lit the ring under the kettle.

"Just your mother being over protective. Sometimes I forget you're all growing up so fast."

"But we wouldn't have you any other way," Joan said, and went across to her mother and hugged her.

"Mrs. Painter, it's Jack Callum, Rosie's dad. I'm sorry that Rosie has let you down today."

"It's most unlike her," Barbara Painter said. "Rosie's usually so reliable."

"You didn't see her on the motor scooter yourself?"

"Not personally. That was Phoebe Russell, one of my regulars."

"Did Mrs. Russell happen to notice the colour of the scooter?"

"If she did, she didn't say."

"Is there any way we can find out? Does she have an address or a telephone number?"

"I'm sure she does, but I don't know either of them. Not that it matters. She only works two doors along in the dressmaker's. I can pop along and ask her."

"If it's no trouble."

"Well, I have a couple of people to attend to, and then I'll go and find out. Can I phone you back?"

"If you would," Jack said, and gave her a telephone number to call. "It's a direct number," he said. "So it bypasses the switchboard and puts you straight through to me."

"I'll call you back as quickly as I can," she said and rang off.

Jack sat looking at the receiver in his hand and tried to control his breathing. Despite what he had told Annie to calm her, he was already imagining the worst.

"Something wrong, sir?" Fuller said. He was sitting at the next desk along and had witnessed Jack making the telephone calls – his boss's face growing darker by the minute.

"It's Rosie," Jack said. "She hasn't turned up for work this morning."

"Perhaps she's taking a sick day," Fuller said.

Jack shook his head. "She's not at home either. That first call was from Annie. She thinks something bad has happened to her. Rosie set off for work first thing this morning as usual, but she never got there. The last time she was spotted was on the back of a motor scooter riding away from the baker's where she works."

"Was it a two-tone blue scooter?"

"That's what I'm waiting to find out. Her boss at the baker\s is going to call me back."

"So it's too early to reach any conclusions," Fuller said.

"That's what I told Annie."

"There you go then."

The telephone on Jack's desk started to ring. He snatched it up.

"Hello?"

"Hello, Mr Callum. It's Barbara Painter."

35

TUESDAY

Jack slapped his hand down on the desk and swore loudly, drawing startled looks from the others in the room.

"Chief Inspector?" Fuller said, but Jack was already storming towards the door.

"Jack!" Fuller called after him.

Fisher looked up from his desk as Jack barged into the office. "Where are you with your search for the motor scooter?" Jack yelled at him.

Greyling and Lymon were rising from their table. "Chief Inspector, I really don't..." Greyling began.

"Get out, both of you," Jack growled.

Fisher looked across at them. "It's all right. Leave us,"

They both glared at Jack and left the office.

"Right," Fisher said. "Do you mind explaining why you burst into my office like a Friday night drunk and start ordering my men around?"

"My daughter's been abducted, ridden away on a two-tone blue motor scooter, probably by the same bastard who took Sandra Duncan," Jack said. "So I'll ask you again, where are you with your search for it?"

"The scooter is just one of the many leads we are following," Fisher said, sticking out his chin pugnaciously. "I'm sorry about your daughter, but it still doesn't give you the right to come bursting into my office, behaving like a madman."

"It seems it's the only way I'm going to breathe some life into this Mickey Mouse investigation of yours," Jack said. "I don't know how you do things down in London, but up here we value good police work, and my team and I know how to get things done."

"And you think we don't?"

"I don't think you and your men could find your dicks in a blackout," Jack said.

"Just remember who you're talking to," Fisher said

dangerously.

"I'm talking to the man who took a perfectly fine investigation and flushed it down the toilet," Jack said. "The man with his head so far up his own backside that he can't see the wood for the trees, and who wouldn't know a clue if it came up and bit him on the arse."

"How dare…"

"That's enough! Both of you!" Chief Superintendent Lane stood in the doorway, his face white, and the veins in his neck standing proud. "Would one of you mind explaining what on earth's going on in here? I can hear your racket in my office, as I'm sure can most of the station."

"Callum's daughter's been snatched, sir, and he barged in here accusing me and my men of not making sufficient progress on the Three Bears investigation."

Lane's face softened. "Is this right, Jack? Has Rosie been abducted?"

"It certainly looks that way, Henry." Jack was breathing hard, and he was trying to control the urge to smash something.

"I'm sorry, Jack. I'm sure Superintendent Fisher is doing his best."

"Well, his best isn't bloody good enough," Jack said.

"I was trying to tell him, sir, that our investigation is progressing slowly," Fisher said. "The way he burst in here and started berating me and my men was insubordination of the worst kind."

"Oh, do shut up, Brian. Jack's daughter been taken. How do you expect him to react?"

Fisher shut his mouth and glared at them both.

"If I can lead the investigation again, sir, I'm sure…"

"You'll do no such thing," Lane said. "Go home, Jack. Your wife is going to need you there."

"But, sir…"

"Home, Chief Inspector," Lane snapped. "That's an order."

Jack held his eyes for a moment and then something went out of him. His shoulders drooped and he walked out of the office and down the stairs to get his coat.

"Where are you going?" Fuller said as Jack came into the

squad room and took his raincoat from the hat stand in the corner.

"I'll be at home if anything comes up, Eddie."

"Do you need a ride?"

"I'll take a pool car," Jack said, shaking his head. "I need some time on my own to think," he said, and left the station.

"Oh, Jack." Annie threw her arms around him as he walked in through the back door.

Joan sat at the kitchen table looking at them pensively. "Will she be all right, Dad?"

"I'll get her back, Joanie, one way or another."

"Is that a promise, Jack?" Annie said as he held her tightly. "Do you promise me that my little Rosie will be all right?"

"You have my word. Be a pet, Joanie, and make your mum and me a cup of tea."

Rosie opened her eyes to sunlight streaming in through the windows. As she blinked furiously to clear her vision, she tried to work out where she was. It only took her a moment to realise that she couldn't move. She was sitting on a wooden chair. Her wrists were strapped to the arms of the chair, and her ankles were tethered to the legs.

She turned her head to look about her, but the dull ache that was throbbing in her cheek roared into a full-blooded assault on her senses and she attempted to cry out, but something was stopping her doing so. Fabric had been forced into her mouth and a gag had been tied tightly around her face, making it impossible to utter any sound except a stifled grunt.

She sucked in air through the gaps in the gag and inhaled deeply through her nose. It was a large room, brightly lit by the full sun pouring in through windows that had been frosted to prevent anyone from looking in, or out. In the centre of the room was an empty artist's easel, and propped up against each of the walls were bright and colourful paintings, mostly life studies, mainly featuring a well-muscled young man who Rosie recognised as David's other friend from the dance on Saturday night.

He wasn't the only subject though, leaning against the far wall were three paintings, two of them pictures of young women, naked, their small-breasted bodies lovingly rendered. The third was of a young boy, a full-length study of his naked body that left no detail to the imagination.

But what chilled her more than their nakedness were their faces. Dead expressionless faces, their eyes and mouths sewn shut, dribbles of blood snaking down from the sealed eyelids and perforated lips.

She struggled against her bonds, but she had been securely tied. After a few fruitless attempts to loosen them she gave up, and collapsed back into the seat. It was then that she noticed the small table standing a few feet away. A table that held a large church candle, a box of matches and a small stainless steel, kidney shaped dish. What the dish contained terrified her.

When she saw the wickedly sharp, curved needles and the small skein of black silk thread, she knew that the paintings of the three young people had not come from the artist's imagination. They had been taken from life. Or rather, death.

It was then that she fainted.

"Did you get to the bottom of why Rosie was so upset on Sunday night?" Jack said as they sat at the kitchen table drinking tea.

Annie was torturing the handkerchief in her hands, twisting it into a knot. "She wouldn't tell me," she said. "I tried a couple of times. I'm sorry."

"I suppose it doesn't really matter now anyway," Jack said.

"David tried it on with her," Joan said flatly.

"What?" Jack said.

"He tried to get into her knickers."

"Joan!" Annie said.

"I'm just telling you what Rosie told me," Joan said.

"You did right to tell us," Jack said. "My first instinct about him was spot on. I should have knocked his block off, the dirty little toe-rag."

Joan reached out and laid her hand gently on her father's arm. "She wasn't crying because he tried, Dad. She was crying because she stopped him."

"Oh dear Lord," Annie said.

"Don't take on, Mum. She stopped him touching her because, no matter how much she wanted it, you and dad have brought her up to respect herself. She's a credit to both of you. I wish I'd had her inner strength when I was her age."

"You came good in the end," Jack said.

"But not before going through the wringer first," Joan said bitterly.

Jack got abruptly to his feet. "I can't just sit here and do nothing," he said. "I'm going to telephone Eddie and see how they're getting on."

"If there was any news they would have called you," Annie said tiredly. "Please, Jack, sit down and wait with us."

Jack stared at her and saw the fear in her eyes. He sat back at the table. "Well, I suppose no news is good news," he said.

"Where did you and the guv get to yesterday?" Fuller said to Myra as they passed each other in the corridor outside the squad room.

"We were trying to track down Peter Lamb. We went to Hennessey's, and then we went to Lamb's house and spoke with his grandfather."

"With no joy?"

Myra shook her head. "The grandfather gave us the name and address of a local artist Lamb poses for to make some pin money, but no luck there either. Apparently he was running some errands in town."

"Do you fancy another trip to the chemist then?" Fuller said.

"There's nothing to lose," Myra said. "I'll get my coat."

They parked outside Hennessey's and looked in through the shop window. "I can't see him in there," Myra said.

"You know what he looks like then?"

The image of the painting of a naked Peter Lamb that Southland had shown her and Jack yesterday was still burned onto her retinas. "Intimately," Myra said with a shudder. "He makes deliveries for the chemist on a push bike. He may be around the back of the shop."

Fuller opened the car door. "Come on. There's an alley that runs down the back of this row. Let's check."

Myra looked at him askance. "Really?"

"It's a long shot," Fuller said. "Indulge me."

"I could have gone in and asked to see him," Myra said as she followed Fuller to the end of the street and down a narrow passageway between two shops that led to the alleyway.

"The element of surprise," Fuller said. "It can't be overestimated."

They emerged from the passageway and found themselves in the alley, bordered on each side by high fences made of feather-edged timber, with wooden gates set in at regular intervals. Beside each gate were large galvanised metal dustbins, each about four feet high, and boxes of rubbish discarded by the shops the alleyway served.

"Which one's the gate belonging to Hennessey's?"

"Probably the one with the bicycle parked outside is my guess," Fuller said looking along the alley.

As they approached, the sound of an engine filled the air, and at end of the alley a figure came into view – a figure riding a motor scooter.

They ducked behind one of the dustbins as the scooter approached and the gate to Hennessey's back yard opened. Peter Lamb stepped out into the alley and looked along at the scooter, raising his hand in greeting.

"Do you think they saw us?" Myra whispered.

"Quiet," Fuller whispered back. "Watch and listen. Let's see what they're up to."

36

TUESDAY

"Any chance I can have a word with Rosie?" David Neville said as Barbara Painter finished serving a customer and looked to him expectantly.

"I'm sorry she hasn't come in today," Mrs. Painter said.

"She told me she was working all week. She said nothing about taking a day off."

Mrs. Painter narrowed her eyes as she looked at him. "I know you, don't I? You've been in here before."

"I'm Rosie's boyfriend," Neville said.

"Are you indeed? Boyfriend now, is it? I thought you'd only been out with her the once," Mrs. Painter said.

"We've been courting nearly a week," he said. "Do you know if she's at home?" Neville glanced around as an elderly man entered the shop.

"Good morning, Barbara," he said.

"Your usual, Ted?"

The old man smiled. "Yes, and one of those iced coconut buns."

"Well, is she?" Neville said.

"Is she what, dear?" Mrs. Painter said, reaching into the window display and taking out two Chelsea buns.

"At home?"

"Not according to her mother," she said. She put the buns in a bag and twisted the top. "Just one coconut bun?" she said to the old man.

"You'd better make it two, Barb," he said. "They're very tasty."

Neville tapped his foot impatiently.

"So you're obviously not the one with the motor scooter," she said to him.

"The what?"

"The scooter, dear. Rosie took off on the back of one, shortly before I opened up this morning."

The blood drained from Neville's face, and he seemed to sway slightly.

"Are you all right, dear?" she said. "Only you've gone very pale."

"I'm fine…thank you," he said, and rushed to the door, pulling it open so hard the bell above it jangled loudly, and then he ran out into the street, looked along it both ways and tore off, away from the town centre.

"Youngsters today," Mrs. Painter said to the old man. "Always in such a rush."

"It'll be a shame when do away with National Service," he said. "They're phasing it out you know? Just when the young people in this country could do with a good dose of army discipline."

"The country will go to the dogs," she said.

The old man smiled ruefully. "Some would have it that it has already, my dear."

"Two shillings," she said, passed the bag over the counter, and held out her hand for the money.

Neville ran across the garage forecourt to the workshop situated at the back of the building. The large double doors were pushed open, and the space inside was taken up by three cars, their bonnets up, each undergoing various types of repairs. Mechanics, wearing grease-stained, dark green overalls, toiled in the warm, oil-laden air, sweating profusely, occasionally mopping the perspiration away from their faces with grubby rags. None of them seemed to notice when Neville ran into their midst.

"Derek?" he called. "Webster?"

A large man with an oil-streaked face and a halo of dirty grey curls looked up from the carburettor of the old Ford Prefect he was adjusting, and wiped his forehead on the sleeve of his overall. "Wrong day, mate," he called back. "He's not here."

"Where is he?" Neville asked him.

"At the dentist, I think," he said. "That's right, isn't it, Bert?" he called to another of the mechanics.

"I think so, man," Bert said. He was a tall, rangy black man whose cheeks still bore the tribal scars of a childhood spent in Nigeria.

"Is he coming back?"

Bert shrugged. "Search me, man. I'm not his mother."

"Okay," Neville said. "Thanks."

Both men shrugged apathetically and went back to their work.

Neville ran from the workshop and to the street that would take him to Ridge Road and Gavin Southland's house. Webster and Lamb had warned him they would take matters into their own hands if he didn't speak to Southland. Now it seemed they had made good their promise. He just hoped he could get there before it was too late. He increased his pace, ignoring the burning in his lungs.

Jack paced the kitchen, stopping to gaze out of the window at the garden for a few seconds before starting to pace again.

He was missing something. Something he had seen or heard in the last few days that would bust this case wide open, but the thought was elusive. It teased his mind, sometimes coming close to the surface before spiriting away again to remain tantalizingly out of reach. He needed to clear his mind, to occupy it with some mundane, undemanding task, to allow his subconscious free rein.

He stopped pacing. "I'm going out to the greenhouse," he said to Annie and Joan, who still sat at the kitchen table, Annie sipping at yet another cup of tea, Joan smoking one cigarette after another and stubbing them out after a couple of puffs in the glass ashtray that sat in the middle of the table.

"Good idea," Joan said.

Annie said nothing but looked at him bleakly, her face seeming to have aged since she heard the news about Rosie. Her eyes were red from crying and deep lines had appeared, etched into the corners of her mouth and around her eyes. He wanted to take her in his arms, to smooth those lines away, to stroke her hair and tell her that everything was going to be all right, but he couldn't even look her in the eyes in case she saw the fear that was filling his.

In the greenhouse an old battered chest of drawers sat opposite the row of tomatoes, its battle-scarred surface testament to years of taking cuttings, re-potting begonias and fuchsias, and the other horticultural tasks he performed to fill his free time.

He picked up a seed tray and filled it with potting compost, tamping it down until he had an even seedbed, and then he took one of his begonias from the shelf above the chest of drawers and selected a plump, sturdy leaf. Laying it flat on the top of the chest, he took out his penknife and started to cut the leaf into small squares, lining them up on the surface of the compost and pinning them flat with thin, wire, hair pins. It was repetitive, mindless work but it helped to relieve the tension in his neck and shoulders that was starting to give him a headache, and it allowed his mind to roam freely.

When he had cut up the first leaf and covered half the compost, he plucked another one and began to trim again, not even noticing when he cut across the top of his finger. Only becoming aware of it when he noticed the blood pooling on the wood.

"Damn!" he cursed and stuck the cut finger in his mouth, with his uninjured hand he pulled open one of the drawers and started rummaging through seed packets, plant labels, boxes of rooting powder and other gardening accoutrements, in search of a sticking plaster.

He taped his finger and had just started putting everything back in the drawer when he noticed a small leatherette box, stuck dawn the side of the drawer, half-hidden by pages from a seed catalogue. He liberated the box from the drawer, laid it down on the wooden top of the chest and opened it

Inside, pinned to a cushion of black velvet was a black, red and yellow striped ribbon attached to a gold, six-pointed star – his Burma Star campaign medal.

For years he had believed it lost and had searched the house for it, turning out every cupboard and drawer, and it had been here in the greenhouse all the time, in the chest of drawers he had plundered from the bedroom years ago.

Just seeing it again sent memories cascading through his mind – memories of friendships made in the heat of battle, of fallen comrades and hard-fought campaigns to capture and recapture positions, of seemingly endless treks through inhospitable jungle in searing heat and bone-drenching monsoons. He took the medal from the box and clutched it in his fist. There was something important here, not just the memories of wartime, bur something more. He closed his eyes.

He was back in Burma, picking over the wreckage of a temple in Mandalay that the Japanese had laid to waste, killing all the monks and leaving their dead bodies scattered amongst the ruins. He was a young man again, weeping at the carnage, mourning the loss of those innocent souls at the hands of a ruthless enemy, and then something came into his mind that made him drop the medal back in the box, shove it in his pocket, and run back to the house.

Myra stepped out from behind the cover of the dustbin and started to walk towards the young men. Peter Lamb was leaning against the fence – his friend was still straddling the scooter, a cigarette dangling from his lips.

"Hello, boys," Myra called when she was almost upon them. "I wonder if you can help me."

Derek Webster's face lit up and he smiled at Myra lasciviously. Lamb tried to ignore her.

She directed her attention towards Webster. "Nice scooter," she said. "Nice colour."

"Custom job," Webster said. "It's a Phoenix 150. You can get them in plain blue, but mine's two-tone."

"I can see," Myra said.

"A mate of mine did it for me especially," Webster said proudly. "Fancy a spin?"

"I'll bet you say that to all the girls," Myra said.

"And they usually say yes."

"Is that right," Myra said. "Did Sandra Duncan say yes? And Rosie Callum? Did you take *her* for a spin?"

Panic flared in Webster's eyes. He kick-started the scooter, twisted the throttle and tore past her.

"Hey!" she called, moving to run after him and Lamb back-elbowed her in the face, splitting her lip and making her head spin. She staggered against the fence as Lamb mounted the pushbike and took off in the opposite direction to Webster.

From the cover of the bin, Fuller watched the encounter with interest. Myra Banks was quietly impressive. She certainly had some guts.

As Webster revved the engine and took off, Fuller gabbed the dustbin and threw it into his path. The scooter's front wheel hit the side of the bin with a deafening clang and stopped dead, the forward momentum lifting Webster out of the saddle, sending him flying through the air to land in an ungainly heap a few feet away. Taking his handcuffs from his pocket he cuffed Webster's hands behind his back, took out his police whistle and gave it three short blasts, and then, leaving Webster curled up on the ground, groaning, he went to see if Myra was okay.

Myra was dabbing away blood from her mouth with a handkerchief. "Lamb got away," she said. "Sorry."

"Not to worry. We'll get him soon enough and we've got the other one."

"He took a bit of a flier," Myra said. "Is he badly hurt?"

"He'll live, but if he's the one who took Rosie and the others, then he isn't hurt badly enough. It's a pity he didn't break his bleedin' neck."

In the distance a dog barked and they turned to see Alistair Kirby running towards them from the end of the alley, Satan, still on the lead, keeping pace with him.

"Keep your eyes on this one," Fuller said to Kirby. "I'll go into the shop and call for a Black Maria."

On the ground Webster was still whimpering. "You've broken my bloody back," he said.

Kirby looked down at him. "It's not your day, son, is it? One wrong move and Satan here will rip your throat out." He turned to Myra. "What's he done anyway?"

"We think he and his friend have snatched DCI Callum's daughter and are probably keeping her somewhere."

Kirby said something to Satan and the dog began barking furiously, inches away from Webster's face. Derek Webster started to cry.

Jack burst in through the back door, ran down the hall and

took the stairs two at a time.

By the time Annie reached the bedroom Jack had yanked a small leather suitcase from on top of the wardrobe, had it open on the bed and had rifled through its contents. In his hand was a small pile of dog-eared photographs and he was looking at each in turn and discarding them on the bed.

"What are you doing?" she said, from the doorway.

He had an old black and white snapshot in his hand and was studying it intently.

He turned to her, his eyes wide. "I know where Rosie is," he said.

37

TUESDAY

Jack reached on top of the wardrobe again and took down a black metal security box. Using a small key from his key ring he opened it and looked inside. The Browning revolver was freshly oiled and pristine. He took it out and dropped it on the bed, and then took out the small box of ammunition, dropped it on the bed beside it and sat down himself.

"Jack? What are you doing," Annie said as he fed bullets into the chamber.

"I'm going to get her back," he said.

"With that?" she said.

He nodded grimly. "I'll make Southland pay for what he's done."

"Call the station, please," she said. "Let them deal with it. They're equipped."

"So am I." He hefted the gun in his hand, stood up and stuck it in the waistband of his trousers.

She grabbed his arm. "No, Jack. Not like this. Let them deal with it," she said again

"She's my daughter," he said, and stormed out of the room.

"She's *my* daughter too," she called after him tearfully.

He rushed downstairs and out of the house, hurling himself in behind the wheel of the pool car. He started the engine, gunned the accelerator and pulled out onto the street, narrowly missing a milk float that was making lazy progress along the road.

"'ere, watch it!" the milkman shouted at the car as it tore away from the house.

Neville ran in through the iron gates and sprinted across the forecourt to the house, hammering on the front door with his fist. "Come on, Gavin, open up!"

He stood on the front step, his heart pounding in his chest, his breath coming in ragged gasps. Finally the door opened a fraction and he threw his weight behind it, bursting it open.

"Where is she?" he shouted at Southland. "Where's Rosie?"

"Hello, David," Southland said calmly. "How good of you to drop by."

Neville stepped forward and grabbed Southland by the front of his kimono. "Where is she?" he screamed in Southland's face, and then made a small surprised sound and stepped back, releasing his hold on the silk robe. He looked down at the front of his shirt and watched the blood spreading out from a small hole in his stomach. His eyes drifted to Southland's hand and the thin, bloodstained knife gripped in it.

His legs buckled and he sank to his knees. "You've stabbed me," he said stupidly.

"You can have an A for observation, you perverted little shit," Southland said and nudged him with his knee, sending Neville toppling backwards onto the carpet.

"Why?" Neville said, his voice little more than a whisper.

"For defiling my artistic statement," Southland said. "For being unable to control your base instincts, your pathetic animal lust."

Neville clutched at his belly, trying to stem the flow of blood. "Help me," he said.

Southland looked down on him contemptuously. "It's not worth my time," he said and, leaning forward, drew the knife across Neville's neck, slicing his throat through to the windpipe and severing the carotid artery.

"What are you doing?"

Southland spun round on his good leg to see Lamb standing in the open doorway, his white face gradually turning green.

"Solving a problem," he said calmly. "Peter, if you're going to throw up please do so outside. This carpet has had enough spilled on it for one day."

Annie listened to Jack's car scream out of the drive and then ran downstairs and picked up the telephone.

"Sergeant Brewer? It's Annie Callum here. Is Eddie Fuller available?"

"Hold on a moment," Brewer said. "May I say, we're all very sorry about Rosie?"

Annie held onto the phone, patiently, biting her lip to stop herself screaming at Brewer to hurry up.

He came back on the line. "Eddie's out on a case at the moment, but Superintendent Lane would like word."

There was a pause and then a more cultured voice said, "Annie, Henry Lane here. How are you holding up?"

"Hanging on, Henry, but it's not me I'm concerned about, it's Jack. He stormed out of here a few minutes ago. He suddenly announced that he knew where Rosie was and was going to get her back."

"Did he say where she was?"

"No. He just said something about making Southland pay for what he's done, but I didn't know who he was talking about."

"Okay then, Annie. We'll take it from here," Lane said, trying to calm her.

"No, Henry, you don't understand," Annie said. "He loaded his old service revolver and took it with him."

"Dear God," Lane said under his breath. "Okay, Annie. I'm ringing off now, and you're not to worry. We'll handle it."

"Where's Fuller?" Lane said.

"Making an arrest," Brewer said, glancing out through the station doors as a Black Maria pulled up outside the front of the station.

"In fact, here he is now."

The driver got out, went around and opened the back of the van.

Fuller and Myra stepped out, followed by a limping and battered-looking Derek Webster. Bringing up the rear was Alistair Kirby and his dog.

Lane rushed out of the station to meet them. "Who is Southland and where does he live?" he said to Fuller.

"I know, sir," Myra said.

"Right, you two. Come with me. We'll take my car. I'll bring you up to date on the way."

Jack screeched to a halt outside Gavin Southland's detached Victorian house. Driven by an incandescent rage, he hadn't

255

really thought what his approach was going to be. All he knew was that he had to get Rosie back safe and sound. He climbed out of the car and, ducking low, ran in through the gates.

He approached the front door and was surprised to find it gaping wide open. He looked into the house and saw David Neville's body lying on the hall carpet in a pool of blood, most of which seemed to have come from the savage wound in the boy's throat. Of Southland there was no sign, but Jack could hear voices coming from deeper in the house.

Taking the revolver from his waistband, he cocked it and moved forward cautiously. The voices seemed to be coming from the direction of the conservatory. Jack crept along the passageway until he was standing directly outside the door.

"Don't panic, Peter. We can get rid of his body as easily as we disposed of the others," Southland was saying.

"But the police…"

"Are no further forward in their investigations than they were yesterday."

"I really wouldn't be too sure of that," Jack said, and stepped into the conservatory.

Southland spun round and hurled the knife at him, but it sailed past Jack's ear, embedding itself in the doorframe.

"You bastard!" Peter Lamb yelled, and hurled himself forwards, arms outstretched, hands reaching for Jack.

Without pause Jack shot him in the leg, sending him crashing to the ground, shouting obscenities, and writhing in pain.

"Where is she?" Jack said.

"Who?" Southland said blandly.

"Rosie. I know she's here."

"Oh, the little tart," Southland said with a supercilious smile.

Jack was across the floor in three strides, pinning Southland against the window, bringing the revolver up and ramming the barrel under the man's chin.

"That little tart happens to be my daughter," Jack said dangerously.

He watched the blood drain from Southland's face and heard him gulp loudly. "Oh dear," Southland said, glaring down at Lamb who was still writhing on the floor, gripping his leg tightly in an effort to stop the bleeding. "There seems to have been a bit of a balls up."

"Take me to her," Jack said, pressing the barrel of the gun deeper into Southland's throat.

"All right, all right, just don't kill me."

"Just give me an excuse," Jack said, and eased the pressure, spinning the man around and stepping behind him, grinding the gun barrel into the small of Southland's back.

"She's in my studio," Southland said. "I haven't hurt her." He started to move forward. "What gave me away? If you don't mind me asking," he said as they passed the shelves containing the orchids.

"Your choice of interior décor," Jack said, pointing to the small brass discs with holes in their centres and embossed oriental writing that separated each pot. "They're coins," he said. "Buddhist temple coins, as I'm sure you are well aware. I've just been looking at a photograph of some. The last time I saw anything like them was in a ruined temple in Mandalay during the war. Your penchant for eastern myth and fable betrayed you in the end."

"Ah, how plans are so easily undone."

Jack ground the barrel deeper into his back.

"Okay, okay," Southland said. "This way."

Rosie's eyes opened wide as Jack and Southland walked into the studio and she gave a muffled sob, straining against her bonds.

Jack pushed Southland forward, keeping him covered with the gun. "Untie her and step away," he said.

From behind him he heard a bellow of rage and glanced round in time to see Peter Lamb barreling towards him. Before he could get off a shot Lamb crashed into him, taking him to the floor. The gun was knocked from his hand and went clattering across the floor of the studio.

Lamb was strong. The boy's hands reached up, closed around Jack's throat, his thumbs pressing into the windpipe, and the sound of rushing blood filled Jack's ears as the room started to spin. Out of the corner of his eye he saw Southland limping across the room, pulling another knife from the pot on the table at Rosie's elbow and moving towards her.

Something snapped in Jack then. Using all his strength, he brought his knee up into Lamb's bloodied thigh and smashed it into the muscle. Lamb cried out and the grip on Jack's throat loosened. Twisting his body Jack rolled onto Lamb, straddling him, and punched him twice in the face. With a groan Lamb collapsed back on the carpet and Jack scrambled across the floor, reaching for his revolver.

His fingers had closed around the butt when he heard Rosie squeal. He turned around, looking desperately in her direction and froze when he saw Southland, crouching behind Rosie's chair, his knife at her neck. Rosie's eyes were wide and she was making small noises behind the gag.

"Is this how it's going to end, Chief Inspector?" Southland said, and then shook his head slightly. "No, I don't think so. You don't strike me as a man who would let his daughter die for the sake of an arrest. Am I right?" He dug the point of the knife deeper, and a small bead of blood oozed from Rosie's neck.

Rosie's eyes grew wider still and tears started to trickle down her cheeks.

"It's all right, Rosie. Don't move," Jack said.

"Do you hear that, Rosie? I'd listen to what he says if I were you."

"If you hurt her…"

"You'll do what precisely? Shoot me? Hardly the actions of a law abiding citizen."

"How do you know what I'm capable of?" Jack said, trying to keep his voice calm.

"I know your type, Callum. My father was a policeman – another bloody gutless wonder like you – and he ran out on us when he was faced with something he had no control over. Coppers, you're all the same." He snorted derisively. "If you can't arrest it and throw it in a cell, then you fall apart."

"You think?" Jack said, leveled the gun at him and fired. The bullet took Southland in the shoulder, the force of it sending him spinning away. At the same time, Rosie rocked the chair, sending it toppling backwards, the back of her skull cracking on the linoleum floor. As Southland, clutching his shoulder with one hand, the knife in the other, moved towards her, Jack fired again, missing him but boring a hole in the lino.

"Drop the knife," Jack said, and for a moment he thought Southland might resist, but then the man's fingers opened, and the knife clattered to the floor.

Still covering Southland with the revolver Jack went across to Rosie and, one-handedly, unbuckled the straps tethering her wrists, and then untied her ankles.

With her hands free she reached up, tore the gag from her face and spat out the suffocating rag from her mouth. Getting groggily to her feet she lurched across to Jack and clutched him. "I'm sorry, Daddy," she said.

"It's okay, poppet. Everything's all right now," Jack said, righting the chair. He twitched the revolver at Southland. "Sit," he said.

Southland did as he was told and, as he limped across to sit down, Jack glanced around at the three pictures of the victims propped up against the wall. Then his gaze alighted on the table that held the needles, silk thread and the half-used candle, and he felt his rage begin to build again. He took a step forward and aimed the gun at Southland's face.

Southland glared up at him defiantly. "Go on then. Shoot me. End it now," he goaded.

Jack cocked the revolver and steadied his aim.

"Do you really think death frightens me?"

Jack's finger tightened on the trigger.

"Put the gun down, Chief Inspector."

Jack turned to see Lane, standing in the doorway, Fuller and Myra behind him, peering over his shoulder. Lane's own gun was pointing at him. The hand that held it was as steady as a rock.

Jack turned back to Southland who continued to glare at him.

"I *will* shoot you, Jack," Lane said.

"Please. Dad," Rosie said. "Put it down."

Jack felt his finger tightening still further on the trigger, but then looked down into his daughter's imploring face and he sighed, lowering the gun. He turned away from Southland, unable to look at the monster any longer.

Lane signalled to Fuller who rushed into the studio, handcuffed Southland and hauled him from the room.

"The gun please, Jack." Lane said, and held out his hand.

Looking regretfully at Southland, Jack handed it to him, and then wrapped an arm around Rosie's shoulder. "Let's go home, pet," he said to her softly as she pressed herself into him.

"Okay, Dad," she said.

38

WEDNESDAY August 20th 1958

"Just give me five minutes with him," Jack said to Fisher.

"I don't really think that's necessary," Fisher said. "You've closed the case. Webster and Lamb are talking to us, singing actually, like the proverbial canaries. It's like a duet between Joan Sutherland and Maria Callas, and they've told us everything. As we speak, my men are picking up Tim Fellowes and Adam Channing. They'll be charged as accessories to murder and will most likely go away for a very long time."

"But I need to speak with Southland," Jack insisted. "I need to know why he sewed the mouths and eyes shut."

"Well, he hasn't told *us*, so why should he tell you?"

"Please," Jack said.

Fisher finally relented. He hadn't come out and admitted that he'd miscalculated the investigation or, in the words of the Chief Constable, made a complete and utter cock-up of it, making himself look a complete idiot in the process.

Callum had been right all along. "Okay," he said. "But you're not going in there alone. Detective Sergeant Fuller will accompany you to make sure things don't get out of hand."

Jack opened the door and stepped into the interview room. Fuller followed him in and took a seat beside him at the small wooden table.

Southland looked up at them. "You're wasting your time," he said. "I've made my statement. I've nothing more to add."

"You know you're going to hang?" Jack said.

"Then I'll hang. I achieved what I wanted to achieve and led you lot a merry dance in the process."

Jack looked at him steadily. "Is that it? You were trying to make a point of some kind?"

Southland smiled enigmatically and said nothing.

"Why the three monkeys, Gavin?"

Southland stared at him, and for a moment Jack thought he

was going to remain silent, and then Gavin Southland began to speak. "You recognised the temple coins," he said.

"I did."

"Would you call yourself a religious man, Chief Inspector?"

"Not especially."

"But you believe in the immortal soul?"

Jack shrugged, wondering where Southland was going with this.

Southland leaned forward, clasping his cuffed hands together. "I used to be a lot like you," he said. "Believing in God was what I had been taught at Sunday school, stories and parables learned as much as a matter of rote than anything else." He paused, his eyes gazing into a distant, hazy past. "When I was struck down with polio I lost any semblance of faith that I'd had. How could there be a God if he could let a boy, an innocent boy, suffer in that manner, reducing him to a cripple to be pitied and ridiculed? I was bitter, but I was determined to succeed in life, to win with the unfair hand I'd been dealt."

Jack raised his palm. "Is this story going anywhere, Gavin? Only I have criminals to catch."

"I thought you wanted to know why I sewed them up."

"I do. Please continue."

"After I left university I was eager to travel. University had whetted my appetite for learning, and I was anxious to continue. I took myself off to the Far East. China, Japan, Tibet, and finally my journey ended in Burma – where I found the coins, in a ruined temple, much like you did. I was searching, you see. I was looking for the one thing my illness had taken from me – my faith, my belief in a higher power, something greater than myself."

"And did you find it?"

"Oh, yes," Southland said. "Oh, yes I found it."

"I'm very pleased for you," Jack said. "It still doesn't explain…"

"Please be patient," Southland said. "In the religions of the East, I found a belief that, at long last, made some sense to me."

"I wish it did to me," Fuller said. Jack hushed him.

"I don't expect you to understand, so I'll try and simplify it for you," Southland said condescendingly. "The issue of the three monkeys has been squabbled over for centuries. Different religions have their own interpretations, but I'll tell you what I believe. The three monkeys represent the *Sanshi,* the three spirits who live in everyone and report good and bad deeds to a God, a higher authority, which can then reward or punish as it sees fit. I was simply making sure they'd have nothing to report."

"And is that it?"

Southland shrugged. "It's what I believe, and who are you, Chief Inspector, to question my beliefs?" Jack stared at Southland for a full minute before getting to his feet and walking from the room.

Fuller caught up with him outside in the corridor. "Sir?" he said. "If you don't mind me asking, what the Hell was all that about?"

"*Hell* was exactly what it was all about," Jack said.

"Well it went over my head," Fuller said.

"He just told us why he sewed their eyes and mouths shut and poured wax into their ears," Jack said.

"Did he?" Fuller said, still looking at Jack uncomprehendingly.

"I read the interview he gave Fisher, and now, after that, I think I understand. After years of living a godless life, a life without faith, he knew his thirst for revenge against his father, a man who had deserted him when he needed him most, would conflict with his recently discovered faith. The three monkeys, Eddie – see no evil, speak no evil, and hear no evil. In his own twisted way, he was stopping the *Sanshi* taking messages back to his god. He painted them, making a triptych – a religious, artistic statement. *He was trying to save his soul.*"

"Do you think he succeeded?" Fuller said.

"I don't think so," Jack said. "I believe that some souls are beyond saving. Gavin Southland is one of them."

Lane was waiting for Jack outside the interview room.

"Chief Inspector, a moment if you please."

Jack nodded. He knew what was coming as he followed the

neatly dressed Chief Superintendent along the corridor and into his office.

Lane sat behind his desk and Jack could gauge his discomfiture from the way his hands were clasped together rather formally on top of the desk.

Jack stood, not quite to attention, but with an erect posture that he hoped conveyed some respect for the man sitting before him.

"Regulations dictate that I have to report the discharge of a pistol by a serving officer, you understand that don't you, Chief Inspector?"

"Yes, sir. I fully understand your position."

"Do you, do you really?"

Suddenly Lane slammed one palm down hard on the desk. "An unauthorized pistol at that. How long have you had it?"

Jack shrugged. "Brought it back at the end of the war and haven't given it much thought since, truth be known."

"Yet you knew where it was, had it in excellent working order, and had sufficient ammunition to make it a viable weapon."

Jack nodded. "I can see your point, sir." He had lovingly attended to the cleaning and oiling of the revolver ever since he'd kept it as part of his discharge uniform. He knew the perils that could befall a copper and their family and he had it in the back of his mind that a working gun might come in handy one day. How right he had been proven.

"By rights I should be reporting this to the Chief Constable. Should have done it already in point of fact."

"I'm sorry for the embarrassment I've caused you, sir. Do you want my warrant card?"

Lane sighed and made an indistinct noise in the back of his throat that in a lesser man might have been an indication of irritation.

"Did you intend to use it?"

"I shot two men, sir, so I think I…"

"Jack," Lane said, and annoyance crept into his tone. "You shot one young thug in the leg to disable him, and you shot Southland in the shoulder to stop him harming your daughter.

That is not what I meant."

Jack noted the change from his rank to the use of his name and hoped that was a good sign. "I think I know what you mean, sir."

"Would you have killed Southland, Jack? That's what I'm asking you. For God's sake the man had taken your daughter, your Rosie, and was threatening all sorts to her. It would be wholly understandable if you had wanted the man dead. He's evil, and we've both seen some bad things in our time. Would you have killed him if I hadn't stopped you?"

Jack let out a deep breath he hadn't even realised he was holding in. Would he have killed Southland in that moment? Without a hesitation. Anything to protect his family and keep them safe.

"I think I should express my gratitude, Henry, that your fortitude probably prevented me doing something I may have regretted after the event."

"I thought that might be the case."

"I killed people in the war, dare say you saw some action yourself. I've shot villains in the line of duty as a serving police officer but I can't say that none of them have come without a price. There are nights, even now, when the night sweats wake me and the heat of the jungle seems to be strangling me again. The cost of a man's life, even in war and even when they are the lowest criminal life there is, comes high when you have a conscience and a moral compass that you live by."

"Quite so," Lane murmured. His eyes had taken a distant appearance as though he too was remembering times spent in actions he might have wished he hadn't had to take.

"Might I ask you something, sir, man to man as it were?"

"Yes, Jack, I would have shot you, to stop you doing something that you would have lived to regret."

Jack nodded and sat down for the first time. "I thought that might be it."

Lane's face assembled itself into a grim smile. "I would have aimed to wound though, not to kill."

"Very reassuring," Jack said.

"Chief Inspector, the mattered is closed. It remains between you and I. There were others present at the scene, but I think we can rely on their discretion. Your…war souvenir will be returned once forensics has finished with it."

Jack stood and clutched Lane's outstretched hand. "Bloody good job, Jack. A first rate investigation and a decent result."

"I just wish I could have acted a bit quicker and saved some of those poor young lives."

"Don't dwell on it, you know better than that. Did you know Southland's father was one of us?"

"A copper, yes I read that in the report."

Lane nodded. "Bit of a bully by all accounts."

"In his own twisted mind Southland was killing those poor young people as some kind of revenge on his father," Jack said. "Fellowes and Channing are both weak men, but Southland had some kind of hold over them. Their statements are going to make for some interesting reading."

"You're due some leave – take a couple of days off. Be with your family. They need you now. I'll see you on Monday, bright and early."

"If you're sure, sir. Absolutely. Thanks, Henry, the garden has been a bit neglected of late. Now if you don't mind I have a certain London copper to evict from my office."

Jack entered his office without knocking and was rewarded with the embarrassed shuffled exits of Inspector Lymon and Sergeant Greyling, both clutching cardboard boxes.

"I'll be grateful for the return of my office, sir," Jack said effusively.

Fisher drew himself up to his full height and glared at Jack. "Think you're the bees knees because your crazy theory had some merits to it do you, Callum?"

"I think the team got a good result…in the end."

"Meaning after I made a monumental foul-up by taking you and your precious officers off the case."

"I think you'll find it was an authority higher than either of us who made that decision."

"Yes, well, I'm off. I'll leave you to your provincial duties."

"Quite so, sir. Get back to the Smoke and the real villains.

Wouldn't want a triple murder to stand in the way of real crime now would we?"

"You really are an impudent man, you know that don't you, Callum?"

Jack got as close to Fisher's face as he could without touching noses. He could smell the scent of whisky and mints on the man's breath. "You are a pompous ass, Fisher, who endangered lives because you had your head so far up your own backside that you couldn't see that we, the provincial coppers you sneered at, might be right and that you, with all your Scotland Yard whistles and bells, could be wrong. At least one young person died because your arrogance took you down the wrong track." If it was possible to do so, Jack leaned in even closer. "Worst of all you nearly got my daughter killed. Lucky for you she's unharmed or else you really would see how impudent I am…sir. Have a nice trip back."

Jack pushed his way past Fisher and sat behind his desk.

"You know the way out," he said.

39

SATURDAY August 23rd 1958

Jack pushed Eric along in front of him, with Annie, Joan and Rosie, their arms linked, following close behind, singing *When The Spurs Go Marching In* with the rest of the Tottenham supporters. Gathering them together, he urged them ahead of him, the protective father, taking his family out to a Saturday afternoon ritual. He led the way through the crowd thronging towards the White Hart Lane turnstiles, and up the concrete steps to the terraces, where they assembled with thousands of others, waiting for the match against Blackpool to get underway.

The stadium pulsed with the sound of partisan cheers and the clatter of football rattles.

"Do you think we'll win, Dad?" Joan said.

"Judging by the way they've been playing recently, Joanie, I think it's highly unlikely. But I'm a Spurs fan, hope is second nature to us."

He looked at his eldest daughter, seemingly lost to him until just a few days ago. She had seen and experienced far more than a girl of her tender years should have done but she seemed untouched by it, at least on the surface. He was looking forwards to getting to know her again.

Rosie was drinking in the atmosphere, as they all were. Judging by her wide-eyed innocence Jack didn't think the awful events in Southland's house would have done any long term damage. He knew from the protective arm that Annie had around her youngest daughter's shoulder that Rosie would be in safe hands.

As Danny Blanchflower led the Tottenham Hotspur team out of the tunnel and onto the pitch, White Hart Lane erupted into a cacophony befitting the first fixture of the season.

"If you can draw crowds like this with your skiffle music, Eric, I'll be very impressed," Jack shouted to his son above the crowd's noise.

"Just you watch me, Dad," Eric shouted back. "Just you watch me."

"Don't worry, son. I'll be watching, and cheering you on all the way."

***

If you enjoyed this book tell me, tell your friends and, if you have time, please leave a review on the site where you bought it. For more details of the DCI Jack Callum Mysteries visit: www.jackcallum.com

Printed in Great Britain
by Amazon